Holder of Secrets
Unrecognised

Chapter 1

Pain woke me. Someone was slapping me, making my head ache. It pierced my brain.

"Stop," I tried to insist, but only a croak came out. It seemed to do the trick. A hand lifted my chin, and water flooded my throat. I swallowed some but most was coughed out. My eyes finally opened and I saw Harry King's face.

"Back with us, little bitch," he greeted me. "About time! I'm in a hurry. You answer my questions straight, and you won't get hurt anymore. Play with me, and you'll get beaten, or worse. Understand?"

He began with, "Where does your Aunt hide her stuff?"

It took me a moment to comprehend the question, and that was too slow. Harry hit me with something and my leg stung.

"She keeps her gin in the back of the larder." It was the first thing I thought of.

Another whack. "I didn't mean her grog, bitch. I mean her money, valuables."

He whacked me again before I could form the next answer, and I wondered what he had done to my aunt if he was reduced to asking me. Did it matter if I told? I had her stuff hidden – all of it, I hoped.

"She kept…housekeeping money in an old sock in her wardrobe."

"What else?"

"I don't know. No, maybe, I once saw a letter peeking out from under a chair in the lounge."

"Who was it from?"

"Don't know. I swear. She came and took it before I could look."

While my legs stung like I had been bitten by a hundred wasps, I heard Harry tell someone, "Go back and check but make bloody sure the local cops aren't there."

Then Harry got into specifics, but he asked about things that I really didn't know about and couldn't answer. I hardly heeded after he claimed Aunt Ida's real name was Annie Simmons.

It had slowly dawned on me that I was tied to a tree, and he had stripped me near naked. Once the other person had gone, he came closer and began to fondle me, and finally removed the last of my clothes using his very sharp knife. Obviously he had wanted me awake and aware when he began to torment me. Then he touched that knife to my skin, and laughed when I shivered. He had the flat of the blade running down from my chin to my chest, letting me know he could easily cut me. His whispered threats of what he could do, making it seem that I should be grateful if he only raped me.

The pounding in my head increased as he hit me over and over. I wasn't aware of him revealing himself and when his powerful penetration jerked me against the tree, the world went black again.

I returned to vague consciousness. My body hurt everywhere. I knew that feeling, but I could not even rouse myself to anger.

"Peg! Wake up. Please, wake up."

The whispered voice was urgent, pleading. I began to shiver. I tried to see who was with me, but it was almost dark. Gentle hands pressed fabric close around me. I tried to speak, but couldn't seem to form words. My lips felt swollen.

"It's me, Stan," the voice told me.

"Wha….?"

"Shh. I need you to get up, so we can get away."

I tried to push up, but I had no strength. Stan half lifted me, and then needed to support me, until my head stopped spinning and my legs solidified from jelly. I began to cough, and threw up a lot of water.

My mind could not grasp why he was still around Matlock. It was enough for me to know I could trust him. He helped me along a path that my eyes couldn't see, until we reached a motorbike.

"I'll put you up in front of me," Stan said, lifting me. "Put your leg over."

I did and gasped with renewed pain.

"Sorry, Peg, but this is the fastest way to go."

"Where?" I forced out.

"Away from here. I will find you a doctor somewhere."

"No. Go to Jack Casey."

"Mad miner Jack? Why?"

"Trust him. He will listen first. Not just take you in."

"Okay, Peg. So long as he will look after you."

I moved in and out of consciousness as Stan drove the bike at near idling speed. He knew the way to Casey's Mine, but not the state of the track. I fought to stay awake. I needed to ask Jack to help Stan. To convince the old man that Stan was not like Mick Devlin. Wasn't dangerous.

"How did you find me?" I asked, trying to stay aware.

"Fluke. I'd been out to check a trap I'd set and heard that bastard. He had another bloke with him and you were unconscious. I thought he'd killed you. You had blood running down from a head wound. Gave me a real shock when I realised it was you."

"How'd you get me?"

"He went off for a bit. I got you free and carried you to my hide out."

"Why'd you come back?"

"I'd thought over what you'd said. I was going to give myself up to your friend York, but I was dithering."

I felt myself fading out again. "I don't know how Aunt Ida is."

"She's a tough old bitch."

"You don't understand. I think Gianni is really mad at her this time."

"We will tell Jack Casey. We aren't far away now."

It hadn't occurred to my foggy mind to warn him about the new gravel Jack had put around his hut. Even going dead slow, it crunched.

I was only vaguely aware that Jack had emerged with a shot gun aimed at us. I heard Stan say, "Sir, I am not armed or intending trouble. I need… Peg needs, your help."

"What did you do to her?" Jack demanded.

I tried to protest, "He did nothing…" but Stan spoke over me. "I pulled her out of Smokey's waterhole. She'd been thrown in there. I saw a body floating and waded in to see who it was, and get them out."

That wasn't what he had told me earlier.

"Bring her in, then hide the bike. When you have done that, will you be coming back?"

"Yes, Sir. You know who I am?"

"I do. Don't be long."

Stan carried me in and put me down on Jack's bed, near the oil heater, and then went to move the bike. Meanwhile, I heard Jack starting up his stove and putting the billy on. While it made its heating up noises, the water on its side hissing into steam, I felt Jack move the cover of the coat that Stan had put around me.

"Who did this?" he asked in his voice of authority.

Part of me hesitated, but Jack urged. "You need to tell me."

"Harry King."

"You mentioned him the other day," Jack reminded me. "Tell me what you know about him."

"He's from Melbourne. Works for Gianni Costa."

"My god!" Jack murmured. "How did you get involved with him?"

"Aunt Ida. She was his pet whore, years ago, and I think still is."

"So Harry King did this to you? Why?"

"He wanted answers I didn't know. Things Aunt Ida probably didn't tell him. He was at the house, had a cop with him, doing what he ordered. He cuffed me, but not tightly enough. I got away, but there was someone else that got me."

Jack had loosely covered me again, and now he moved off to take the billy from the fire and then I heard him rummaging through a cupboard.

"Lucky that someone stuffed my first aid box with stuff," Jack told me as he pulled a stool close to the bed. "I am going to have to do something about the open cuts. The water in Smokey's Dam isn't the cleanest. This will sting."

I only felt the first few, and then the blackness took over again.

When I next woke up, I was warm, and until I moved, nothing hurt. The hut was dimly lit – just one hurricane lamp on Jack's table. I could hear him talking softly, and when the other spoke, I recognised Stan's voice. Their conversation was too quiet to hear and I didn't try. I was just relieved that Jack was giving Stan a hearing. No one had done that when we had all been arrested.

Finally, Jack spoke a little louder. "I am going to have to talk to Vic Maddern, see if he can arrange to take you somewhere, incognito. I think you need to talk to the Organised Crime task force."

"What about Peg? And my mother if she is still okay?"

"Yes, Peg too…"

"I don't want to talk to the police," I said. I was thinking of Jack's uncle, being with Harry King. I thought he'd actually let me go, but then Harry had found me.

Jack seemed to have second thoughts. "If what you said is true, Stan, and King thinks she is dead, she would be safer staying out of sight. However, if she know anything that might help the task force, I need to get her to them."

"No!"

Jack looked over at me. "Peg, do you want King to stay free?"

"I want him dead!"

"I will tell you what, child, I will think on this until morning. Meanwhile, you get what rest you can. I cannot keep you here. Will you trust me?"

I thought on that. He was a judge, sworn to uphold the law…

"Okay, I guess."

I drifted off to sleep again until near morning when a minor disturbance erupted.

Jack can't have slept. He was still sitting in his chair at the table when someone approached and knocked on the door.

"Who is it," Jack called out grumpily.

"It's Mike Scott, and a friend."

Jack stood up, picked up the shot gun again and went to the door. He opened it a fraction, and then wider – letting two people slip inside.

"Who is your friend, Mike?"

The friend answered. "Jack Dawes, Sir. I am a friend of Peg Jessup."

"Jack!" I exclaimed, and two heads turned my way. This was going to be awkward.

The elder Jack sighed, and sent the younger over to me.

"Does anyone else know she is here?" Casey demanded.

"Sir, I didn't know. I just came here to get your help," Mike told him.

"Go on," Casey invited.

"Sir, they think Peg killed her aunt. Maddern and York had me at the station for hours. Grilling me."

"Tell me what you know," Casey insisted.

I shushed my friend Jack Dawes, so that I could listen to what Mike told Jack Casey. I began to shiver. Maddern had told Mike his reasons, and even I had trouble believing my innocence. Mrs Bernstein had reported the screams, and seeing me run off. There was the broken gin bottle, and that had been used to kill her. It had my prints on it. My Aunt's face had been bruised and grazed. Maddern had seen me hit her before, and there was how I had fended off those louts last week. I wanted to be sick.

He finished with, "Jack, she was trying to get her Aunt to leave the house. She wouldn't kill her."

Casey stared at me for a long time and seemed to make a decision.

"No doubt Maddern and York will be up here today. They probably know that Peg often visits. It will be better if they start investigating without her help."

He studied his young namesake. "Young man, I need you to get Peg away from here, so listen carefully. Stan hid a bike near here – use it to go to Benalla – 10 Grosvenor Street. The owner is Nell Bricknell. She's a former nurse and a good friend of mine. I will sketch a rough map for you."

While he did that, both Mike and Jack Dawes glanced at the silent man leaning against one of the walls of the hut, guessing that it was Stan Jessup.

Casey finished his sketch and handed over the paper. "You will have to be careful to draw no attention. Peg had better cover her hair. That two tone look is distinctive. The fading facial bruises are bad enough. Peg, can you move around? You can borrow one of my shirts and a pair of shorts and a beanie."

"Stan, can you bring the bike to the back of the shack?"

"What can I do?" Mike asked.

"Hold up this table cloth so that Peg can get dressed," Casey said. "Do you know the way to the main road from here? Or to the uphill back road?"

"Both."

"Okay, you can direct my namesake to the back road."

Casey went and fetched the promised clothes and tossed them onto the bed. Mike helped Jack Dawes hold up the cloth.

"Are you going to tell the police where she is?" Mike asked.

"Not right away. I want to find out what is what first. There is a lot I know now that I am not going into. Best that you stick to what you know now. But – do not tell anyone that Peg was here. You came asking my help. That's all."

"And I didn't see Stan Jessup?" Mike asked.

"I will be going with him to Maddern anyway, so yes, you can mention that Stan was here. That way, maybe they won't ask about Peg."

Chapter 2

Jack Casey knew that dawn was not far off, and if Mike had come straight up after leaving the police, they would probably be up at first light. As soon as Peg was dressed, he gave her aspirin for any pain, and hurried her out to the bike, where Stan was giving Jack Dawes a brief lesson in riding it. They wouldn't be going very fast at first, both because the track was rough and so the engine noise would not travel very far. Mike set off with them, able to keep up with them on foot.

Once they were gone, he and Stan covered the tracks with dirt and leaves and trampled on them. They had just gone back inside when the sound of a car engine working up the incline, was heard.

"They will have to park five minutes down the track, and walk the rest. Are you ready?"

"Yes, Sir, I am. Thank you for listening to me," Stan told him.

"Thank young Peg. She had already put her opinion in. I really can't fault the family loyalty – even if she isn't a blood relation."

"She's a good kid," Stan agreed.

"Well, don't mention having found her at the waterhole, okay?"

Stan nodded.

Then Casey asked, "Do you know who her parents were?"

"No. Ma told everyone here she was her brother's kid, but I'd never heard her mention any relatives. To Harry King, she made out Peg was hers – but Ma just turned up one day with her, and she had not been pregnant. I resented Peg back then, for all she did for the first few weeks was cry all the time. Ned and Jasper didn't mind, they were younger and liked the idea of a little sister."

The gravel outside crunched under two pairs of feet.

"Ahoy, Jack," Vic Maddern called.

Casey went out. "Vic, Steve, what brings you here so early?"

"Can we come in?" Vic asked, but it was more of an order.

"Of course. I have someone here who I was going to bring to you today."

Maddern walked in and looked around. His face betrayed surprise when he saw Stan Jessup, sitting on the edge of Casey's bed.

While still watching the escapee he had been on the lookout for, he said, "We came to see if you had seen Peg Jessup."

"Or know where she might have gone," Steve York added, also keeping an eye on Stan.

"Peg came here after the court case to tell me of the result," Jack Casey said smoothly. "What's the matter? Wouldn't she be at work at the moment?"

"She didn't turn up to work," Maddern explained. "She also left work early yesterday. Owens said it was something to do with her aunt."

"I see. How is Ida Jessup? Is she alright?"

Maddern looked at Stan as he said, "Ida Jessup was found dead, late last night."

Stan rose, as if the news was a shock. "How? What happened?"

"It looks like murder. Had you been to see her?"

"No," Stan shook his head. "I almost did, a few weeks back. But I figured you'd go there first and I didn't want her in trouble."

"Considerate," York commented. "How long have you been in the district?"

"Not long, Detective York. I was wanting a couple of things and then was going to go interstate. Peg got the things for me."

Maddern frowned, and Stan hurried to say, "Sir, I don't want to get her in trouble. I thought she'd hate me, but she didn't. She said I ought to give myself up and finish my time. Promised to help me get a new start. No one else has cared enough about me to do that."

"When was this?" York asked sharply.

Stan thought back and estimated the date. "I did go off, but I kept thinking on what Peg had said. So, I came back. She'd also said I ought to talk to Mr Casey."

"You are voluntarily turning yourself in, then?" Maddern stated.

"Yes, Sergeant, I am."

Casey spoke up then. "I am going to request that his recapture is kept quiet until I have spoken to the organised crime task force."

"Will you share your reasoning, Jack?"

It was Stan who answered. "Because Gianni Costa is my father, and he was the reason why I escaped."

"Did your sister, Peg I mean, know this?" York asked, and when Stan nodded, he merely shook his head, and began to move around the shack towards Stan. "We will need to hand cuff you."

Stan turned and placed his wrists together.

"Can I catch a ride, Sergeant?" Casey asked. "I am going to be acting as counsel to Mr Jessup."

Chapter 3

Jack Dawes had never ridden a motorbike before and he had only Stan's brief instructions – but he felt the urgency to get Peg away.

While the engine was just idling, he didn't think the sound would carry. In fact, he could hear a car revving up the lower part of the track. He couldn't go any faster, since Mike had to walk, and Peg had decided to do the same for that part of the track. At least he was getting a feel for keeping his balance, and while doing so, had no time to wonder what Peg and Mike were discussing.

Finally, the twisty, winding track emerged onto a graded dirt track that was wide enough for a car. He stopped the bike.

"This is the Upper Candowie fire track," Mike told Jack, and indicated their position on Casey's rough map. "Go to the left, and you will come out onto the main highway beyond Burrabri."

"Right. Peg, are you ready to get on? You had better use the helmet."

"What do you want me to do with the stuff you gave me, Peg?" Mike asked.

"That feels like a lifetime ago. Where is it?"

"Still in my car, and that is back in town. After Maddern had finished with me, I went back to where I am staying, and then snuck out to meet Jack."

"I have two other bags stashed away too. More stuff from Aunt Ida's place, and the bag of spare clothes and cash I'd got ready for my getaway."

"Do you need it?" Mike asked.

"Mainly the money. If I am 'dead', I can't exactly go to the bank, and they will probably stop paying in that allowance anyway."

"I've got money," Jack assured her.

"Yeah, but how long will that last?"

"For a while."

Peg thought for a bit. "Can you meet us at that address, or somewhere part way? And bring the stuff?"

"Ah, there's a roadhouse near Myrtleford, before the turn off to Benalla," Mike recalled.

"Ok, there," Peg decided. "Bring what's in your car. Not that album though. I don't need that. But I'd like the other stuff retrieved, to get the money out of it."

"Why did you take what you did?" Mike asked.

"I thought that if it was whatever Harry King had been sent for, if he couldn't find it, Aunt Ida would be safe."

"What was it?"

"Damned if I know. Might be documents, might be photos. The stupid bitch tried blackmail and way back when, probably took stuff Gianni wanted. And I really can't see why anyone still cares. Still, I don't want to chuck it out, and I don't want to haul it around."

"What about a storage place," Jack suggested. "I know of a couple of places that will store old business documents. They are in Melbourne though, or just out of it."

"You tell me where they are," Mike offered, "and I can put the stuff there and send you the details."

Peg leant from her seat on the bike and gave Mike a hug. "That's thanks for being such a good friend."

Jack held out a hand to Mike. "Thanks, I owe you one."

Mike shrugged. "Be careful, both of you."

Mike half ran, half walked back towards town. He reached the start of the dirt road at the bottom of the hill where he'd left the car. This was one Jack Dawes had borrowed. They'd used it rather than his, because he hadn't wanted the local police to know he'd gone out again after they had let him loose.

Jack had given him the keys to drive, since he knew the local roads, and told him to call his mate to come and get it. Mike, however, decided to drive it back to Melbourne when he went to store the stuff Peg didn't want with her. Then he would catch the train back. He wished he could have slept more, for once he was back at his digs, he'd only had about an hour when Jack called him to say he had arrived in town. He had to have been over the speed limit all the way from Melbourne.

Mike told himself not to speed, he didn't need to be stopped by any of the local cops just now. He went past his lodging house and parked around the corner. Then he used the lane that ran behind the lodging house to get back there. He had the idea to collect a few more things that might be useful for Peg and Jack – spare clothes, a torch and battery radio. Perhaps a few cans from his land lady's pantry. He need something to wrap that photo album in too.

On his way out with his packed bag, Mike remembered that he'd need to let Mrs Brewster know he wouldn't be in for a few days. She would soon hear about Peg, if she hadn't already, so it wouldn't hurt to tell her. He would mention that he'd been trying to help the police last night. She would probably guess that he wouldn't want to face anyone today. He'd give her a call, and then get going to find where she had stowed the packs and get to the roadhouse.

He discovered however, that Maddern had all the police in the district out searching. He couldn't get near either place Peg had mentioned, without attracting attention. As it was, they had already stopped him twice to ask what he was doing. His answer was that he was looking for Peg. Each time, he was told to go home, but he'd promised Peg. Finally, he figured that the best he could do was take what he had, and bring the rest later. So he headed for the highway.

Jack Dawes had to stop at the first petrol station they saw, for the bike was almost out of fuel. Peg almost fell off the bike and only managed to stay upright with him holding her.

"Are you alright?"

Peg tried to make a joke of it. "No. I have never ridden a motor bike before." Her attempt was spoilt by her grimace of pain that wasn't only from sore muscles. "I will take some of the aspirin that Jack Casey gave me."

"It isn't just from the ride!"

"Forget it, Jack. We need to keep moving. You get fuel while I find the ladies room here."

Peg took off the helmet, and made sure her hair was still under the woollen hat.

"Looking like that," Jack commented. "You should go to the gents!"

"No." Peg couldn't control a shudder at the idea. "I won't be long."

Jack found the pump attendant, an old man with a trimmed grey beard, and then had to endure he casual small talk, like, "Where are you off to?"

"Not sure yet?" Jack evaded. "Do you know of any work in the district?"

That got the man talking, instead of asking questions.

"Bit early for fruit picking," he mused aloud. "And most of the planting is done..."

Jack ignored the muttering when a police car pulled in. He had hoped to be long gone before the local cops started a man hunt. The pump stopped and he pulled out his wallet to pay the man – interrupting his talk. "Do you have an air pump? I ought to check the tyres while I am here."

The man spotted the police car and quickly pointed to the pump. It was closer to the toilets and partly obscured by a delivery truck.

"Thanks, mate," he said as he began to wheel the bike that way.

One of the police officers got out to talk to the attendant. The other came in Jack's direction.

"Damn!" Jack cursed under his breath. He shouldn't be scared of cops. Not now. He was straight, and working for his uncle who was a high ranking cop. Not that he was going to mention that!

"G'day," he greeted the policeman. "What's up?" He kept on with checking his tyres after that initial look up.

"Where are you from?" the policeman asked.

"I'm up from Melbourne. Looking for work," Jack said.

"Have you travelled far today?"

"Couple of hours. Stopped at Matlock last night."

"Seen anyone walking or hitch-hiking?"

"Not this morning. Why?"

"We are looking for a runaway. Girl about 18, tallish, has hair that is bleached at the ends."

"Wouldn't have thought that you'd bother if she were 18."

"Matlock CID have questions for her. If you see her, don't approach her. Just call 000 when you can."

"Okay, I'll do that," Jack agreed amiably. He turned his full attention back to the tyre, which had enough pressure. He knew the policeman was watching for a moment, and saw from the corner of his eye that he was moving off towards the toilets. He was glad now that Peg hadn't come out, and hoped she wouldn't yet. He moved around to work on the other tyre, and made sure he could watch the policeman. He groaned when the policeman knocked on the door of the ladies toilet and then went in. He was half rising to go over when the man re-emerged, alone, did a cursory check of the men's toilet, then returned to his car.

Moments later, he saw the door of the ladies toilet opening a crack. He looked fully that way and shook his head. It wasn't safe yet. When the police had finally gone, he went over and knocked on the door.

"How did he not see you?" Jack asked as they walked to the bike.

"Old trick. I stood on the seat and the door was only loosely closed. He just poked the doors to see if any were locked, and maybe checked to see if there were any feet in any of the stalls. I think he was afraid that some woman would find him in there."

Jack laughed. "Stay out of sight. They were looking for you."

"I heard. I think I need to do something about my hair."

"I have an idea about that. I just need to find a shop."

They next stopped by a river, just out of another small town. Jack walked back there and returned with food, bottled drinks, some aspirins, as well as scissors, black hair dye and a newspaper.

He found Peg resting, her back against a tree, while her legs were stretched out on the ground. She had removed the beanie, and the borrowed shirt was open to a point just before indecent. She was in shade, but the day was warming up.

"I'm back," he announced, but he got no reaction. He walked closer. Peg seemed to be asleep.

"I have food, drinks, and some of the stuff Uncle uses to hide grey hair," he chuckled.

Peg groaned, and moved slightly. It was enough to set all her aches and pains off again. The aspirins Jack Casey had given her had long since worn off. Not that they'd done more than take the edge off it.

"What's wrong?"

"You got more of those aspirins?"

"Yes, I'll get you some. How are you feeling?"

"I'll live."

Jack put his bag of purchases down, found the pills and took out one of the drink bottles. Kneeling next to Peg, he carefully prised the cap off. He had the idea of refilling the bottle with water when it was empty, so they had some to take with them.

As Peg swallowed the tablets, Jack noticed something else. "Heck, you've got blood on you."

Peg looked down, not totally surprised. Her lower regions were still sharply painful as a result of Harry King's attentions, and she had been bleeding when Stan had got her to Jack Casey's shack. He'd placed a rolled up pillowcase between her legs, and she'd tried to keep it in place, but his spare shorts were too big, and she'd had to get on and off the bike. At the previous stop, she'd found some toilet paper and added that inside the roll, but she didn't want her Jack to worry.

"Damned rotten time for my period to start," she said to distract him. She hoped it was, since it was actually due in a week's time. In any case, she obviously needed to change what she had on. It must be soaked. "Did Stan leave anything in the saddlebags? I can't exactly go and get what I usually use."

Jack went to look and ended up pulling out a shirt. "Will this do?"

"Yeah. I can stuff some dirt in the sleeve. Can you tear it off?"

"I have scissors," Jack told her.

"Whatever. Can you cut a couple of strips off the bottom too? I will have to tie the other bit on somehow."

"Can't you just hold it in place with your…you know…underwear?"

"Ah, no. I kind of don't have any on."

Jack stared at her, not comprehending.

"That's why Jack Casey leant me some stuff. When Stan found me, I was kinda…" Peg couldn't go on.

It recalled past memories and made her think about what King had done to her after she blacked out.

"Help me up," Peg asked. "I'll go and do what I have to do."

Taking the sleeves and torn strips with her, she went down near the river to find soft dirt to use in the sleeves. Something that should absorb the blood. Since there was no one around, she took out the blood soaked pillowslip and eventually figured out how to keep the new makeshift pad in place. Then, moving carefully, she knelt by the water's edge and rinsed the blood from the shorts. There wasn't that much, and it was fresh, not dried. Once they were back on, she decided to rinse the pillowslip, she might need that later.

Jack was reading the newspaper when she returned, feeling somewhat better once the aspirin had begun to work, While Jack had been away, she'd felt hot and light headed. She had not noticed either when they had been riding along with the wind in their faces.

"Want something to eat?" Jack asked, looking up.

"I don't know. I really don't feel like eating." She went and sat back at the tree.

Jack moved so he could sit next to her. He brought the rest of the bottle of drink. "At least finish this."

Peg reached for it.

"Peg, what happened?"

After taking a long drink, she answered. "What Mike said, that you told him? I knew some things from the aunt. I tried to get her to go away, but the stupid bitch wouldn't. So I made her tell me where anything was they might want. Damn woman, told me there wasn't anything before, but this time – gods! I went off with a pile of stuff, left her packing a case. When I got back from hiding it, Harry King had her tied to a chair, and when I tried to smash a bottle on his head, I was grabbed from behind. King told that guy to tie me up and he put handcuffs on and dumped me on the floor. I managed to crawl away, and the cuffs weren't real tight. I was running off to get to a phone, when something tripped me. I blacked out then."

"But your aunt was alive?"

"Yeah. She helped distract the guys."

Jack closed the paper, so Peg could read the headline. The murder of her aunt was all over the front page.

"Bastards! Blood sucking bloody bastards!" she closed her eyes, feeling tears welling. She had forgotten about what Mike had said when he turned up at Casey's place. Now it came rushing back. She turned away from Jack.

"I know you wouldn't have killed your aunt…"

"I didn't," Peg said, her voice unsteady. "Harry King must have. When Aunt Ida wouldn't tell him what he wanted, and his mate had me, he tried to make me tell him – but I didn't know the answers."

She pushed up the shorts she had on. They were way big on her, and came below her knees. She showed Jack the welts from Harry's belt. "I'm sore all over, but he…didn't stop at hitting me. He…I blacked out and came to with Stan slapping me awake."

"Did King rape you?" Jack demanded.

"Probably. The bastard's done it before – when I was 15. That time my damn aunt let him. Said I would never be any good for anything and I might as well learn a trade."

"You have to go to the police and tell them. I'll call my uncle."

"NO!"

"What? Why? You can't let that guy stay loose!"

"I said, NO! Have you forgotten? The police think I killed my aunt."

"Tell them what happened. They'll know that you didn't do this to yourself."

"NO!"

"Because you are an ex-con? Don't you think they'd believe you?"

"It isn't that. Harry King had someone with him at Aunt Ida's place. Someone I know is a cop. If the Matlock police want me for murder, that guy obviously hasn't said anything about King bashing my aunt. It will be his word against mine."

"You're not thinking straight. Uncle will be discreet and if there is a crooked cop, he can deal with him."

"Jack, it was your uncle that was there. Just watching as King did what he wanted, and roughed up Aunt Ida. He caught me and took orders from King to tie me up. It was just lucky I could get free."

"You have to be wrong. I have been working for Uncle for the last month. I just can't believe he is crooked. He must have tied you loosely so that you could escape."

Peg squashed that idea. It still didn't explain why he was even there. "Didn't help. Did it?"

Jack didn't know what to say – he just stared.

"So he knows that I didn't kill my aunt."

"You might not know all the facts."

"Maybe not, but if King thinks me dead. I would rather it stayed that way."

"Can he be sure?"

"Stan said he pulled me unconscious from Smokey's waterhole. He'd seen King toss me in. Likely he thinks I ended up drowning and sinking."

Jack nearly gagged, but he forced himself to take deep breaths and when he could talk again, he changed the subject.

"The hair dye is a cream, you massage it in. I thought if we both use it, we could pretend to be brothers."

"Fine."

They spoke little. Jack was still unsettled by her accusation of his uncle. He helped her dye her hair and she helped dye his. They took turns rinsing out the excess dye by leaning over the river and pouring water from refilled water bottles.

Before they left, they refilled the water bottles and pressed on the flattened caps to be carefully stowed in the pannier bags.

"Peg, I'm sorry."

"What for?"

"Trying to make you go to the police. It's your choice, even if I can't agree with you about Uncle."

"It's not just my preference to run. I trust Jack Casey – he's been like a father to me – and he decided that I should too."

"Did you tell him what happened?"

"Yes, but not all of it. I blacked out again soon after I got there. He's trusting me, so we'd better get to this friend of his. And Jack, we'll talk more then, okay?"

"Yeah. At least I was able to come and help you."

"And I have never been so glad to see anyone in my life. This is the second time you have helped me out since I was released."

"I guess. Finding you in such a state rattled me. I was half out of my mind when Mike rang me and told me what the police thought."

"Obviously, you didn't tell your Uncle where you were going?"

"He wasn't around, and no, I didn't tell anyone else either. He wouldn't be impressed if he finds out I have run off to help you. I haven't forgotten that threat of having us charged with consorting if I went near you. He'd probably add something about interfering with a minor just to get his point across."

"I will be 18 soon, and then I will be able to do as I please."

"There's still his other threat."

"You see – he's a sod."

Jack didn't want to discuss his uncle any further. "Let's get going. We still have a couple of hours ride to go, and we may have to wait for Mike to meet us."

Chapter 4

Stan Jessup tried not to imagine what would happen to him now that he had given himself up. He had been tarred with the same brush as Mick Devlin – everyone thought he was dangerous. In gaol, the other inmates had kept away from him, knowing that he was mates with Mick, who had soon begun to terrify everyone he met.

In the month he had been free, he had read occasional newspapers, and they had all said, that he was dangerous, and to be avoided. He wasn't like that! He had never used a gun. Never even handled one.

In the past year and a half, he'd had plenty of time to think – too much time. He had got his brothers in trouble, and the kid. She hadn't deserved to be sent to that girl's place. She hadn't deserved what his whore of a mother had done either.

If he could have his life over again, he would kill Harry King as soon as he was strong enough. The man was perverted. He had nearly killed the kid, after torturing her. It had been the sheerest fluke that he had decided to go back just when he had.

The kid had given him a present – forgiveness. He hadn't expected that. And she had helped him – risking her own new freedom to do it. For a kid, her advice so far had been sound. Jack Casey had listened to him and was even going to help him. The two detectives too, were trusting the old man's opinion. He doubted that they would be able to keep his recapture secret though.

He was too full of his own thoughts to notice where the police car was going, and was startled to look out and see that they had stopped at his Ma's place. He hadn't been there very much in the past twelve years.

"Jessup, are you willing to come in and see if you can see anything out of place?" Maddern turned as he spoke.

Stan gulped, knowing that his Ma had died there and they thought the kid had done it.

"I'll try, but I haven't been here much since I walked out, years ago."

Jack Casey helped him from the car, still handcuffed, and they all went in via the back door. York had gone ahead to move the tape meant to keep people out.

Stan stopped in the kitchen, and looked around. Trying to recall his most recent and ill-fated visit. In response to a glance from Maddern, he shrugged. "Furniture and stuff looks the same. Was it like this when you found Ma?"

"Pretty much," York told him. "The fingerprint people have been over everything."

"Find many different prints?" Stan asked.

"Why do you ask?" Maddern asked sharply.

"Ma used to have a lot of male visitors. Wondered if she still did, and if one of them did her in."

Stan caught a brief look passing between the policemen. Good!

York spoke up. "Your sister, Peg, claims she was drinking too much."

"Can't say about that. She liked a nip of gin, but I can't recall her ever being drunk. She did keep a stash of the stuff, along with the odd bottle of the better stuff."

"Where was her stash?" York queried, interested.

"She had a false back in the lowest shelf of the pantry, and another in the laundry behind a bag of rags."

Maddern gave York a signal to go look. He knelt down and checked the pantry first, and stood up shaking his head.

"False back is open. Two bottles are there. That's all."

From his vantage, Stan could see that the lower shelf had been emptied and the stuff shoved onto the next higher one. Well, if they hadn't known of that place, looks like someone beat them to it, since they left the place taped off.

York went out to the laundry next, but came back moments later, pulling some electricians tape from his trousers. "Nothing there either."

"Where else did your mother hide things?" Maddern asked.

"Probably in her room. We kids weren't allowed in there, and once we got tall, she couldn't hide things in the top of the pantry or cupboards."

Maddern moved towards the front room, but Casey caused him to pause by asking York a question. "Where did that tape come from?"

"Must have been on the floor near the laundry cupboard."

"Did you look to see if anything was taped under it?"

York shook his head.

"Later," Maddern decided.

Maddern was watching Stan as they entered the front room, where the drying bloodstains were all too visible on the fading grey carpet, and other places nearby.

Stan closed his eyes and took deep breaths. "Do….do you think the kid did it?"

"It looks that way," Maddern said neutrally.

"You haven't been around. Peg has changed. She is not a mouse anymore. You forget, she's been in Meredan with the Shaw girl. Devlin's girlfriend. She fought off five boys, only last week," York told him.

"That was defending herself…" Stan began, then shut up.

"Look around. Does anything look odd to you?" Maddern changed the subject.

He tried to avoid looking at the floor as he thought back to his last visit – just before Mick had decided to rob that truck. "Furniture looks more knocked around than it was."

"We'll go back to the kitchen," Maddern decided.

Once there, Stan was told to sit at the kitchen table, and York went back out to the laundry.

"I decided to talk to you here, rather than at the station," Maddern revealed. "Are you going to co-operate?"

Stan nodded. Casey added, "Within reason."

"Do you have any idea where Mick Devlin is?" Maddern began.

"I hope you make it known that Stan is co-operating fully with you," Casey inserted before Stan could answer.

Maddern's face hardened, but he nodded.

"He said he was heading for Perth, but I don't know if that is true. Said he would get on a freighter there and go overseas. He was full of stories and I reckon only half were true. I slipped away from him at the border – he probably guessed I would head this way. I'd mentioned it and he called me a fool, but if I wanted to do as he claimed, I'd need a passport and to get one I would need my birth certificate."

"Where was that kept?" York asked.

"Ma had it originally, but I found it and took it. It was in my wardrobe. Peg said she'd found it after some bikies wrecked it."

Seeing the expression on the faces of the two detectives, Stan thought, Damn, I've just got the kid in more trouble.

"You said that Gianni Costa is your father. Do you know who he is?" Maddern demanded.

"Now I do. Then, I had no idea. I was startled to learn that my father wasn't Albert Jessup."

"How did you find out about Costa?"

After a sick sounding laugh, Stan said, "I'd heard the name mentioned inside. Asked Mick who he was and he told me. Then he asked why I needed to know and I told him. He whispered the info around and used it to make the others obey his demands."

"And you? Did you use the knowledge that way?"

Stan gave an involuntary shudder. "No. The more I heard of Costa, the less I wanted to be related to him."

"So why did you escape? What changed?"

Stan found it hard to go on. Casey gave him a nod of encouragement.

"It wasn't my idea. It was Mick's and he can make even an abysmally stupid idea sound reasonable. Word gets around inside…and I heard that Costa didn't want his son in jail, and was going to break him out. Mick wanted out. Anyway, I was cornered by one of the greenies – a first timer. He told me that Costa was proud of his son and wanted him – me – to work for him. So he was going to get me out and protect me."

"You could have told the warden," Maddern suggested.

"Mick warned me not to. Said we should get out ourselves and go to him on our terms and not as people indebted to him."

"Did he say how he would contact him?"

"No. Just that he had contacts."

"We've been trying to find Costa for over 20 years," Maddern said.

"Well, he never showed any interest in me – all these years. The idea that he was pleased that I was a criminal made me ill. I wondered what he wanted me for now that he had a hold over me."

"What indeed," Casey murmured. "Sergeant, all this is interesting, but I am quite concerned about young Peg Jessup. I agree with Stan in thinking that she wouldn't have killed her aunt. I am aware that her aunt was frustrating her, but she did not seem to be mad enough at her to kill her."

"If she is innocent, why doesn't she come to us?" York asked. "Running away makes it seem that she is guilty. She should come and tell us what happened."

Casey kept his face impassive. Stan admired him, but couldn't match his calmness. He didn't need the old man to tell him not to mention seeing and rescuing her. Maddern didn't know King like he did. Better that King thought her dead.

"What if she is in no condition to come to you?" Casey asked.

"There is no sign that she has been hurt," Maddern pointed out. "So if she ran, where do you think she might go?"

"I would hope that she would come to me," Casey began. "However, she knows that I am a judge, and all that means. She does know this part of the hills very well. Perhaps you might check the Lomax place or the section of Tom's Gully where the old mine adits are."

"What about your mine, Jack?" York suggested shrewdly.

"I haven't been down there for several days. She may have thought of that. There are a lot of other mines around."

"Where were you hiding, Jessup?" York asked. "And did Peg know where you were?"

Stan nodded, but only said, "I was around Smokey's waterhole."

"Did you stop there before seeing Jack?"

"No, Sir. Not this time."

"Right! We should be getting back to get back to town," Maddern announced.

Maddern and York hustled Stan from the car to the station, hoping that no one was close enough to recognise him. Inside however, Sergeant Kennedy certainly did.

"Stan Jessup. Well now…"

"Have him taken to one of the cells, Bert," Maddern directed. "And if anyone asks. Jessup is still at large. I will explain later. I'd like this kept to just the four of us, and Judge Casey, for now."

Maddern looked towards Gary Hogan, who nodded that he would. Then he asked, "Bert, can I borrow two of your men to check out some places where Peg Jessup may have gone to hide?"

Kennedy turned to Gary who stood up quickly. "Get Talbot in to help you."

Maddern was about to go upstairs when Kennedy went on, "The local news station has put a broadcast out for us and we have had several calls already."

"Anything likely?" Maddern asked, keeping the conversation cryptic.

Kennedy shook his head. "My guess is that these came from friends of those who came in last week."

"We will go and interview those five again," Maddern decided.

Once Stan had emptied his pockets and removed his belt and shoes, Kennedy escorted him to the cells and removed the handcuffs. York followed, collected his handcuffs and gave Stan a word of thanks.

"I would like to think that Peg is innocent of all this too. We will check out the places suggested."

Casey watched the proceedings and then followed Maddern upstairs. He accepted a seat opposite Maddern.

"What's on your mind Jack?"

"You might also try around the lagoon near the base of the bluff. It is closer to Ida's place and there are some small caves there."

"We will, thanks." Maddern turned his attention to a file on his desk and then used the phone to dial a number. Casey listened as Maddern explained to the officer in charge of the Organised Crime Task Force about Stan Jessup, and requesting confidentiality about his capture until the taskforce could question him about Costa.

Then, he saw Maddern's head nodding as if he agreed with what the other officer suggested.

Casey did not reveal that he knew the personnel who were involved with the task force. He was in fact a consultant for them, although he had been more active earlier in its history.

Maddern replaced the receiver. "They will bring a truck up to get him as soon as they have arranged a secure safe house. What will you be doing?"

"I think that I will stay here and go to town with him."

"What if Peg decides to go to your place?" York asked.

Jack frowned. "You have a point there. When might that truck come for him?"

"It will take several hours to get it here."

"Well, I will head back there and pick up some things and see. Now that you have left, if she has been nearby, she might come."

"I'll send Steve to take you back," Maddern decided.

"Thanks. Just give me a few minutes to go and arrange a bed in town."

Chapter 5

Mike strolled into the road house and glanced around. He spotted Jack, nursing a coffee and reading the afternoon paper. Before joining him, he brought a drink and snack for himself.

When he sat at Jack's table, his first question was, "Where's Peg?"

"Down near the river. She thought it better not to come here. Besides, she feels worse after being on the bike. She's had more aspirin and has found a good place to keep out of sight and try to sleep. Get your car, I'll lead the way."

Mike was not used to driving on unmade roads, and the track Jack took the bike along wasn't even graded. It came out in a little clearing that showed signs of having been used as a campsite before. When they had both stopped, Peg emerged from behind some bushes, and came over.

"How are you?" Mike asked. He had noticed her walking awkwardly. Peg only shrugged.

"Well enough," she finally told him, when she noticed a glance between him and Jack.

Mike quickly said, "I brought the stuff I had in the car, but I couldn't get near the other stuff. The police were everywhere."

Peg shrugged and took the things Mike gave her. The money and the change of clothes would have been useful. She took out the box and letters that she'd snatched from the house aside, but handed the album back as it seemed melted shut. "I can't do anything with that."

"I'm going to get the rest tonight," Mike told her. "When the police go off. When do you expect to get to Benalla? I could bring them to you there."

Jack frowned. "I'm not sure. Was there much police activity on the road to here?"

"Not really. I took the main highway but I did see a police car at the Burrabri turn off."

"They were checking at the Shell servo just past there," Jack said. "That was this morning."

"You both look quite different with black hair," Mike reminded him.

"I know, but I don't think riding the bike is helping Peg. I'm thinking to stay here tonight. It's likely to stay hot, and we can finish getting to Benalla tomorrow."

"Wouldn't Peg be better off with Old Jack's nurse friend?"

"Probably, but she needs a break from the bike."

"So, when and where do you want to meet to get the stuff?"

Jack glanced at Peg, not yet ready to voice what he was thinking. "What say I give you a call when we get to where we are going?"

"Okay. I'll leave then and come to meet you."

Jack gripped Mike's shoulder. "Thanks mate. Can you find the way out?"

Mike nodded and moved to give Peg a quick kiss on the cheek. He felt how hot her skin was and hoped she really was okay. He could tell that she wasn't her usual self.

Jack and Peg watched him turning his car in the small area, and Jack had a few final words before Mike drove off.

"You really should see a doctor," Jack said when the sound of Mike's car had gone.

"No. I'll be right if I can rest for a bit."

After a sleepless night, traipsing through the bush, Mike returned to his car with the second of the packs that he had promised to find. Peg had done a good job of hiding them.

When he had spoken to Jack just before leaving their little camp, he had suggested he'd call in the morning and arrange the meeting. That way, they could look at the stuff privately, and not at the house of Jack Casey's friend. If they had moved from where they were, he'd find out then. Mike privately agreed it would be better.

Meanwhile, he'd keep the partly burnt album hidden, and hide it with whatever else Peg didn't want immediately until he got it to the storage place Jack mentioned.

He slipped into the Church's house without disturbing anyone, and set an alarm to wake him at about his normal time. He had already arranged with Mrs B to have a few days off from the café, but he wanted to get out and get a few things from the shops that his friends might find useful, and be back before Jack called.

Mrs Church was in the kitchen when he got up, so he told her he'd get his own breakfast. She merely nodded. Her pantry had a range of cereals for her guests to help themselves. If they wanted a cooked breakfast, they knew to request it the night before.

Once back from the shops, and in his room, Mike took everything from the paper bag and put it in an old pack of his, then wrapped the album in the paper bag, making a note to ask Mrs Church for some string to tie it. He left it on the chair when he went down for breakfast. Idly, he wondered if he should mention it to Jack Casey. Was it even relevant to anything? Probably he should check with Peg first. He hadn't mentioned it to the police, nor the other things either. All he'd said was that he'd had a really weird call from a friend of Peg's, and that had caused him to go to the Owens' place to pass it along. They'd asked what the message was, and he'd just said about Peg needing to get her aunt away.

Surely that should have given the police the idea of an outside threat, so why did the newspapers keep implying Peg had killed her aunt?

Deciding that he couldn't really eat much, Mike made his breakfast small, and hurried back to his room. He couldn't sit around and spent the next hour either pacing, or staring out the window. He started to grow worried, and decided to check with Mrs Church that he hadn't missed a message.

He entered the sitting room and stopped short at the sight of Jack Casey reading the local paper with a cup of tea beside him.

"Jack! I thought you'd still be in Melbourne."

"I got back quite late," Jack Casey admitted. "I pulled in a few favours and fixed up a proper lawyer for Stan Jessup, though I stayed until the Task Force finished questioning him about his mother. Once they took him off to Pentridge, there wasn't much more I could do."

"Are you going to be staying in town?" Mike asked then, ambivalent about Stan Jessup.

"I thought I might. Have you been in town this morning?"

Mike nodded, scowling. "I had a few things I wanted to get, and went and saw Mrs B for a bit. At least she seems concerned about Peg. Must be the only one."

"What did you hear?"

"A whole lot of ignorant idiots spouting nonsense," Mike blurted, moving further into the room. "I don't know how long after she arrived that you went into town, but as soon as people knew she had, they were blaming her for every little irregularity. They were finally starting to change their minds, when some bastard killed her aunt. Mrs B had the radio news on, and they are making it sound like she's a murderer. Oh, I know it was phrased as 'police are concerned for her safety', but I'd go past people and they'd start making comments to each other – no one believes she's innocent."

"Do you think we did the wrong thing?" Jack Casey asked, looking up at Mike, who shrugged. "What do you think we should have done?"

"Told Maddern. He's s decent guy. Or York! If they saw how she is now, they'd know she didn't do it."

"Take a few moments to think it through," Casey suggested, just as their landlady came through to warn them that lunch would be ready in half an hour.

Disgruntled, Mike stalked from the room, deciding to take a quick shower. He tried to figure out Old Jack's reasoning for suggesting Peg hid and didn't mention the attack she had survived. His mind got stuck on the idea of the bastard walking around, strutting arrogantly, and feeling confident he had framed Peg for murder.

Peg had told Casey who it was. Surely the police would look for him. An image of the man in the phone booth returned to his mind. Peg must have expected someone to be there. Was that King? He still thought the police should look for the guy – but did they even have a picture of him?

It ought to be obvious to anyone with eyes that the beating she'd endured wasn't self-inflicted. Nor the rest of it, but the cuts and bruises would heal and within a couple of weeks the evidence would be erased.

Right now though, she was really hurting, He felt her flinch when all he did was give her a light kiss on the cheek, and her skin was feverish.

He mentioned it to Jack, but he'd said Peg had refused doctors and hospitals.

Mike sighed to himself as he turned off the water. Peg's Jack had agreed with the old man. Maybe he knew more about things than Jack Dawes had told him. He supposed that if King knew Peg was still alive and could identify him, he'd go after her to finish the job.

He mentally wished Peg and Jack the best of luck, and squashed any other wish he'd had. He could judge the depth of the attachment between them by the way Jack had raced up from Melbourne, and Peg's delight in seeing him. He had known, because Peg had said right off, that they could only be friends. Yet she was the only girl he'd met that he was comfortable with.

Dressed in fresh clothes, Mike went back to the sitting room to wait for lunch.

"Any further thoughts?" Jack Casey asked casually. He was being cryptic because his landlady, Mrs Castle, and her husband were both at the table.

"Drat you, Jack. You are probably right as usual."

Jack gave a faint grin. It wasn't that he was amused, but rather that he wanted to mislead his hostess. "I will be heading down to Melbourne tomorrow and I am not sure how long I will be away. If you have time, can I get you to go up and keep an eye on my place? I know that York will be checking to see if Peg goes there, but I have just got those new herbs to grow and they may need watering."

"Surely that girl will be long gone from here," Tom Castle stated. "She'd know you wouldn't be able to hide her."

"What have you been hearing, Tom?" Casey asked mildly.

"The talk in the pub was about how she had beaten those five boys."

Mike wasn't going to add to the gossip. He kept quiet and let Casey tell him that Peg Jessup wasn't dangerous.

It was an uneasy meal though, for Mrs Castle knew he had been taking Peg out.

At the end of the meal, Mike stood and went to his room. He was not surprised when Casey followed, for the Castles had only two spare rooms and the other was next to his.

"Mind if I have a word?" Casey asked as Mike pushed his door open.

"No, come in." Mike guessed that the old man wanted to be sure Peg had got away.

He gestured to the single chair as he closed the door. Then he recalled the grocery bag that was there and trotted to grab it, but Casey was already lifting it. He didn't know how, but the bottom of the bag gave way when he took it, and the scorched album dropped out, filling the room with the smell of burnt synthetics.

"Is that something I should know about?" Jack asked as Mike snatched the album from the floor.

"I…Peg said not to mention it to anyone, just to take it and hide it. That was just before she sent me off to find her aunt. Told me then that I'd better not come back."

"The girl has more intelligence than anyone here would credit her with. Tell me how this was burnt."

"We found it in the kitchen stove. Her aunt must have put it there, expecting it to burn up."

"And what do you think that might mean?"

"It's something she did not want anyone to find."

"Was there anything else?"

"Just a shallow box, and a letter she'd grabbed from under the laundry cupboard."

"Do you have them?"

"No."

Jack's expression suggested that he was waiting for more information.

"I met up with them at Myrtleford, at the road house. Or rather I met Jack. Peg wanted those two things, specifically. She didn't say why."

"Was there anything else?"

"If you mean, from the house? I don't know. I promised to find a pack that she'd hidden near your place with clothes and money in. She said it was for a quick getaway when she turned 18."

"Or…something was going on that she didn't mention," Casey mused. "All she mentioned to me was the expected friction between her new self and her aunt. You met Ida Jessup did you?"

Mike laughed faintly, "Twice, yes. She was a character. One minute she was giving me the Victorian parent act, and the next, insisting that Peg went to the dance with me."

"You will let me look at that album?" Casey asked. "Since we both agree that someone else had to have been at the house."

"Yeah, okay." Mike loosened his grip on the album, and placed it on his bed. His bedside table was too small to open it on.

Casey pulled the chair closer, and firstly examined the cover. Although blackened, there were a few patches where the plastic had only melted. Once, the cover had been pink.

Very carefully, Jack lifted the cover. The inner plastic had softened with the heat and it had stuck to the front. With care, it separated. The photos on the first page were relatively unscathed, as were those further in.

On the first four pages, the photos were of a fashionably dressed young woman, or rather in clothes that were the height of fashion 20 years ago. She was pictured in the city, out riding, in gardens and other places where rich people went. Then, on the following pages, as each were revealed by unsticking the plastic over them, the woman seemed different. Less care free, the eyes dead looking, the smile more wanton. All the woman's original vitality had gone, and her clothing was lacier and suggestive.

"Was that Ida Jessup?" Mike asked, even though he saw no resemblance.

"I don't think so," Casey said absently as he turned over a couple of blank pages. Then he came to where some cut out news articles were preserved.

The faces, the names mentioned and the places meant nothing to Mike, but it only took one glance at Casey's rigid posture and intense concentration, to know that the same was not the case for the old man. He looked more closely at the headlines, and tried to read the articles over Casey's shoulder.

"Heiress missing", "Guitarist arrested", "Lead singer/guitarist of The Roman Candles sentenced for drug possession", were some on the first page. Then, a noticeable change of tone, "Blair Industries new CEO" and "Blair Industries to build new high rise apartments."

His attention was riveted when he read, "Former heiress, marries news photographer, Albert Jessup."

"So that was Adelaide Jessup when she was younger," Mike said, pointing to the picture. "She wore that same dress when I took some groceries home for Peg. And that must be Albert Jessup. He must be tall."

Further articles seemed to be more haphazard. They mentioned robberies, deaths, new building projects, and various prominent people. The photos with these seemed to be of people, taken from a distance – just talking.

The final photos were of various people, clothes disarrayed, close to or kissing women. One showed a man of medium height and European decent, with the girl who had been in the initial images. That man did seem vaguely familiar to Mike, but he couldn't place the resemblance. Then there was another photo of the first girl, taken when she was standing side on to a mirror and looking at herself in it. She might have been admiring how she looked in that particular dress, but her hand was on her belly. This photo was on a page by itself.

A couple of pages further on was an envelope and within it were negatives.

"You know some of those people," Mike commented as Casey looked up.

"Yes." Casey didn't explain. "I will take this to Maddern. I think there is a need to investigate the past of Ida Jessup. Having this will, I hope, help us keep Peg Jessup out of the investigation. Certainly, I would like to see if we can get new prints taken from those negatives."

Mike turned the pages back to the news clip of the Jessup wedding, and tapped the groom's picture. "You know, take the glasses off the groom, and age him 20 years and that could be the bloke I saw in the phone booth yesterday."

"Peg told me that Ida's marriage was a sham, that the groom was actually Harry King dressed up to look like him."

"Huh? So does that mean Ida was married to Jessup, or to King?"

"I doubt that it matters now, but my guess it was probably to mislead everyone into thinking Jessup was still alive."

Mike couldn't make sense of that, beyond the obvious. "So, why must we not mention Harry King? I thought that I had it figured that if he knew Peg was still alive, he'd go after her. Is it more than that?"

Casey met his eyes and nodded.

"Just for now," Casey said after a while. "Peg doesn't deserve to be mixed up in this. However, I think she might know more than she realises – or why would King want to kill her? She could at the very least, testify to what he did to her. She may even have seen King kill her aunt. If so, that is a nasty surprise that I want to keep in reserve. Meanwhile, he might give us a lead to his boss."

Mike went and sat on his bed, sick at the thought of what King might have done to Peg. "He raped her, didn't he?"

Casey nodded. "And beat her quite severely. I think he has underestimated her though. She has always been a tough little thing, and now, she is not so easily dominated."

"I thought she was hurting, and when I gave her a parting hug, she was burning hot," Mike revealed to Casey.

"I'll give Nell a call and check on them," Casey promised.

"Jack thought they might stay where they were and move on sometime today," Mike told him.

"If they haven't arrived, I will try again later."

Next morning, when Mike went, still yawning, into the Castle's kitchen to get breakfast, he saw the worry lines on Jack Casey's face. His own sleep had been poor, and his dreams full of dire things that might have happened. Jack should have called him yesterday.

When he sat at the table, Casey said quietly, "Nell says they haven't arrived yet."

"If Peg was really ill, perhaps they had to stop?"

"I hope that is all it is. She might just have needed to rest for a bit. However, I am going to go back to Melbourne again this morning. If Nell calls, I have asked Mrs Castle to tell you. Will you let me know? I will ring when I have sorted a place to stay."

"Yes, of course," Mike agreed readily. "How will you explain the book to Maddern? You will be telling him?"

When Casey shook his head, he silenced Mike's look of protest by saying, "I spoke to the Organised Crime Taskforce leader, CI Tarrant. He wants me to bring it straight to him, as a matter both of secrecy and urgency. He will determine if the local police need to know anything and if so, what to tell them."

"He will have to tell Maddern, or he will keep thinking that Peg is guilty and ran away."

"Be patient, Mike. Things will work themselves out."

"I hope you are right. I will keep my ears open here for you."

"You're a good lad," Casey said rising.

The breakfast lay heavy in his belly – heavier than the guilt on his mind for keeping secrets from Casey, and even more secrets from the police. He was going to have to keep in mind what he had told who. He had half planned to drive to Melbourne after seeing Jack and Peg with the packs, but unless they called him and told him where they were, he wasn't sure where to go since they hadn't arrived where Casey had sent them.

He was on edge, hoping for a phone call. So, instead of going to his room, he finished the dish washing for his landlady, who had gone off shopping, and began to vacuum the sitting room.

The sudden shrill sound of the phone ringing, made him jump. He glanced at the clock as he ran to the phone. Mr Castle was out the back in his workshop. If the phone rang for too long, he would answer on the extension outside.

"Hello, Castle residence, Mike speaking," he answered formally.

"Mike?"

"Jack! What's going on?"

"I rang to say don't come and see us. Just go and put all the stuff where you said. Peg said to use some of the money in the bag to pay for the storage."

"How's the kid?"

"Okay. I think the fever has finally broken. We had to stop – she couldn't hold on. I had her half in and half out of the river all night to try to cool her down."

"Will you be going on?"

There was a long pause, and Mike heard people talking in the background of where ever Jack was using the phone. "We are not going where we planned. I came into Benalla early – to go to the chemist. The police had road blocks out – even on the back roads. They are after Peg – for murder, and supposedly other things. Peg has no idea of what the other things could be, but they mentioned 'perverting justice', 'receiving' and accessory to fraud."

"Oh, gods! That might be my fault," Mike groaned, and he explained about the album.

"Never mind. The police having that is probably the best compromise. All those other charges might just be a smokescreen – because they want to know what she knows."

Mike considered that, Jack might be right. "Won't you need the money?"

"We'll make do. Peg and I talked things over. We are going to change our names and go interstate. As soon as she is 18, we're getting married. We will need to be careful, because my uncle is sure to decide that I have gone off with her. He might even try to carry out his threat of arresting me for carnal knowledge of a minor, or something."

"What about Jack Casey? Will you tell him what you are doing?"

"No, and we feel bad about that, but with what you said, he would be obliged to turn us over to the task force. Peg is adamant that she doesn't trust my uncle. I still don't agree, but we have to assume he will find things out and he or someone will tell Gianni Costa, who uses Harry King as a hitman."

"How can we keep in touch?" Mike asked.

"For now, I'll try to call you or send you a letter every so often."

"Jack, I've got all the stuff Peg hid. I'm still willing to meet you somewhere. Peg will need more clothes, and she can take the money. What she can't use I will get stored."

There was silence for a few moments. "Okay, you have a point. I'll get to the roadhouse outside Benalla. When? Tonight?"

"Yes. I'll aim to be there just on dusk."

Mike saw how pale Peg was and frowned, but he said nothing. Jack was right. They needed to lose themselves. He had picked Jack up from the petrol station and driven him back to their tiny camp – that was well hidden from the main road and the nearest houses, and right on the river.

Peg greeted him with a grin, but he was sure it was forced. "Let me go through my stuff."

At that, Mike fetched the two bags and the box, a locked steel deed box, from the boot of his car.

While Peg was pulling everything out of the bags, Mike spoke quietly to Jack about what had been going on in Matlock. He watched as Peg pulled a key from somewhere, and tried it in the lock of the deed box. It didn't fit.

Of the other odd stuff, Peg put aside the letters and envelopes she had found, or which had been in Ida's car on her return, but not the shoebox, which looked to have piles of old letters and several diaries. That and an old handbag were shoved back into the bigger of the emptied packs. She pulled money from various outer pockets of the packs, and put the lot of it into a plastic bag that had some items of jewellery in it. She glanced at an old photo, and put that into the small pack followed by a change of clothes.

"I'll keep this stuff," Peg announced. "The rest I don't have time to go through. If I don't want the stuff I kept, I'll send it to you, Mike, and get you to add it to the rest, okay?"

Mike readily agreed. "I'll get going then. I'll head to Melbourne tomorrow. Casey went down there today, so when I get there I'll try to find out from him how things are going with your brother. The old man said the OC Task Force had questioned him about your aunt."

In reality, he was reluctant to leave them, but he couldn't help them further. It was better that he be their eyes and ears in Matlock.

"All the best, you guys," he said as he returned to his car.

Chapter 6

Mike wandered into town and found himself outside the police station. He wanted to stride in and demand to know why they wanted Peg for murder – but he realised that wasn't a good idea. He didn't dare say too much, or he might let slip something more than he'd told them. Surely, he thought to himself, it would be safe enough to ask if they had any news of her.

Sergeant Kennedy greeted him neutrally. "How can I help you today?"

"I just wanted to know if you'd had any news about Peg Jessup."

Kennedy's expression softened. "I haven't heard anything. Sergeant Maddern may have. He's due back soon. Do you want to wait?"

"I might, for a bit. I feel too fidgety with worry to do much."

He wandered back out into the short passage outside of the office. From the seats there, he could watch both the front and back entrances to the station and listen to Kennedy if he took any calls. He tried not to think of anything, just to appear worried. Well, he was worried. Jack had said Peg should be fine now, but what if she wasn't?

He heard the front door rattle and looked up to see two men hurrying in. One had a camera, and the other a notepad. Mike stood quickly and walked to where the toilets were, just down towards the back door. He didn't want to give the reporters any chance to recognise him. He edged back when they confronted Kennedy.

"We're from the North West Journal. Is it true that Peg Jessup is wanted for the murder of her aunt, Ida Jessup?"

Kennedy's voice was lower, but Mike heard, "We need to ask her questions."

Just then, Maddern and York came in the front door. They both saw Mike hovering, but went into the office.

Maddern settled the journalists by saying, "We would like to question her as she was probably the last person to see her aunt alive, except for her killer. We believe that Ida Jessup was involved in some questionable activities and her niece was aware of them."

Mike decided that could be taken both as they thought her guilty, or as a possible second victim. Certainly, if the press printed that, the real murderer would be wanting to be sure Peg was dead.

"Have you heard anything from Peg?" York startled Mike by saying. Somehow he had come around and approached from the back part of the station.

Mike glanced behind him, and merely shook his head. He was still listening to the reporters and their questions.

"You heard?" York asked gently.

Mike nodded and kept listening.

"I'm sorry Mike, but we have been unable to find any evidence that anyone else but Peg and her aunt, was at the house after you left there."

Mike didn't respond to that. He kept looking towards the office where Maddern was saying, "You can print a request for anyone who knew Ida Jessup well, to come and talk to us."

The two journalists left, happy to have been given something to print. Maddern emerged and said to Mike, "If we have any news we will let you know."

"I'll do the same for you, Sergeant. But I never heard Peg say anything about her aunt doing anything illegal."

"No, I expect not," Maddern said with a wry smile. "The Jessups have always covered up for each other."

He nodded, and muttered, "Thanks."

He decided he ought to turn up at work, and do something to take his mind off things. He'd delay going to Melbourne for a couple of days.

The gossiping customers were full of the news of the presumed charges against Peg Jessup. Mike though, was almost sure that no formal charges had been laid. Some of the people hearing the 'news' were shocked. Many were vocal in their relief that she had run off.

The younger patrons, those about Peg's age were snickering. Mike listened to their talk and thought that some of them should not cast aspersions when their own reputations were not so pure.

He was beginning to agree with Peg's opinion of the town. It was a gigantic rut. Peg was better off away from here.

Near lunch time, someone came in with a flyer and pinned it to the business board near the door. He idled that way and saw it contained Peg's image, probably a mugshot with the background blanked out and her normal hair colour touched up to appear bleached. The text was a simple request to let the police know if anyone knew her whereabouts. He decided that the paper was going to 'accidentally' end up in the rubbish bin later in the day. In the meantime, he would observe the reaction of the café patrons who looked at it.

Part way through the afternoon, he saw a tall blond man come in, and seem to catch sight of the flyer. When he continued towards an empty table, he had a smirk on his face.

Mike continued on his way to deliver a tray of tea and cakes to a group of ladies, but watched the newcomer weaving between tables with a lithe grace. He wore a dark jumper, but it was snug enough that it didn't hide the muscles in his arms.

The man chose a table at the back, and gestured for attention as Mike turned to return to the kitchen.

"Coffee. Strong and black," the man drawled.

"Yes, sir. Would you like anything with that? We have a range of home baked cakes and biscuits."

"Just the coffee!"

"Yes, sir." He went over to Mrs Brewster, and gave her the order to prepare. He had the man's features imprinted in his memory and he checked his recollection as he delivered the man's order and passed him the slip of the bill. He received no thanks from the man, who merely reached for the complimentary local paper on the table and began to read.

Mike wondered if his guess was correct and this was the same one that he had seen in the phone booth, and who Peg hadn't said, but she must have thought had called her aunt when she had been there. It just didn't make sense though, for the guy to be hanging around if he had killed Ida Jessup. Or if he had raped Peg…

He considered telling the police of the man, but he had no evidence that he wasn't just someone passing through town. Moreover, the man looked more like a professional soldier, with his solid physique. Mike didn't want to draw especial attention from the man. It didn't stop him covertly observing him, as he glanced around the tables to see if any of the customers wanted him.

The Friday after school crowd should descend soon, Mike wondered if the man would stay and listen to the uncensored conversations.

For a while, Mike was too busy to keep watching the man, but once the initial flurry was over, he saw that the man was still at the far table, seeming to be reading and occasionally sipping from his cup.

"Hey, Mike!"

He turned to the table he was passing. The speaker was one of the girls who were persistent in trying to get him to take her out.

"You ought to consider yourself lucky that the Jessup trash ran off. If you'd got her mad, she might have cut you to pieces. You need to get yourself a proper girlfriend."

He'd heard enough aspersions about Peg, that he had forced his mind to ignore them.

"I heard that she used to be a bit of a mouse before," he said casually. "So had that been the case still, what could you have done for me? Cut me up and eaten the pieces?"

The girl began to laugh, then seemed to sense Mike had meant it as an insult.

"Bastard," she muttered.

That particular epithet was only new in her use of the word, but he replied with the old comeback he had used from a young age.

"I might well be, since I don't have any rich parents, so what does that make you?" He added, "It didn't stop you trying to get in my bed."

The girl turned her head away, but the back of her neck was a bright red. Her two friends, who had also tried their charms on him, simply glared. All three stood abruptly, left enough money for their milkshakes on the table, and stalked out.

Good riddance, Mike thought to himself as he collected the money.

Jack Casey called up from Melbourne that evening, seeking news about Peg. Mike didn't mention Jack Dawes' last conversation, just that he had heard nothing more from Nell Bricknell to say she'd arrived there.

Instead, he mentioned that the man he had seen in the phone booth, was still hanging around Matlock.

"Now, that is very interesting," Casey admitted. "If this is indeed Harry King, it suggests that he hasn't found what he was looking for. I will mention it to the task force."

"I'm thinking of coming down to Melbourne," Mike found himself saying. "I am sick of the way everyone is talking about Peg."

"Well, I am staying with an old friend. I will ask him if he minds another guest."

Mike hadn't expected such an offer. "Thanks Jack. That would be great."

Mike drove down to Melbourne the following day, having arranged a week off with Mrs Brewster. His first stop was one of the storage places he'd been told about. When Peg's stuff was safely stored, he went to the address of Jack Dawes' friend to return the car. From there, he took public transport to the small terrace house in Fitzroy where Jack Casey was staying.

The man who opened the door looked vaguely familiar, but Mike couldn't place him.

He introduced himself nervously. "I'm Mike. A friend of Jack Casey."

"Hi, I'm Ian. Jack told me about you. Another of his strays, he said."

"Yeah, that's what he calls me."

"Come in."

Casey was in the front room, relaxing in an armchair, with his feet on a stool. "So, how are things in Matlock?"

"Poisonous."

Ian inserted, "Do you want a drink? Water, beer, soft drink?"

"Water will be fine, thank you."

Ian went off, and Mike decided to ask, "I saw at a paper stand that they have recaptured Stan Jessup. What's happening with him?"

"He's been held in Pentridge, but will be kept out of contact with the other prisoners. It was the best I could do."

"Did he help the task force at all?"

"I believe he did. He could tell them all he knew of his mother. Nothing that could be used as evidence, but they are now going to investigate her further. I mentioned your theory about Harry King being in Matlock, and that was of great interest. He is some kind of enforcer for Gianni Costa. They have told Vic Maddern to confiscate everything that is not part of the structure of Ida Jessup's house. The stuff will be put in secure storage down here until the forensic team can go over it."

Ian returned with water in a beer glass, and handed it to Mike. "I like to stop in Matlock for a change of pace," he remarked. "Odd that you came to Melbourne for the same reason."

"I'd had enough of snide remarks and knowing looks. I like Peg Jessup and I am sure that she didn't kill her aunt but the majority of people there are perfectly ready to believe it of her. I just wish I knew she was alright."

"Jack tells me she is missing."

Mike glanced at Casey, not sure if the old man had told his friend the full story. He compromised with, "The police are looking for her."

Ian had settled onto the couch, but now he stood up and walked to a side cupboard that had a lot of photos on it.

"I know how that feels," he admitted. "Not knowing what happened to someone you care about."

"Before I took that scorched photo album to the Task Force, I showed it to Ian," Casey said. "I recognised him in one of the photos."

Mike tried to recall, but he hadn't tried to memorise any of the faces.

"I was a guitarist back then...into drink, drugs, and so on," Ian admitted.

"Women?" Mike found himself asking.

"Groupies? Roadies? No. I have only ever loved two women. The first walked out on me. The second, was the one I lost touch with. She was one of the young women in the album."

"Not Ida Jessup?"

"No, but I now realise that my Megan Pearl must have been another like her. She wasn't a whore when I knew her, but then I was set up and the police arrested me. Someone wanted me out of the way. When I got out of prison, Megan was gone and Ida had gone."

Mike fell silent, feeling that he had been too intrusive. Ian was taking a glass from the cupboard and pouring from a bottle of spirits.

"I traced Ida, Adelaide Swan as she was known then, to Matlock, but I didn't speak to her. I sent a man to check her out. As far as he can tell, no one in Matlock ever saw Ida Jessup with a girl like Megan. They would have noted her if they had seen her."

"Ridge Road is quite isolated," Mike suggested. "How long ago was this?"

"Twenty years almost," Ian admitted.

"And Ridge road isn't insulated from nosy neighbours. Ian's man found Elfrida Bernstein an excellent source of information. She has been a busybody since she moved to Matlock."

"Ian, Sir, I am sorry for your loss back then," Mike apologised for bringing it all back.

Ian swallowed his drink in three gulps. "It's okay, lad. It's been a long time, but seeing that album, brought it all back. Have you plans for your time here?"

Mike was startled by the abrupt change of topic. "Ah...not really."

"Perhaps you would like to come to a concert with me? I write articles on up and coming musicians, and singers. I can easily get another comp ticket. Jack is coming."

"I would love to come," Mike decided.

42

Chapter 7

Mike was only waiting for Ian to return, and then he and Jack Casey were heading back to Matlock. That morning Ian had gone to talk to the Organised Crime Task force, who had begun to investigate Ida Jessup. How long they would keep him with their questions was anyone's guess.

To while away the time, Mike had turned on Ian's radio and he was examining all the band posters and photos on display in the spare room of Ian's three bedroom house. The previous night, when he had gone with Ian to the launch of an album by an ultra-popular band, he'd learnt that Ian still played a mean guitar. The best part had been when Ian had asked the band to let him, Mike, sing with them, at the party afterwards.

When the posters lost interest, he went back to the front room and looked amongst the multitude of photographs. Ian had pictures of him with all kinds of important people, even politicians. It seemed that his stint in prison had not made him a pariah.

The cadence of the tune leading up to the news caught Mike's attention and he paused to listen. Stan Jessup's recapture was the first item, but all that was said was that he was being taken to Pentridge. He hadn't expected there to be any mention of the task force investigation, nor in fact to hear Matlock mentioned.

Some news reporter had learnt of Ida Jessup's murder, Peg's disappearance and was speculating. However, the next statement froze him in place.

"Police are going to drag a deep waterhole as they believe that the clothing found nearby belongs to the missing Peg Jessup." Further speculation had it that Peg Jessup had committed suicide.

"Of course she bloody hasn't," Mike exploded aloud, unheard in the otherwise vacant house. Then doubts overcame him. *Had she decided to go back there for some reason?*

"No! She wouldn't. Jack wouldn't let her do anything so stupid. They were going to hide themselves."

King must have taken her there, and she had escaped. And that was why she had no clothes.

How had King known of the waterhole? He wasn't a local and that dam was technically on private property. Maybe, Ida Jessup had mentioned it to him?

Still stunned by the news, Mike was staring at some of Ian's private family photographs, nearly oblivious. He heard the front door opening and closing, and his mind was jarred back to the present. His eyes focussed on one photograph and his mind went into another stunned state.

"Mike?" Casey asked, coming to see what was causing his young friend to be both white and rigid. Robot like, Mike reached to pick up one particular framed photograph, that had central pride of place. "Who are these people?"

"Ian?" Casey summoned, and he gestured towards Mike when his friend entered the room. He took the frame from Mike and repeated the question.

"My ex-wife and her parents," Ian said, needing only a glance. "I don't know why I even kept it. Helena went off and married some jerk with three uni degrees."

He stopped speaking, wondering why Mike was searching his wallet, with hands that were shaking so much that he dropped it.

Cursing, Mike let Ian pick it up, but grabbed it again, and finally found what he had been looking for. It was a folded up photo graph, with folds almost rubbed into holes. He almost tore it as he opened it, so he could hold it wordlessly out for Ian to see.

All his concern for Peg was washed away – this moment was so unexpected. Was his lifelong dream about to come true? Could Ian Sinclair know his parents? Could Ian be his father?

"Where did you get this?" Ian asked, incredulously comparing the faded rubbed photo with the protected one.

"My foster parents got it from the department. It had been with my grandparents' stuff when they died and I became a ward of the state." Mike was staring at Ian, as he handed both pictures to Jack Casey.

"Sit down lad," Jack Casey suggested. He put the photos down and fetched a shot of spirits for his older friend. To Mike he continued, "Your photo is faded, but the house, the style of the clothes on the people are similar. I don't know if we can get your photo touched up and if that would help anyway. This is quite a shock, coming as it did right after having to recall events of twenty years ago. I know you are on your own, Mike, but why don't you tell us of what you know of your child hood?"

"I don't know that I remember all that much. It's more what I was told. I know I was living with my grandparents for a time and they never wanted to talk about my father. If I asked, their faces kind of got tight and they said he wasn't a nice man. Then I'd get a homily on the sins of drinking too much. If I couldn't live with my father, I wanted to be with my mum, but she rarely visited and when she did it was never for long."

Mike found that he was beginning to remember more and more, and only now, as an adult, realising how much of his grandparents strait-laced beliefs had been forced on him.

"They died when I was ten, and at the time, they could not find my mother. I was fostered out to the Scott's and they later adopted me."

"What was your previous name," Ian asked, leaning forward. "Do you remember it?"

"It was Sacco," Mike said.

Ian turned his face away. "After years and years of fruitless searching...."

"Ian? What is it?" Casey asked with concern.

"Helena's maiden name was Sacco."

"Well, why the gloom? I think this calls for a celebration," Casey announced. "Didn't you always say that 21 was your lucky number?"

Ian twisted back to stare at Casey. "What?"

"Well, it's been 21 years, give or take."

"Since my life hit the skids," Ian growled.

"Hardly that," Casey argued. "But I am going to see if I can find anything out. Mike, are your foster parents still around?"

"No, not anymore. Why?"

"Might make things easier. Mike, lad, do you mind staying here another day or two?"

His first reaction was, "No," and then he remembered other things. "Jack, Oh god! Have you heard the news?"

"Heard what?"

Mike told him.

"Drag the waterhole? For Peg's body? I doubt they will find her there. But, yes, I see what you mean. We need to go back."

"Peg? That youngster I met at your place? What happened to her?" Ian demanded. His mind was whirling with too many conflicting concerns.

"Later, Ian. For now, why don't you two get better acquainted? Even if you are not two ends of a broken string, you're definitely compatible. I will just go and set some enquiries in motion."

Chapter 8

At Mildura, Jack Dawes found a bank to get more money from his savings, and decided they would hire an on-site van at the caravan park for two nights. It would give them access to a laundry and decent showers. It would seem like luxury compared to the rough camping they had done over the past week.

"While you wash our things, I'll head into town. I will look to see if I can get a small tent and some cooking things. Maybe a map and some food," Jack told Peg.

"Get a newspaper," Peg suggested. "I intend to get a shower after I do the washing. My hair feels like gummed string."

"You'd better take the cream. You will need to darken it again."

"Yeah. So don't be too long, okay?"

"I'll aim not to be, but I had another thought. Do you think I should try to trade the bike in on a car?"

"Don't you need the rego papers for that?"

"They were in one of the panniers. Bike belonged to a guy called Bluey Adams."

"And how can you claim to be him? I know that Stan found that bike hidden in the bush near Matlock, but if you want my opinion, we'd be better off ditching it."

"Then how would we get around?"

"Dunno, but if you must know, I think that Adams guy is probably dead."

"Shit! You never mentioned that!"

"I can't remember everything at once," Peg said. "And I haven't exactly been thinking straight. Why don't we stay here for a bit and see if we can find work?"

"You? You'd be better off staying out of sight."

"I will call myself Margaret Blair," Peg decided. "Sounds better than Peg Jessup and Peg's a diminutive of Margaret, did you know?"

"I didn't actually, but what made you decide on that name?"

"I think Aunt Ida was using that name for something. I saw it on an envelope."

"Peg…do you think…that if she was using the name…that you ought to? No doubt the police will be investigating her if only to see if she had any enemies."

"Well, I hope they are," Peg said sourly. "But I am not convinced they are. Didn't you say they'd decided I was guilty?"

"All the more reason not to use the name."

"Well then, what about Megan Blair then?"

"Better. Oh, have you forgotten that stuff Mike brought us?"

"Uh! I had. Where is it?"

"On the bike. I'll bring it in."

"Bring everything in, so the bags are empty. If you think you might ditch the bike, we'd best try to clean all fingerprints off it."

"Maybe I should do that first, and leave the bike at the train station or a truck stop. That way, if they connect us to that bike, it will look like we have hitched a ride or got a train somewhere."

"Great idea."

Peg was taking clothes from the dryer when Jack returned from town. He'd already put his shopping in the van, but had the newspaper in his hand.

"I was asking about work in town," Jack greeted Peg, keeping his voice low, since there were two other women in the laundry area, waiting for clothes to either wash, or dry.

"Yeah? Anything?"

"They've got a race meeting here on Friday and they hire a lot of casuals – mainly for cleaning up and stuff."

"I've never been to a horse race," Peg murmured, restraining herself from jumping up and down like a child. "Mr Owens, the guy I worked for, had a horse he was going to race. Why don't we both see if we can work there?"

"That would mean paying for another couple of nights here," Jack reminded her.

"If money's the problem, we'd be getting something for working… please?"

Jack looked at the hopeful look Peg was giving him. He couldn't say no – after all she'd not had a very good trot lately. "Alright, I'll go back into town and put our names down. Want me to carry the bag back for you?"

Once back in the privacy of the van, Jack slipped into the bench seat next to the table and opened the paper. He actually had two – the NE Journal, and the previous days Herald from Melbourne. "Peg, read that!" He pointed to an article in The Herald. He twisted the page around when Peg slipped into the other seat.

After reading for a few moments, Peg blurted, "I knew it! I bet those two bodies they found were the bikers that roughed up Aunt Ida."

"Huh?" Jack queried. It was not the reaction he had expected. "When was that?"

"About when I started working for Mr Owens," Peg told him as she continued to read. "I bet that Bluey Adams is one of them. I think they pissed off Harry King."

"Peg…"

"Megan, remember?"

"Whatever! Where do these bikies come into it?"

Peg looked up. "I guess it can't hurt the stupid bitch now. Aunt Ida was hiding a package of something the weekend of the biker rally. Two bikies tried to steal it. I think King went after them."

"How did you get involved with him anyway? Do you know who he works for?"

"The fat and unlovely Gianni guy."

"Gianni Costa? How on earth…"

"How? Well, Aunt Ida apparently used to be his favourite mistress, years ago. The idea I got from her was that she was still in love with him. I assume he decided to start up with her again. However, I don't think he cared if Harry had his go with her. Ned and Jasper are King's by blows."

"Does Mike Scott know all this?"

"No, I didn't mention any of that. He didn't need to get involved."

"Who does know?"

"About Gianni Costa and Aunt Ida?"

"Yeah."

"Well, I only told Jack Casey just before you arrived. But I reckon the police have the idea. That time I met you in Melbourne, the cops asked me, I assume because my name was Jessup. If I knew a list of people. Gianni Costa and Harry King were two of them, but I only knew of King then."

"Perhaps that's why Uncle didn't want us together. He's working to get enough on Costa for a conviction."

"I have a different view of that," Peg reminded him.

Jack growled. He wasn't going to argue that point. "What kind of work would you do?"

Happy to be distracted, Peg considered. "Mucking out stables? I don't mind that. I might even see my friend the horse."

"Is that a good idea? What if Owens is there? And he sees you?"

"Do I look like I used to?"

"No, but I don't know if people who saw you regularly would still recognise you."

"A point, but I doubt if anyone would expect me to be there. However, I will do anything that's needed, but preferably somewhere where I don't have to deal with millions of people. What about you?"

Jack had been thinking about that. "Might try for something to do with catering. I've washed dishes and waited tables before. Like you though, I'll take on whatever is offered. I can even cook!"

"More than just opening a can and eating stuff cold?" Peg had never seen any hint that he might have such a skill.

"Yeah, I can empty them into saucepans and heat the stuff. I bought soup, baked beans and tinned vegies."

"Sounds like a feast. If we are going to have all that I will need to go for a walk before I try to sleep."

On race day, Jack and Peg presented themselves at the staff gate an hour before the first race. Jack was neatly dressed in black pants and a white shirt, since he'd been okayed by the caterers. He'd also had proof that he was over 18 with his driver's licence.

Peg had no such proof, but looked old enough for cleaning work, and was readily assigned to work in the stables. They thought she was a boy, since she had mumbled her new name and they thought she'd said Martin Blair.

So Jack went off with the caterers, and Peg was directed to a different area. Arriving there, she was immediately put to work, to ensure the watering troughs in each area were full.

Most of the horses had arrived during the morning, particularly those that had races in the morning, or stable mates that did. Horse floats were still arriving, and manoeuvring into their assigned places. She guessed that when the main gates opened, the carpark would fill up - possibly blocking access for the trucks. That wasn't her worry.

Peg concentrated on her work, catching snippets of talk between owners, trainers, lads, jockeys and drivers. The atmosphere was one of excitement and high hopes. This meeting was, apparently, the most important one on the racing calendar for the course.

She had soon learnt her way around, introducing herself as Martin, when challenged or noticed. Whenever someone asked her to help, she was agreeable and conscientious.

The simple fact of being accepted as part of the stable crew, gave her a feeling of personal freedom and she was relishing it.

The smells typical of stables and horses, the sounds of horses stomping, and whinnying was familiar to her now, and she was feasting her eyes on the cream of horseflesh that was all around her. Approaching time for the first race, she took time to watch the runners assembling, and walking around until they were led down to the start.

She didn't get to watch the race, for she was called on to help muck out the stables that some of the runners had used, and to make sure there was water when they returned and had cooled down.

The roar of the crowd as the horses approached the finish was stimulating, and she made sure she was where she could see the first four horses entering the winner's enclosure. She smiled, seeing the owners and trainers strutting proudly.

On her way back, she had to wait for a horse float to back into place. The name on the side meant nothing to her. It was from a stud farm in Shepparton, but horses had come from all around, and even NSW for this meeting. However, two of the men who alighted from the float she did know. Neville Owens and his father didn't look her way, and she ducked out of sight, but still able to see the stomping horse that was being led down the ramp. She sighed unconsciously. The brown horse looked every inch a champion – someone had groomed him well, but there was no mistaking that the horse was the oddly named Black Diamond.

Owens let Neville lead the horse to their assigned place, and he was followed by a small man who Peg guessed was the jockey. Owens then helped a second horse down the ramp – also brown, but with white hocks. Another man led that one off while the truck driver closed the ramp and climbed back in the cab to go off to park the truck. Only then did Owens go off after his horses.

Peg slipped away, but she really did want to watch her friend the horse, in his race.

Jack came looking for her during his first break. His serious expression gave her misgivings. Peg moved out to meet him and asked, "What's up?"

"I've seen my Uncle. Here!"

"Has he seen you?"

"Not sure. But why is he even here? How could he have found me?"

"Maybe he is using cop tricks and found out you used your bank account up here?"

"What if he demands I go back to Melbourne? I can't say no, because you're here. I am meant to be doing work for him."

"Tell him you quit. You're over 21. You have a mind of your own."

"What if he figures that I am here with you?"

"Look, if he thinks you came up from town looking for Peg Jessup, maybe you did, but no one knows where she is. If he gets wind of you being with some female, then I am just a girl you met on the road. At worst, we are sharing expenses."

Jack shuffled his feet and glanced around. "You don't know him like I do. Anyway, how are you doing?"

"Great, and I saw Mr Owens, Neville and Horse."

"What?"

"Oh, they didn't see me, and they won't know me. I am imitating how the other lads move and walk."

"You'd better keep away from them."

"I have no intention of fronting them and saying hello! But can you put a bet on Black Diamond for me? To win?"

"We don't exactly have enough money to just throw away? Do you even know how good the horse is?"

"No, but Horse is a really sweet creature."

"And you're a daft woman!"

"Then you'll do it?"

"I'll put a dollar on him."

"Ten dollars?"

"I will think on it. I have to get back to work, but I am in one of the general race goer food places, and it is near some of the bookies."

Peg watched him go, relieved not to see the hulking figure of Jack's uncle anywhere around. She turned to return to filling water troughs, but a voice called to her.

"Hey, Martin! Give us a hand here, will you?"

Brian, one of the lads she had been talking to, gestured her over. He really only wanted help to finish his cleaning task sooner, but that was fine. The supervisor only yelled if he saw workers idling, and she hadn't tired of hearing Brian's version of what went on during race meetings. "Did you see that last truck come in?"

"Yeah, two brown horses."

"They are from Garamond stables. That's where I usually work. The boss has five runners here today, including those two. One of his horses won the second race."

"Was that Garamond that came in the horse float?" Peg asked, even if she knew it hadn't been.

"No, that was Owens. One of his owners. His Black Diamond is in the second last race. One of the maiden races. It has a good pedigree, but it hasn't won a race yet. It's high strung."

Peg had never heard of a 'maiden race' and had to have it explained.

When she'd finished helping Brian, Peg decided to go find the portable conveniences again, and then find somewhere to cash in one of the food chits they had been given.

The main rush was over for a while, as there was a race about to start. Peg went looking for Jack, and when she spotted him, found a chair at a vacant table. He came over when he spotted her.

"I'm due another break. Want to grab something to eat and wander around?"

"Okay. Do you know when the second last race is?"

"Yeah, about 3.30, but they will call the horses up about ten minutes before that. Are you thinking of watching that race?"

"That's my plan."

"I put a bet on him for you, but do you realise that the horse has been in five races so far, and hasn't done better than third?"

"Well…he's due for a win."

"Well…" Jack copied her tone, "my advice to you is don't take up betting for a career."

Peg chuckled. "What time do you finish?"

Jack shrugged. "They will want me to finish with the clean-up. What say we meet up where the buses go from?"

"Fair enough," Peg agreed, since she didn't know when she'd be finishing either.

Peg would have liked to have visited 'Horse' but she knew Jack was right in warning her to keep away. However, she thought it safe enough to mix with the crowd when the runners for the second last race were called up. There had been some drama in the previous race, one of the jockeys had fallen. Peg guessed it happened every so often, but had simply shrugged to herself, hoped he wasn't too badly hurt and forgotten about it.

However, she realised that behind her in the stable yard there was currently a rather subdued commotion. When she looked, part of the problem was the nervous behaviour of Black Diamond, who was trying to pull away from the lad with the reins. The rest was an urgent discussion between Owens and another well-dressed man. Dragging her eyes from them, she saw Brian looking her way, and seemingly pleading for her to come over to where he was holding Black Diamond. She did, keeping herself from looking at Owens.

"Here, take a hold of this prima donna."

"What's going on?" Peg asked as she went to the far side of 'Horse'.

"Blackie's jockey can't ride. He fell in the last race and the doctor has vetoed more rides. I'm going over. I have my jockey's papers, and this might be my big chance to get a ride."

"Go for it," Peg encouraged, taking the reins firmly and hauling Black Diamond's head down. The horse's state was obvious from the quivering muscles and the wild look in his eye.

"What's gotten into you, horse?" Peg murmured as Brian made his offer to his boss. "I can see you are raring to go and all, but at this rate you'll wear yourself out before you start."

Peg would have sworn that 'horse' recognised her voice. He stopped trying to pull free of her, and turned his big head to sniff her. "Yeah, horse! It's me, but don't you go telling anyone."

Owens came walking around to Peg, seeing only that the strange lad had his horse under control. "Can I get you to hold Black Diamond for me until I get back and then walk him to the starting line?"

"No worries, Sir," Peg said, trying to deepen her voice. Owens merely nodded thanks and went off after Brian.

Peg patted Black Diamond with her free hand. "So, horse, this is your sixth race?"

The horse nuzzled her hair.

"Only got to third, huh? You must not have kept your nose in front." Peg patted the horse's nose as she said it. "The idea, horse, is to have your nose in front at the end, when everyone starts yelling like idiots. It's a great feeling, leading the herd, and you were born to do it."

Bryan came running back, dressed in green and gold silks and carrying a saddle. Horse already had one on, but now Owens was back, beginning to remove it. No time was wasted swapping the one Brian held onto the horse.

The trainer was giving Brian instructions, and then hoisted him into the saddle. Then Garamond spoke. "Come on! This way."

He led the way to where the other runners for the race were circling, and one of the stewards spotted Black Diamond, came over and took the reins and slotted Black Diamond into position.

"Run like the wind, horse," Peg told the creature in parting.

Garamond distracted Peg when she was watching the string of horses going down to the start. "Can I ask you to be available after the race to take Black Diamond back to his stall?"

"I'm hoping he will have to go to the winner's enclosure first. He's a bonza horse."

"Maybe he will. He has settled down much better today."

"Um, Sir? Where will I need to be at the end of the race?"

"Why don't you come with me to the rails to watch the race?"

"I'm meant to be mucking out the stalls and hauling water," Peg explained.

"This is only a short race. It won't take long."

Peg allowed herself to be persuaded, and was relieved that once the race started, the trainer ignored her. When Owens joined the trainer, Peg slouched over the rail, ignoring both of them. From snippets of conversation that she pretended not to hear, she gathered that Garamond didn't expect Black Diamond to win against two other particular horses. But she also got the feeling that Owens really wanted his horse to win. Probably because he needed the prize money.

Once the race was underway, Peg was caught up in the excitement. She could make out the green and gold silks, even when the horses were on the far side of the circuit, and they were near the front. She hoped Black Diamond would still be there when they neared the finish, where she was. Then she couldn't help herself, Black Diamond and another horse were neck and neck, a length in front of the other nearest runners.

"Stick your neck out, horse!" she yelled, even though her words were drowned out by thousands of other yells.

The horses went passed so fast, that she couldn't have said which horse was leading. Nor it seemed could the race caller whose voice was coming over the PA system. The result was going to have to wait for the photo. Peg hurried after Garamond to the winner's enclosure. She wasn't needed there immediately, as stewards were holding the reins of the first three place-getters.

Black Diamond, despite sweating from the effort, still held his head high. By contrast, the horse he had been neck and neck with had his head drooping. It seemed to Peg that 'Horse' knew he had won, and the broadcast result of the photo confirmed it. Black Diamond had beaten the favourite in the feature race of the day.

Garamond thumped Owens on the back and a girl in an elegant white dress and a fancy hat breezed up to them. She only had to open her mouth to speak and Peg recognised her. Cecily Owens wanted to bask in the reflected glory of 'Horse's' win, and Peg moved back behind Garamond to be out of sight. She glanced up at Brian, and gave him a huge grin. The guy positively glowed with exultation. He dismounted and was told to go and weigh in.

After the presentations, Cecily gladly handed the horse's reins to the 'lad' without a look or word. Peg smirked, both amused and glad that her former classmate did not recognise her. Then, with instructions to walk Black Diamond back to his stall, and until he was properly cool, then groom him, Garamond and Owens went off to celebrate.

Peg was just finishing with Black Diamond, when she heard someone walking up behind her. She turned, expecting it to be Brian, but it was Owens. He was taking money from his wallet, and glanced up to see her looking at him. She quickly looked away.

"Martin, is it?" he asked her.

"Yes, sir," she agreed, flashing him a look and then turning away to pat the horse's neck.

"You've done a good job there," Owens told the shy lad in front of him. "I want to give you a bonus, your help was appreciated."

"You don't need to, Sir. I am getting paid to help where needed."

"That may be true, but I saw how Blackie settled as soon as you took over from Brian. I think that made a great deal of difference in how he ran."

"Maybe it was having a different jockey," Peg suggested.

Owens didn't reply and she turned to look at him.

"Let's leave it at that, shall we? You still deserve the bonus."

Owens passed her a fifty dollar note and turned and walked away.

"Damn it, Horse! I think he knows I'm not a boy," Peg said softly. She was sure that Owens knew exactly who she was, but he hadn't challenged her.

Peg pushed the money deep into her pocket. It would certainly come in handy, and anyway, Owens owed her for the few days she had worked before disappearing. She went back to grooming Blackie, using the time to calm herself.

Neville Owens appeared as she was putting the brushes away. "You can nick off now," he told her, taking Blackie's reins.

"Great! That's a bonza horse you have there."

"Today he was," Neville grinned, not recognising her. "Won us twenty grand."

"Was that the amount of the race prize?" Peg asked, although she reckoned he'd had a bet on.

Neville jerked slightly before he said, quickly, "Yes."

Peg figured he was lying, and fast on that idea was who the rest of the 'us' was.

As the day had progressed, the number of horses in the stables decreased. The trainers tended to leave once all their horses had run. For a while, Peg was at a loss what to do. She decided to go and find Jack.

He wasn't where she had found him before, so dared to ask where he'd gone – claiming she was his cousin. The chief of that catering stall looked her up and down and said, "Someone came asking for him, and when I told him he went off to see him. Not ten minutes ago."

"Which way did he go?" Peg asked.

The guy pointed, and Peg looked that way. "You two aren't in trouble are you? The guy looked like a cop."

"Tall guy, buzz cut, dark hair?"

"Sounds right."

"That'd be our uncle. He's not police, but the next best. Ex-army."

"Sounded like your cousin was a crim he'd found."

"Yeah, well, he's like that, and we were meant to be back home a week ago. I guess I had better go find him too and show my nose."

"He headed towards the bookie stands," the guy decided to say.

Peg went that way, but she was on the alert for Jack's uncle. The last race was due to start in fifteen minutes, so the bookies were busy. She moved along the line, seeming to be comparing the odds being offered, but actually looking for Jack. She spotted him, moments before she spotted his uncle, and moved to where Jack would see her when he turned.

Relief was plain on his face. "Here, look after this. I'll just keep a twenty."

"How much is here?"

"Two hundred, we got. The damn horse was at twenty to one odds to win."

"Your uncle is heading this way," Peg warned.

"Go! If I don't get to the gate, I will meet you in town, okay?"

Peg immediately wriggled between groups of people, and moments later, Jack felt the vice-like grip on his shoulder.

"I want a word with you, Jack."

Chapter 9

Peg didn't go back to work, but followed Jack and his uncle at a distance. They went to the management office, probably so Jack could sign off and get his pay. Then they went to the official's carpark, to a white falcon. When it drove off, she went slowly back to the stables. Her mind was furiously active. There was no use being angry at Jack's uncle – that was a waste of time. She needed to consider how things might go.

Jack won't mention me, she was certain. But what would he say about where they had been staying? Did the bastard have ways to find out?

A sardonic voice in Peg's head said, *probably*.

"I need to leave," Peg said aloud to herself. That meant telling the stable manager that she had to go.

"You've been a good worker, Martin. I hope you come and help again."

"Thanks. Sir. I hope so too. Today was exciting. However, my uncle showed up. I have to get back home."

"Well, don't forget to sign out and get your pay."

"No worries there," Peg assured him.

She was going to ask about busses to town, but that would be odd if her relative had met her. So she went back out to where the busses had dropped people in the morning. There was one waiting there, and once she was on, hoped it would be leaving soon.

Back at the caravan park, there was no sign of a white falcon, so she went to their hired van and set to work. First packing all her stuff in a bag, and then starting on putting Jack's in another. Trouble was, there was now more stuff in the van that they'd come with. Jack had bought a small tent. He'd said it would be cosy for two, but she hadn't cared. She liked snuggling close to him when they slept. He hadn't tried to take that intimacy any further, and she was glad.

Peg pulled her mind back to the present, and decided to go out of the park and come back in as if just arriving. She'd ask about a campsite. It should be safe enough as the owners hadn't seen her when she arrived with Jack. Then, if Jack got back, all was well. Well, maybe it would be better to leave Jack's bag, just for now. If his uncle was going to drag him back to Melbourne, he'd have to come here to get it. If it wasn't in the van, it might be odd. That made carrying things easier.

An hour later, she had finally sorted out the tent and got it up, all her gear and the extra stuff Jack had bought were out of sight. From on the blown up airbed, she could peek out the front opening, straight across a section of lawn to the van. If Jack didn't show, she'd have to fetch his bag in the morning. They were meant to be out by ten o'clock.

Peg dozed off, tired out from the day's work, but woke when it was dark, shivering with cold. Before she moved to get out a thicker jumper, she glanced out of the tent.

Stopped outside of the van was a police cruiser, its strobe lights reflecting off the nearby windows. She was in time to see a uniformed policewoman bringing Jack's bag out.

In the night stillness, she heard the woman's partner thanking the manager and requesting that he did not have the van cleaned until given the okay.

"Shit!" Peg swore softly. She realised that she needed to be sure no trace of her remained – fingerprints especially. When things quietened down, she'd use her key to get back in. To occupy her mind until it was safe to move, she concentrated on thinking of everyplace she might have touched, and then rummaged in her pack for something to use to wipe or smear them. She found the torch Mike Scott had given them and mentally thanked him.

She began to wonder what Jack's uncle was doing, and whether he had expected her to be hiding in the van. He might not be sure that she hadn't run off. She doubted that Harry King would boast to him about raping her and killing her.

Jack Dawes was led out of the lock up at Mildura police station and directed to a small interview room. He hadn't been handcuffed, but he didn't have his shoes, either.

"Have you decided to be civil this morning?" his uncle greeted.

"You had no effing right to have me locked up," Jack exploded.

"Why did you run off to Matlock? You are legally obliged to keep away from that Jessup girl."

"As if you give a stuff if anything happened to her! I do! Someone has to."

"You are twenty-four, she is only seventeen."

"So what? We're friends and we have never had sex!"

"Do you know who she really is?"

"She is my friend!"

"Her brother, Stan Jessup, apart from being in prison for his part in a violent armed robbery, is actually the son of Gianni Costa. I know that you know who that is. For all you know, your friend could be his as well."

"Peg isn't anything like Costa, and even if she was his, he hasn't had anything to do with her."

"Irrelevant! You are not to be associating with her."

"Well, you may have no need to worry. No one seems to know where she is. She could be dead for all you care."

"Who were you sleeping with in the van this week?"

"What?"

Chief Inspector Taylor, glared at his nephew, forcing him to speak.

"No one!"

"The park manager said that you arrived on a bike and booked for two people."

Jack suddenly had a way to answer and annoy his uncle. "Are you trying to imply I am queer now?"

The faint frown on his uncle's face told Jack that his answer had indeed been unexpected. The bastard had hoped to trick him.

"What do you mean?"

"What do you? I arrive here with a friend I met in Benalla, and you assume I am fornicating with him."

"Tell me about your friend, then."

"I was asking about work, I met this bloke, Martin Blair. He told me about the race meet here and offered me a lift on his bike. Let me drive it too. I booked the van and offered to let him share it. He stayed there a couple of nights, worked yesterday, and was going to leave from there."

Although the story was fiction, Jack saw the pensive expression on his uncle's face change. It must have fit well enough with the information he'd got from other sources.

"Where was your friend headed?"

Jack shrugged and named the first place he thought of. "Heyworth, I think."

"I'll have him checked out," Taylor said bluntly. "And I am having that van you were in fingerprinted."

"So you are assuming that Martin is a crim, then?" Jack stuck with his story. "And if he is? What then – you stick a false charge of consorting on me?"

"Settle down!"

"Why?"

"Maybe you would like to explain how you knew to make a beeline for Matlock before word of Ida Jessup's murder hit the media."

"No I wouldn't."

"Then you might explain why you did."

"We've been through that."

"And why you walked out of the job I had entrusted you with."

"I quit, alright! I am an adult! I can make up my own mind. And for your information, injunction or no, Peg and I were going to get married as soon as she turned 18."

"She would have to prove her age. Can she do that? Does she have a copy of her birth certificate?"

"No, damn you. I tried to find a record of her birth, but didn't find any mention."

"Probably because her mother, Gianni Costa's mistress, was known as Adelaide Swan."

"Ida Jessup was her aunt!"

"That was probably to appease those rustic gossips in Matlock. Who else could have been her mother?"

"It doesn't matter," Jack insisted. "She was going to get a stat dec signed attesting she was 18."

Taylor didn't betray any reaction to the news that Peg Jessup and his nephew had an unofficial engagement. However, his next comment was less hostile.

"You are mistaken in your belief that I didn't care about Peg Jessup's safety. I asked the Matlock detectives to take a special interest in her. York offered to be a kind of mentor."

"So?"

"So, he is concerned by her disappearance. They found clothes that he recognised as hers near one of the local waterholes. They are afraid she killed her aunt and then drowned herself. They are getting the water hole dredged."

"I read about that, but they found two male bodies, didn't they?"

"True, and they are likely to be the two bikers who went missing a month ago. I heard this morning that they have also found the remains of a woman, believed to be 16-20 years old."

Even though he knew it wasn't Peg, Jack could only stare at his uncle, stunned.

He forced himself to ask, "Was it Peg?"

Taylor shrugged. "The body had been forced deeper by a rock tied to the feet. The fishes in that hole had been eating…"

"No! It can't be her. I won't believe it!"

"I hope it isn't too," Taylor said. "But, either way, it looks like she killed her aunt, and if it isn't her body, then she is on the run."

"No, damn it, I don't believe that."

Jack's anger was apparent and he knew his uncle was trying to provoke him, and play with his head. His uncle wanted to find Peg that was for sure, but why? Ida Jessup's murder wasn't his case.

Peg had said that she knew she wasn't guilty. Her aunt had been alive when she escaped and according to Peg, his uncle knew that because he had been there. There might have been a window of time, his uncle might have left, King, the likely killer, could have finished Ida Jessup.

He doubted that his uncle would be so keen to find Peg if he was sure she was dead. Was Peg right about him? Did he really not know who the murderer was?

"Look, Uncle. If Peg is alive, and on the run, I am going to find her."

"You are a fool, boy. Always have been."

"No one else cares about her! If I find her, I'm going to get her a lawyer."

"You will advise the police, immediately!"

Jack phrased his next comment carefully. "I will tell her to talk to the police, okay? I am sure she's innocent, and we can't get married until this is sorted, okay?"

"I will accept that as a promise. However, if I find out that you have been hiding her, don't expect me to speak for you."

Jack merely glared, keeping his thought of, when have you ever spoken up for me, unspoken.

"Are you finished? Can I go?"

Taylor made a dismissive gesture. "I had your pack collected from the van. Ask the desk sergeant for it."

Jack went and signed to recover his belongings, donned his shoes and strode from the police station without looking back. He debated going back to the van park, unsure if the owners would welcome someone 'known to the police'. Well, he'd have to go and tell them he'd mislaid the key. He could pretend his mate had taken off with it or something.

Since there had been no mention of another pack there, it meant Peg had got her stuff, and she'd have the tent and extra stuff he'd bought. If there had been, his Uncle would have argued his made up story. He'd hoped that Peg would figure out what might happen and get her stuff away, but where would she be? And had she thought of fingerprints? He had played down that threat, but if they found even one of hers, his uncle would come after him again and crucify him.

He suddenly recalled the tent again, and began to smile.

The park manager was frowning when she emerged from the private quarters behind the desk and saw him, but Jack simply smiled at her.

"I just wanted to check if I still owed you anything for the use of the van," he said quietly. "Particularly since I can't find the key amongst my stuff."

"Perhaps the police still have it?" the woman suggested, letting him know she connected him to their visit. Possibly it was a subtle ploy for more information.

"They may have," he admitted. "Though I thought they would have returned it to you. They probably did go through all my nicely cleaned clothes and stuff."

"So what did they want with you?" the woman felt it was safe to ask.

"To ask about the guy I arrived with. We met down south, and he offered me a lift. He seemed okay to me, but I guess it is hard to tell sometimes."

"They had their people check the van for prints," the woman told him. "Left a mess all over it. We can't rent it tonight, since it is still like that."

"Um, I was going to ask if you had a spare van for tonight. I'd be happy to help clean the mess, since I was inadvertently the cause."

"I shouldn't...in that state...but yes, very well. Just for one night?"

"Yes, Mam, I had best be heading back home but it is a bit late today to get started."

"I've only got the spare key, until I get another cut. There will be a ten dollar fee for the lost key."

"That's fine," Jack agreed and finalised the transaction. "I appreciate your kindness."

Jack went directly to the van, with some cleaning materials supplied by the owner. For the next two hours, he made good on his promise. After that, when he had done the best he could, and cleaned anywhere the sooty powder was visible, he was happier. He had seen very few prints and all were smudged.

After returning the cleaning stuff and allowing the owner to check his work, he took a look around the park. He wouldn't put it past his uncle to set someone to watching him. He strolled, somewhat aimlessly, so any watcher might think he was thinking things, but that wasn't true. He was alert for anyone taking an interest in him, and looking to see if he could find the tent he had bought.

He didn't need to go far for that, and as he idled past it, looking away from it, he heard a hissed whisper, "Jack!"

With his hand he made a gesture meaning 'not now', stopped to look at a noisy flock of birds that had just taken wing. When their raucous noise had receded into the distance, he heard, "You're being watched. I'll come to you later."

Jack moved on, going via the men's amenities before returning to the van. If he was being watched, the person might be in a van or tent.

When the sun had set, Jack went for a shower and spent the time wondering how Peg would get into the van unobserved. She had a key, but there were the watchers.

He discovered, when he entered and turned on the light, that she was already there. He made sure the door was locked behind him.

He would have gone at once to the bed where Peg was curled up under a spare blanket, but she said, "Just pretend you are having tea by yourself and then go to bed."

Peg had returned some of the tinned food so he set about preparing to warm some tinned spaghetti and make coffee.

If he sat on the bed and removed his shoes while he was waiting, would not be out of the ordinary, if anyone came up to the van to watch his shadow. He told himself he was being paranoid.

While sitting on the edge of the bed, Jack shared the food with Peg. Neither of them spoke, but Jack let his relief show by gently rubbing her cheek. Later, when he had cleaned the few things they had used, and turned on the small black and white TV, he lay down on the bed next to Peg so that they could cuddle and speak in whispers.

They had a lot to tell each other. Peg began with what she had done before the police visit, her suspicion of people in two campsites, and her utter relief that Jack wasn't being hauled back to Melbourne.

"I missed you last night," Peg finished, as she pulled Jack's arms closer around her. "Why do you think he let you stay here? Do you think he was hedging his bets in case I came to you?"

"You did, you fool," Jack reminded her. "Are you sure, no one saw you?"

"Positive. Now listen, I've got more to tell you," Peg insisted. "While I was waiting for you, I had a look at the stuff that I took from Aunt Ida's house. The stuff Mike brought up."

When Peg fell silent, Jack urged, "What was in it?"

"Well, in one envelope, which had been hidden by itself, was my birth certificate. And I found a second one with other stuff."

"I couldn't find any record of you."

"Shh, you were looking for the wrong name. You were looking for Jessup. However, do you remember I mentioned that I thought Aunt Ida was using a fake ID for something and calling herself Margaret Blair?"

Jack nodded, and Peg felt rather than saw it.

"She was. Margaret Blair was my real mother. And Aunt Ida had her birth certificate too."

"Huh?"

"Shhh! There was also a document, something called a power of attorney. It authorised my aunt, known then as Adelaide Swan, to act on her behalf, and if she died, to be executor of her will."

"Did you see a will?"

"No, but I got from the envelope it was in, the name and address of the solicitor. He's in Burrabri. He has the actual will, I think. I am going to have to find a way to see him. However, if he is the guy I think, he took off because someone was asking about him."

"You're not going back there…"

"No, I will ring and suggest another place."

"What about your Aunt's will?"

"I have a copy of that too, but that is problematical. She appointed me her executor, and had me sign one of those POA documents. I can't exactly do anything there, can I?"

"Why don't you just walk away from it all?" Jack suggested.

"Because aspects of this are nagging me. Aunt Ida finally admitted that

I wasn't a blood relative and now I have seen my birth certificate, which doesn't name my father, I want to know what happened to my mother. She must have died about when I was born."

"It's past! What imperative reason is there to dig it all up?"

"Because, I think my mother had something that Gianni Costa wants very much. I think, that she gave it to Aunt Ida before she died. And I think my aunt knew how she died. Was maybe even involved. She had some cases under the house for years, before bringing them inside while I was away. She admitted they weren't hers, but belonged to a friend who had gone away. I looked in the case when she wasn't around. It was full of frilly clothes and a few trinkets and a photo…"

"Ah, Peg," Jack interrupted, "I may know what happened to that woman."

"What's that?"

"Something my uncle said. They were dredging that waterhole, remember? Well they found the remains of a young woman there too. Which made me think the body had been there a long while. I don't think he knows more than that, or wasn't telling, but he wanted me to think it was you."

"SOD," Peg muttered before she went silent.

"Look, Peg. I think we need to get away from here. Wait a while before seeing if you can find that solicitor. See what the police dig up."

"Yeah," Peg agreed, more readily than Jack had expected. "And I had better see what else my aunt had, but that is with the stuff Mike took to Melbourne, and I am not going there either."

Jack hugged her tighter in agreement. "Where will we go?"

"Do you have any preferences?"

"Only somewhere with you. Do you still want to marry me?"

"Yes! Yes!" Peg wriggled around in the confined space on the bed and faced Jack. In moments she was kissing him, and he was all too happy to keep it up.

They finally moved slightly apart.

"You are my best friend, Jack. I can't think of anyone else I want to spend the rest of my life with."

"What about Mike?"

"He's sweet, but he isn't you."

"You going to stay all night?"

"Better not, although I want to. And tomorrow, I think we need to leave separately and meet up out of town somewhere."

"North or south," Jack asked, having the idea Peg had a destination in mind.

"North. I want to go to Tamworth. They had a music festival up there this year, and will be having another in January. I want to go and see if I can take part. I probably won't win any of the comps, but…"

"Maybe you will," Jack finished for her. "Okay, let's do it."

Chapter 10

York sat at his desk and reported, "No. The bikie group had taken off as soon as the local police left. All they gave them was confirmation of when the two bikers went missing and who they were. I put a request through to see if they had their bikes registered. How about here?"

"Nothing new. The divers did find a large boulder about 20 feet down, and some chain but we probably won't get anything useful from it. The police divers and the dredge master don't think there is anything else in there to find."

"Well, if Peg Jessup's body isn't in there, she must still be alive?" Steve York wanted to believe that.

"We can hope so," Maddern agreed, "But there was a lot of blood at the scene. The pathologist and the forensic team believe that victim there was beaten, possibly also slashed. The blood type does match Peg Jessup's. So if she was alive, and able to get free, she might have stumbled into the bush."

"Have searchers found any indication of that?" York asked. He had been away almost a week trying to locate the bike gang.

Now Maddern growled. "It's been a damn circus. Once the press announced that we were dredging the water hole, we've had a horde of people tramping around. A lot were locals, but quite a few were from the papers. The area has been well trampled."

The phone on York's desk rang and he answered it. He spoke in monosyllables as he jotted information down, then thanked the caller before hanging up.

"That was vehicle registrations calling back. The two dead bikers hadn't renewed their bike registrations for some years. They checked older records and came up with a few licence numbers for each. I can crosscheck against the registrations we got from them all when they were here."

"Put a call out for each of the registrations," Maddern suggested.

"I did that, and we've had a bit of luck already. The police at Mildura had been asking about one of those registrations. A bike was reported dumped or abandoned at the railway station."

Maddern twisted to stare at his colleague. "When was it noticed?"

"Yesterday."

"That's interesting," Maddern noted, and he considered things for a while. "Stan Jessup mentioned two bikes hidden at Smokey's waterhole. He rode one away when he left here the first time, and maybe he rode it back here. He didn't say where he left it, but it wouldn't have been this past week. We didn't find the other one."

"I wonder if Jessup rode one back here, but someone else left on it, and that's the bike found in Mildura. Or that bike is the second one?" Then York had an idea. "Maybe while they are here, we should get the dredge and divers to check Smokey's."

"Are you expecting to find more bodies there?"

"I hate to think. I was considering that the second bike might have been sunk there."

"The media are beginning to suggest we have a serial killer in the district," Maddern said. "So far they haven't printed such nonsense. I pointed out that the two bikers were connected, but a young woman, twenty years ago, is unlikely to be related."

"They might be if they all got in the killer's way," York suggested. "Though it just occurred to me that if the killer had a reason to move that bike, and heard something to cause that action, he could still be watching around here."

"And be the killer of Ida Jessup?" Maddern suggested, to York.

"Peg, couldn't have killed the bikers, nor the woman. And if we consider her the owner of the blood, there had to have been someone else in the picture."

"I don't disagree, Steve. But we still need to talk to her, if she is alive. It is quite likely she knows more than we do about her aunt's life and her murder."

"Any more reported sightings?" York asked.

"Nothing credible. I am considering putting a piece in the paper – with a call to Peg to come and talk to us or at least, call us. And I think we need to alert the police in other states to look out for her."

"You look like the cat that found the cream," Steve York remarked when he met Mike Scott in the café.

Mike, who didn't realise he had a wide grin on his face, finished re-setting a table as he asked, "Are you here for the coffees?"

"Yes, and two extras. We have visitors from Melbourne."

"I'll go see if they are ready," Mike offered. He returned quickly. "Five minutes, Detective."

"So, what has got you so happy? Heard from Peg?" York asked.

Mike shook his head, and his expression sobered just a bit. "No, but I am glad you no longer seem to think she is a killer."

"You've been listening to the town gossip?" York asked, neither denying nor confirming what he believed about Peg Jessup.

"Occupational hazard, working here. The rotten part is the number of people relishing the idea that Peg might still be in the waterhole, or dumped in the bush. Is it true that the blood you found there matches her type?"

York nodded. "So, where have you been these past few days?"

"Down in Melbourne. I just had to get away from the poisonous tongues. I met up with Jack Casey, and stayed with him at the home of a friend of his."

"It must have been a good break."

Mike knew what York was getting at. "It was! I finally met up with my father!" his grin was back at its widest. He told York about the amazing fluke.

"Good for you," York said with genuine delight. "I'm surprised that you didn't decide to stay in Melbourne."

"Ian and I will be keeping in touch, but he has his life and…I wanted to come back here in case Peg did."

Mrs Brewster brought out a tray with holes for six cups of coffee, and also a bag of freshly baked biscuits. "Here you are Detective York. I've put the bill on the station account."

"Thanks, Mrs B," York said as he took the tray.

"Mike, help him with the bag," Mrs Brewster suggested.

Mike returned to find his employer still looking from the door and watching the police car disappearing down the street.

"Nasty business," she commented, talkative now as the café was empty. "Three bodies were found in that waterhole."

"But not Peg," Mike said, to see how she would answer.

"I pray she got away," was her admission. "Not that I intend to say so to any more reporters who turn up. Vultures. And they are starting rumours that we have a serial killer around here. It's bad enough that there have been a lot of break-ins around here in the past week."

"Not here?" Mike was concerned. He'd not heard this news as it hadn't reached the Melbourne papers.

"No, not here. The post Office, the solicitors – both of them. They tried to break into the bank, but they failed there. The sooner this business with dredging places finishes, the better."

"For sure," Mike agreed, "I wonder what the thief, or thieves were after at those places. I doubt it was money."

"Could have been," Mrs Brewster decided. "Or why target the bank? Anyway, what I've heard…well, let's say that the people who don't think your Peg is dead, are saying that she is doing the breaking and entering. I don't understand how otherwise sane and intelligent people can parrot that drivel."

"Yeah." Mike agreed whole heartedly. "Do you need anything from the grocers? I might as well go before we get busy again."

An hour later, York came back and Mike was surprised when he was asked to come back to the station. He didn't have a guilty conscience, so he told Mrs B, and went out with the detective. The few customers in the café then, stared after him – wondering what he had done, or the police thought he had done.

During the short ride to the police station, Mike asked, "What's up?"

York only said, "We'll explain when we're there."

Mike controlled his curiosity and the niggle of worry. Surely they didn't know he'd taken some stuff to Melbourne for Peg? Or helped her to get away?

Up in the detective office, Maddern introduced Mike to two Melbourne detectives, and sat back to let them begin. York found another chair for Mike to sit on.

"I understand that you know Jack Casey," one of the detectives began. He was Nolan

"Yes, Sir." Mike settled onto his seat.

"Are you aware that he has been liaising with us on the Organised Crime task Force?"

"Yes, both he, and his friend Ian…"

"Right! Well, Jack mentioned to us about a man you had seen here, who has become a person of interest to us."

Mike was only too pleased to tell all he could about the man he was convinced was the Harry King that Peg had mentioned. He even referred to the album that Peg had rescued from the kitchen fire. The second detective, was, he then discovered, a sketch artist. Mike worked with him for a short time to help build a likeness of the man.

The mention of the album led to questions of what he thought of Peg's behaviour the last time he had seen her, and also what he knew of Ida Jessup.

That hadn't been much, and he was startled when he was asked, "Do you think Peg Jessup knew her aunt was mixed up in something illegal?"

Mike considered what he recalled of that horrid day before answering. "I don't know why Peg wanted to get her aunt away. I got the impression she expected someone to be coming after them. When we got to the house and her aunt wasn't there, she sent me to find her."

"Did you?"

"Yes, I found her coming out of the post office."

"How did she react to your message?"

"Asked me what the little bitch was up to now."

"Did she seem worried?"

"I couldn't really say."

"What about Peg Jessup?"

"I think she was concerned for her aunt."

"And herself?"

"Indirectly, I guess. She had to live with her aunt until she was 18. She didn't want to go back to Meredan. That was why she was trying to keep her aunt off the gin."

"You went to where Peg worked and she came back to the house with you. What did you tell her?"

That was one question Maddern and York had asked him that he hadn't answered fully. He decided he should say more.

"I had a call from a friend of Peg's in Melbourne. He uses me as a go-between because his uncle has warned him off Peg. His Uncle is CI Taylor. He overheard him saying something had been traced to Ida Jessup in Matlock. Dividends or something. Jack wanted me to tell Peg, so I did."

The two Melbourne detectives glanced at each other.

Mike decided to test a guess he'd had by asking, "Seems that someone wanted something from her." He wanted to suggest that someone had been the killer.

"The question is, did they get it?" Nolan commented.

"I don't think so," Mike blurted. "I heard someone has been breaking into places around here. The Post Office, the solicitors and other places. Unless that was just gossip."

Maddern confirmed, "No, there have been break-ins."

There was not much else he could tell the Melbourne detectives, or more correctly, was going to tell them. He was not going to mention that he knew Peg was alive. He had promised Jack Casey that much, and Casey knew these men.

"A final question," Nolan said after thinking for a time. "Did Peg tell you that she wasn't related to Ida Jessup?"

"She isn't?" Mike asked, suddenly interested. "I know she wondered. Her friend in Melbourne had tried to find her birth entry to get a certificate for her, and he couldn't find anything."

"Neither could we," Nolan admitted. "Which raises the question of where Ida Jessup found her."

"It does," Mike agreed. "I spent a few years trying to trace my own father. My mother didn't put his name on the birth record. I only just met him a few days ago. And you might know him. Ian Sinclair. A friend of Jack Casey."

Chapter 11

Peg stopped the trolley outside the door of room 30, straightened her uniform and then knocked on the door.

"Room service," she called and waited for a response.

Further down the passage, she was aware of Jack up a ladder pretending to check a light bulb. She didn't glance his way. He wasn't happy about her going to see the man who had requested her, known at the hotel as Megan Dawes, by name.

She was pretty sure that it had to be the solicitor from Burrabri that Ida Jessup had been seeing, but she had never met him. Her only contact had been the one letter she had received in reply to her own, sent when she and Jack had settled into working.

The door opened, and the grey haired man gave her a head to toe glance before saying, "Thank you. Are you able to set things up? I am expecting a lady friend for lunch."

"No, trouble, Sir," Peg agreed. "It won't take me long to do that."

The door was opened wider and Peg wheeled the room service trolley inside and heard the door shut behind her.

"You don't look like your mother," the man said as she stopped the trolley by the table near the window.

Peg hadn't expected that comment, and did a quick rethink of her approach. "I believe that I take more after my father, but I never met him so I can't say. Are you Mr Stanton?"

He nodded, but Peg asked, "You have some ID then?"

With a faint smile he produced his driver's licence. She looked closely at it and memorised his home address in Malvern, Victoria and handed it back. The check had been Jack's idea.

"And I believe you do as well?" Stanton counter-commented.

In turn, Peg removed a bundle of papers from her slacks pocket. She had copies of her birth certificate, her mother's birth certificate and her marriage certificate. These were scrutinised by Stanton before he passed them back to her.

75

"No driver's licence?" Stanton queried carefully.

"Not yet. I only turned 18 a month ago."

"Is your mother here with you?"

"No. She isn't."

"I am sorry that she couldn't make the trip," he said quietly. "However, she told me that once you were 18, I could deal with you directly. Has she told you anything?"

"Not much. All I really understood was that she had stocks or shares that she was handing on to me when I was 18."

Peg was busy preparing the table as he went on.

"That is true. She has had me dealing with them for almost twenty years. The dividends have been accumulating in an account. I have all the records with me, and I will be giving them to you." He walked over to a side bench and opened his brief case. "Everything is up to date, so whoever you choose to take over your portfolio has all the information needed."

"I understand from your letter, that you are retiring," Peg commented. "Am I also right in inferring that you have been approached about these shares?"

Stanton didn't reply at once, just frowned slightly before saying, "You will need to ask your mother for the details, but it was my understanding that these shares were gifted to her before her father disinherited her. I sensed that the enmity still existed and that was why I was instructed not to deal directly with Blair Holdings in relation to them."

Peg nodded, this was new to her, but she wouldn't be able to ask her mother, or her aunt, for more information. "Was it a representative from Blair Holdings that approached you?"

"That was what I was to understand, but as instructed, I proclaimed ignorance of any such shares. Since then, I believe that I have been followed. My Burrabri office was broken into, but I had already ended the lease there."

"So…should I assume that person who spoke to you wanted the shares? To buy them?"

"Wanted them, yes. He claimed that they had been stolen and demanded the name and address of my client. Naturally, I had no authority to give them those details."

Peg had finished setting up and needed to leave.

"Is there anything really vital that I need to know? I have to get back to work."

"It's all in the folder."

"I can't take that right now. I have no way to disguise it," Peg pointed out, and saw Stanton jerk slightly. "When you've finished, I will come and get the trolley…"

"You need to take it as soon as you can."

"Why? Do you think you were followed here?"

He shrugged.

"I can have my husband, Jack Dawes come and get it. Is there something worrying you?"

Stanton's frown became more pronounced. "I have heard that Costigan Consolidated is working to take over Blair Holdings. The latter need to have control of your shares to have a hope of holding them off. You will need to decide which side you want to be on. Costigan Consolidated are offering a price that is well above the current market value of the shares. If they win the takeover, those shares may become devalued. They could pay you out at whatever negligible rate they chose. On the other hand, Blair Holdings will be holding a shareholder's meeting in the first week of February. If you choose that side, you need to reply two weeks before, either granting them your proxy vote or stating that you will attend. The forms are in the folder."

"I will think on what you said. Can I contact you if I need to?"

"No. Once you have the folder, I am finished with the account."

"Okay. Do we owe you anything?"

"No, your mother attended to that."

"I will see you later then." Peg was happy to accept his assurance of no fee to pay him.

"I will say, that I am glad to have finally met you, Miss Blair. Sorry, Mrs Dawes."

Peg felt herself blushing. She was finding it strange to be called by her new surname, almost as much as being called Megan. She nodded and quickly let herself out.

Out in the passage, Peg walked briskly back the way she had come. She glanced at the man on the ladder, as if she were only checking the way was safe. Jack had moved two lights closer to Room 30 during her talk with Stanton.

Jack Dawes, for his part, merely grinned down, as if seeing only an attractive maid, and then went back to replacing the shade on the light he was working on. Only he would have heard Peg say, "Can you go in and get the folder?"

He glanced in the direction of Stanton's room, and in that instant a man in a brown suit came into the passage, and approached at a stroll. He decided that the suit was the same colour as that of whoever it was that had been loitering around the corner in a side passage just down from Room 30 when Peg had arrived. So he descended the ladder, with his borrowed work bag slung over one shoulder. He gave the man a casual, "Good day, and got a good look at the man's face before moving the ladder along to the next light – the one that just happened to be right outside room 30.

He began the same routine with the next light, placing his ladder under it. The man had gone from sight, but Jack wanted to be sure he wasn't loitering around the corner. He contrived then, to have a roll of electrical tape, roll off along the narrow section of polished wood between the carpet and the wall. He cursed, and after a slight delay, trotted after the tape. He caught up to it as it bounced off the wall where the passage made a t-junction. He looked both ways; brown suit was not in sight. Just because he was being paranoid, he went to the other end of the passage and checked there as well. He returned to near his ladder, and knocked on the door of room 30, adding, "Room service."

Jack kept back so that Stanton could see him through the peep hole. He wondered if the man would open the door. After a while, he heard the bolt slide in the safety chain and the door opened an inch.

"What is it?"

"Megan sent me. I am Jack Dawes."

"You have identification?"

Jack slipped his driver's licence and a photocopy of their marriage certificate through the gap. Stanton examined them and undid the safety chain.

"Come in. Wait by the door."

Jack obeyed, watching Stanton go to his briefcase and remove a file. He walked briskly back.

"Megan said she would get it later."

"I was watching outside in the passage. I think there is a man in a brown suit interested in you. It seems to me, better for you, to pass it on sooner rather than later."

Stanton's face paled. "Yes. I agree."

Jack took the file, pushed it carefully into his borrowed work bag and with a nod, slipped back out the door – relieved to see that the passage was empty. Still, he didn't leave immediately. He finished 'fixing' the dead bulb before closing the step ladder and heading back to where he had borrowed his gear from.

Jack found Peg in the kitchen washing dishes and sidled up next to the sink.

"Are you here to help?" Peg asked him with a grin.

"Nah! What time do you finish?"

"Another hour."

"Want to go shopping? I still have to get you a birthday present."

"Yeah? So what else is new?"

Peg's boss moved away with a faint smile on her face. All the staff knew she was a newlywed and had been teasing her.

Jack spoke in a lower voice, "The file is in the hotel safe. I reckon Stanton is going to flit – if he hasn't already. There was a man watching his room and I told him that. I think the man heard what Stanton asked you before you went in. He is seated in the lobby watching the door. I assume it is for Stanton's lady friend."

"You are probably right." Peg bit her lip. "He told me he had been approached by someone from Blair Holdings, but that he had heard that Costigan Consolidated were trying to take them over. He didn't explain much, but I assume the shares are in my real mother's family company. Having said that though, I know Gianni Costa wants them badly. I wish I knew more and what connection if any that he has to the other company."

"And who that man is really looking for – and working for," Jack added. "I will see what I can find out about both companies."

"I've heard the name Costigan in the news," Peg mused.

"There's a Reg Costigan who drives V8s," Jack told her. "Youngish bloke in his early thirties."

Peg shrugged. "Let's discuss this later, huh? Stanton said a few other things that got me thinking. I can do that while I am mindlessly washing dishes."

"If you get sent back for the trolley, be careful, okay?"

"I will. Where will you be?"

"Keeping an eye on brown suit."

Peg was not really expecting to be asked to collect the trolley from room 30, since she agreed with Jack's appraisal that the man wouldn't stick around now that she had the file. Perhaps though, he wanted to be sure Jack had given it to her.

"Don't people usually just dump the trolley in the passage?"

Her boss shrugged. "Some do, some don't. Off you go."

While removing her coverall apron, Peg wondered if she had time to go via the lobby to see Jack. She felt a slight tinge of apprehension. Then she decided, if brown suit had come up, Jack would be nearby anyway. It didn't stop her keeping aware of her surroundings. No one seemed to be paying her any attention.

"Room Service! I've come to collect the trolley."

The door opened abruptly, but the man facing her was not Stanton. She repeated her reason for coming and the man gestured her in. Once beyond the door, her mouth dropped open. The room was a mess – bed stripped untidily, cupboards and drawers open, spare blankets in a heap on the floor, the lunch trolley overturned, and the stuff from the table on the floor.

"What happened here?" Peg asked, relieved that there was no sign of blood or a body.

"That is what we are trying to determine," a second man said. He had just emerged from the bedroom, and came over to show him his ID. "Pearson, Hotel Security. I understand that you bought up the trolley."

"Yes, Sir, I did. Seemed that he asked for me. Knew my mother or something, and wanted to catch up with her."

"Did you know the man? Stanton?"

"Never met him before," Peg said with perfect honesty.

"What time was it when you bought the trolley up?"

"I was up here just before half past one."

"And all was fine?" Pearson probed.

"Of course. If I had seen a mess, I'd have reported it."

"Naturally. Perhaps you could look around and see if anything is missing."

Peg took a more careful look. "I didn't really notice too much, since we are not meant to seem nosy, but I saw some kind of brief case next to his suit case."

The clothes from the case were also on the floor.

"Anything else?"

"No, I mean, not that I can tell. Except for the bloke, obviously."

"Did you notice anyone hanging around the passage?"

Peg decided it would be better if she mentioned Jack. "Just Jack." Just by recalling her first few days of being married, she felt her face grow hot. "He was fixing some lights on this floor."

"Jack?" Pearson queried.

"Jack Dawes, Sir. Um, he's my mate. We've only been married a couple of weeks." Let him think she didn't have any attention for anything else. Pearson nodded.

"I don't think that there is anything else, unless he mentioned anything that might be relevant?"

With a glance down at the floor, Peg pretended to be thinking. "Well, he asked me to fix up the table, since he was expecting a lady friend for lunch."

"Did he ask you about your mother?"

"Yes, but I had to tell him that she wasn't around anymore. She died a while back – pneumonia. He said he was sorry to hear about it and all that. Didn't seem too broken up, and he was expecting some other lady."

"Did he say how he knew your mother?"

Peg shook her head. "Ma knew lots of people. I assumed he was a travelling rep with a girl in every town."

"You have been very helpful, Mrs Dawes," Pearson told her. "Are you staying here in the hotel?"

Peg nodded.

"I will let you know if you can help further."

The man who had opened the door and was silent throughout, straightened from leaning against the door frame to let her leave.

Peg went back to the kitchen in a thoughtful mood.

"Where's the trolley, girl?" her boss demanded.

"Uh, I didn't get it. A guy from security was there. The room looked like it had been trashed."

Such gossip interested the kitchen manager, so Peg described the mess, but not all of the conversation. When she had milked the subject for all Peg was willing to tell her, she said, "Finish that last lot of dishes and get yourself off. I have had that young bloke of yours in here three times looking for you."

Her boss, and the kitchen manager, both chuckled knowingly. No doubt thinking that Jack couldn't wait to get her into bed again. Peg blushed. She and Jack had done a fair bit of bed activity since their quiet registry office wedding.

Jack found her on her way back to their room and trotted up to walk with her. They didn't talk until they were alone and the door was closed.

"Where were you?"

Peg knew he meant when he had looking for her in the kitchen. She explained her encounter with security. Jack whistled softly, as she had come to know he did when he was thinking.

"The bloke I saw didn't go to the lounge and wasn't around when I went back. I don't know where he was, but I think it was just as well that I got that folder from Stanton."

"Do you think he will come looking for me?" Peg asked.

Jack shook his head. "He followed you back to the kitchen, and in that uniform, it is quite obvious that you weren't carrying anything."

That she was at that moment only in her underwear, caused her to blow a raspberry. Jack looked at her and blushed in turn.

"I meant when you were dressed, idiot! Hurry up and get decent again. We can walk around the shops for a bit to see if anyone is interested in us. Then we will go where I want to take you."

"Just a little hint, Jack? Please?"

Now Jack grinned. "Nope. It's my surprise."

Chapter 12

"I love it! I love it!" Peg iterated as she ran her hand over the smooth, red lacquered veneer of the guitar. "But we were only going to hire one until after the festival was over."

"And I wanted to give you the best birthday present you ever had," Jack told her. "And it's not just for you. I like hearing you play and sing. Although you are going to have to sing louder if you are going to sing at the festival."

"They have microphones, you know! Anyway, where did you find this?"

"It isn't brand new, if that's what concerns you. However, I did get it serviced, or set up – whatever they call it. I think a lot of music sellers are coming here to sell stuff."

They were sitting at a small café, having a very late lunch after traipsing all over Tamworth and visiting a number of music shops. Peg had her guitar in its case beside her and was looking through the books of country music scores that she had bought. She was intending to practice some of the songs to play during her turns. She had already registered her interest in participating in some of the competitions.

"I am going to find it hard to repay you with a great Christmas present," she said after a while.

"Do well at the festival," Jack told her. "I already have my Christmas wish." He reached across the table and grabbed her hand. "And I intend to have more of them tonight."

Peg sat back and grinned at him. Christmas was only a bit over a week away and the festival was going to start early in the New Year, and running through most of January. She was both looking forward to performing, and scared out of her wits. All her life, she had never sought to be the focus of attention, but to be a popular singer/musician, people had to see her.

The lingering fear was that someone would recognise that she was once Peg Jessup. It didn't matter that the past two months had been drama free.

Mike Scott's letters had told them that the police still wanted to talk to her, and that they had not found any clues to her aunt's real killer. For now it seemed that they had successfully put the past behind them.

As if aware of her thoughts, Jack changed the subject. "Had another letter from Mike. It seems that Ian is intending to come here and cover the festival."

"Mike too?"

Jack nodded.

"It would be good to catch up…but chancy."

"That's what I told him."

"You know, I still can't get over the fact that Ian and Mike are related. I mean, what are the chances? Mike happens to meet and make friends with Casey, who happens to know Ian. Though that one time that I met Ian Sinclair, I thought he seemed familiar, but I didn't know from where."

"He heard you play, didn't he? Do you think he will recognise your style?"

"I am one amongst who knows how many wannabee country and Western stars," Peg shrugged. "If I had to give an opinion, then, yeah, he might. Perhaps I'd better not play any of my stuff."

Jack considered that. "No…let's say if he confronts you we deal with it then. Being able to compose and sing, puts you ahead of a lot of the other wannabees."

"I doubt that I will be doing gigs at any of the main venues. They'll be for the people who have been singing for years. I am really looking forward to hearing Slim Dusty and Tex Morgan playing live."

With a chuckle, Jack agreed. "So am I, to be honest. Have you had enough yet? I'd kinda like to head back."

Jack waited until the full on bustle of Christmas was over before retrieving Stanton's folder from the hotel safe. He took it to their room and had a quick look through it before Peg arrived at the end of her shift. Some of his questions about the two companies that Stanton had mentioned to Peg, were answered. Blair holdings was headed by CEO David Blair, a dynamic magnate who had made a fortune in building and transport. His bio mentioned a son, who was already being groomed to take over the business, and made little mention of a daughter.

In his mind, that daughter had to have been Peg's mother, and was probably the skeleton that had been dredged from the water hole in Matlock. She was listed as a shareholder.

Costigan Consolidated was headed by John Costigan, a second generation magnate whose business was importing and exporting, as well as having a trucking company and owning roadhouses. He had an impeccable reputation, was well known and liked, and sponsored lots of sporting events. He probably was indulging his son and heir with V8 racing.

All in all, the information in that folder was way out of his league. They would need to find someone who knew about shares to advise them. Should they sell? Each share was currently worth a lot – especially now. They really could use the money to set themselves up.

Jack glanced up when he heard the door open. He had a momentary flare of alarm until Peg sidled in. They both had keys, since their work shifts didn't align exactly.

"Got it all figured out?" Peg asked when she saw what he had open in front of him.

"Nope. We need an expert." Having said that, he pointed to the bottom line figure, on the top of the next page. "Look at that. If we sell those shares today – if the figures are still the same as when the report was made – that is what they are worth."

Peg read it and whistled. "Who was offering that much?"

"Costigans."

"I am not planning on selling. What are they usually worth?"

Jack found a graph and studied it. "I'd say, that before the takeover began, they were probably about a third less. That is still a lot."

"Yeah, and we could certainly use it to get a house and stuff, but we couldn't do that yet anyway."

Jack knew that. They had to be ready to pack up and go without much notice – just in case. "What do you want to do?" he asked.

"I am still in two minds, and I don't know how Gianni Costa fits into the picture. I would like to know more about the Blair mob too, although I don't reckon I owe them anything either. I have been toying with the idea of attending the shareholders meeting that Stanton mentioned. Have you found the info on that?"

Jack flicked through the pages, found one with a note attached, and quickly scan read it. "If you plan to be such a damn fool as that, you need to send this off pronto. And we would need the share numbers."

"That info should be in the folder."

"Yeah, but I'd bet the accountant at Blair Holdings will know exactly who they belong to. How are they going to react when you, a stranger, walk in with them?"

"I won't have them on me."

"You could just send in your proxy vote," Jack suggested.

"Or I could do nothing, keep them guessing, and let them slug it out with Costigan."

"What if your shares could make a real difference?"

"Then I would have a great deal of power, maybe even a controlling interest. My mother's kin kicked her out. If she was friends with Aunt Ida, she might have sunk to being a whore. Maybe they don't deserve my consideration."

"They probably don't know about you."

Peg moved and went from looking over Jack's shoulder, to flopping on the double bed. "No they don't. Aunt Ida was very careful not to mention that to anyone."

"How do you mean?"

"Well, everyone in Matlock thinks that she was my aunt. Gianni assumes I am one of Harry's by blows like Ned and Jasper. But she told me that I am neither, but we know that now. If anyone recalls not seeing her pregnant before I appeared, people might start putting things together."

"Hmmm," Jack murmured.

"What will those shares be worth if the other mob takes over?"

"Dunno," Jack admitted. "That's why I said we need advice."

"I don't disagree. Stanton told me not to contact him."

Jack said, "I think he was scared off."

"Anyone we find to act for us is going to come into the limelight. Can they be forced to tell who we are?"

"Again, I dunno."

"I wish I could ask Jack Casey," Peg finally admitted. "Let me look through that stuff and I will try to decide what to do. And then I think this stuff will be safer back in the hotel safe."

Chapter 13

"Who is in charge here?"

The loud voice received the immediate attention of Sergeant Kennedy and Gary Hogan. Kennedy stood and went to the bench where the large, solid, greying man stood. He was flanked by a well-dressed grey haired woman and a younger man, their son obviously, due to his likeness to the older man.

"What is your concern, Sir?"

"I want to speak to the senior detective in charge of the case of the woman found in the waterhole up here."

"Your name, Sir?"

"David Blair."

With a nod, Kennedy returned to his desk and spoke into the internal phone. "Vic, a Mr David Blair to see you in regard to the unidentified woman." He listened and then replaced the phone. "Sergeant Maddern will be right down."

Indeed, he was emerging from the stair case in moments, closely followed by Steve York.

Maddern went directly to the visitor and offered his hand. "Do you think you might know who our mystery woman is?"

Blair, loud and gruff as he had been, now seemed reluctant to say anything. His wife drew breath to speak, but Blair finally spoke first. "I cannot say with surety. I would like to examine the objects that were found with the dead woman."

His wife dug into her hand bag and drew out a folded piece of newspaper. It still had the header of the Melbourne Herald, as well as pictures of several distinctive pieces of jewellery.

While Maddern examined the article that he had requested to be circulated by the media, Steve returned upstairs for the box holding the originals of the items. When he returned, he carefully drew out the delicate items, placed them on a sheet of paper, and opened up the attached forensic report that described the metal and gems.

The woman glanced at her husband before leaning closer to examine the pieces. With careful fingers, she twisted a reddish gem and held it up to her eye in the direction of the light from a window.

York commented, "The jeweller who examined the pieces described that gem as having an inclusion…"

The colour faded from the woman's face and she trembled. Hogan quickly moved a chair over to her.

"Thank you, but I will be fine," she told him. "David, bring out the insurance pictures."

The older man gestured to his son, who leant down and produced a brief case. From it he removed a folder, extracted a sheet and passed it to Maddern without a word.

"Were these the only things found?" the woman asked.

"Yes. If there had been anything else, say in the woman's clothes, they are probably still in the water. The clothing had rotted, and the bottom of that waterhole is mud."

The woman went even paler, but spoke with only a faint tremor. "This pendant belonged to my daughter."

Maddern hid his elation at finally having information about the dead woman. He kept his voice and face neutral. "If you would come upstairs to my office, I'll get some details from you. Steve, organise some coffee."

"Tea, please," the woman requested. "If you would be so kind."

Once the two older visitors were seated, the son used the front edge of Steve's desk for a seat.

Maddern began, "When was the last time that you saw your daughter, Mrs Blair?"

"Oh dear, It was nearly twenty years ago now. Not long after her 21st birthday."

"I told the little tramp to stop seeing the trash…" Blair spoke over his wife. "She was always following some band or other with their doped up musicians. She broke off her engagement to a perfectly nice young man – a policeman – for no good reason. Told her she'd end up a drug addict and a whore, and she did."

Mrs Blair brought out a hanky and dabbed at her eyes. The son kept quiet, his face deliberately blank.

"Did you see her again after she left?" Maddern queried.

"No we did not! We heard about her debauchery," Blair stated. "Told her to get out. That she wasn't a daughter of mine. Told her she wouldn't get a penny from me, then or ever. The impertinent tramp said that she didn't care, loved whoever it was and didn't need me."

"You had no contact after that? Or attempts at reconciliation?" Maddern prompted. "Any news of where she went?"

"I wouldn't have answered her if she tried. She stayed in town with that drugged out guitarist and his band."

"What was the name of the man she went with?"

"Ian something," Mrs Blair spoke up. "The band was called the Flaming Candles, or something like that. I recall he was arrested for selling drugs and went to prison. I hoped that Margaret would come to her senses and come home."

Maddern didn't need Blair to say, "I'd have left her to rot," to understand why the girl hadn't.

"Well, can I get some details about your daughter?" Maddern suggested. "We can start with her date of birth and a description."

Blair clamped his mouth shut and let his wife give the details. Maddern patiently extracted everything that he could think of that might help confirm the dead woman's identity and to trace her last movements of twenty years before.

"You asked if we had found any other jewellery. Did your daughter have other pieces that you can describe?"

Without being asked, the son took another folder from the case and passed it to his father.

"Little tramp stole some of her mother's trinkets," Blair commented. "The details are here."

Steve York returned with the refreshments and passed them around. He retreated to his desk, and perched next to the younger Blair, who greeted him with a grimace caused by his father's hostile tone. York decided to talk to the younger man, away from his father.

"She also had some jewellery of her own. Details of those are on the reverse side."

Blair put a series of photos on Maddern's desk that were enlargements of the small ones shown on the detail sheet.

"That gold necklace is worth several thousand dollars. The silver one, over a thousand. The cameo is a family heirloom, worth over five thousand."

"I will have copies made of these photos and have them circulated. Something may come of it," Maddern said, in spite of his doubts. If the pieces had been sold two decades ago, they might be anywhere. He paused to contemplate his next questions, never pleasant ones to ask grieving relatives. "I need to ask if you daughter had any injuries to bones that you know of."

"No!" Blair stated, but this time, his son spoke up.

"She fractured a finger once – playing netball. The little one on her left hand."

Maddern added to his notes. "What about dental work?"

Blair took another folder from his son. "Gave the ungrateful tramp the best dental care possible – her teeth were perfect."

The folder contained file cards showing teeth and the dentist's cryptic notations. Maddern had seen enough of these to know that the owner of the teeth described had indeed had fillings done.

"I'll keep these if you don't mind, and have a copy sent to Melbourne."

"Why Melbourne?" Blair asked, startled by that revelation.

"The remains were sent there for forensic examination, and will be kept there until an identification is made," Maddern explained.

"So, what happens now?" Blair demanded.

"Will you be staying in town over night?"

Blair frowned. "I hadn't planned to. Is there a need?"

"I should be able to return your records by late morning," Maddern explained. "In the meantime, I will be instigating a new line of investigation and may have more questions that you can help me with."

"We don't have any overnight things," Mrs Blair said with dignity.

Maddern smiled. "I will ask Nell Kennedy to organise what you need. Steve can do the same for your husband and son."

"Thank you Sergeant," Mrs Blair said, rising from her chair. "I do feel the need to go and rest."

Blair's thanks were terse. "It will be gratifying to put an end to this whole sordid episode. What is the best hotel in this town?"

York spoke up. "The Grand, on Main Street. I am happy to show you the way and get you settled."

On the way down, York heard Mrs Blair say to her husband, "I really don't know how Margaret came to be here. It's so far from town."

It was an excellent question.

York didn't return to the police station until after dark, some four hours later. He wasn't surprised to see Maddern still there.

He was greeted with, "Get anything useful out of the son?"

"Confirmation of what the parents said for the most part," Steve reported. "He apologised for his father's bombastic behaviour. Claimed that the family business was having problems and he hadn't wanted to come here."

"I wonder what else his daughter did to anger him. Surely, after all this time, he could have forgiven her."

"The son, his name is Rick by the way, told me that he hadn't mentioned his sister all this time until recently. Anyway, from the hints he gave, I had the impression that Blair Holdings is fighting off a hostile takeover and it is close. He only agreed to come and see if this mystery woman was his daughter to try and find the parcel of shares that she had."

"Shares?" Maddern echoed.

"Rick and his sister both received a quarter share in the company when they turned eighteen. Their father retained fifty percent. Over time though, they created more shares, although, in theory, the family still owns the controlling interest."

"We should try and find out if any activity, related to those shares..." Maddern began, but York indicated he had more information.

"I think that's part of the reason why they took so long to come here. Someone has been actioning the shares. For a long while, Blair was convinced that his daughter was still alive."

"I wonder what he has done to try and trace them," Maddern mused. "If he hated his daughter so much, and promised her nothing, she would have been getting some dividends from the shares."

"Well, it appears that she wasn't. Somebody else has been," York pointed out.

"True. Did Rick Blair mention if he tried to help his sister?"

"Yes, but he admitted that he and his sister weren't particularly close. He said she was a spoilt princess. He did see her a few times during the first year or so, but she refused to try to make things right with her father, or even her mother. Apparently, her ex-fiancé was trying to straighten her out too."

"Did you get his name?"

"Taylor. I think it is Chief Inspector Taylor now."

Maddern's eyebrows rose. He would need to approach the CI with care. "I asked Nell Kennedy to see if she could get Mrs Blair to open up about the rift between her daughter and husband. There has to be more to it."

"According to Rick, the old man is rabidly anti-alcohol. When I suggested a drink to Rick, he opted for a walk instead." York's shrug indicated that may have been another part of the rift.

"Bert will let us know if Nell discovers anything. I want you to see what you can find about Blair, his company, and whoever is behind the takeover bid. I am wondering if there could be any connection between the girl's death 20 years ago and this takeover bid."

"That's a long shot," York protested. "We haven't even had the ID confirmed yet. Maybe someone planted that jewellery on her in case the body was found and we would think it was her. Perhaps the Blair girl is still alive."

"No, there was that rock and chain holding her down. I don't think that whoever put her there wanted her found. But you are right though, we need to be sure. I have faxed the dental records to Melbourne. They should have a report by the weekend."

"Did you go home and sleep last night," Steve greeted his superior when he found Maddern already in the office.

Maddern grinned. "I did, but I didn't sleep that much. I kept thinking of more questions."

"Like what?"

"Well, we probably know why Blair took his time coming here, but would you agree, that he had no reason to come until he saw the pictures in the paper?"

"York nodded. "Your point?"

"If he is looking for his missing shares, and thinks his daughter came up here, what do you think his next moves will be?"

"Same as ours. Look for bank accounts, safe deposit boxes, rental agreements, etc in her name," York supplied. "But if we found nothing, he won't."

"How about that spate of robberies when we were still dredging the waterhole? Lawyers, banks, real estate agents…."

It was York's turn to be enlightened. "That can't have been Blair."

"I tend to agree. Take it a bit further."

York thought before answering. "We found two bikers in that hole. Two bikers terrified Ida Jessup. Someone tried to kill or succeeded in killing, Peg Jessup near there, and that girl. Do you think it is all connected?"

"It is possible, even if I can't see how," Maddern admitted. "The catch is, why wait 20 years to come looking for what they wanted?"

"Something must have happened and they realised who might know things. But What?"

Chapter 14

Most of the people who worked with Peg knew she was entered in the contests that were part of the music festival. When her first gig was on, those who were off duty came along to cheer her on. Jack was there too, but he hovered back stage and gave her a good luck kiss after the make-up girl had finished.

The first round of competitions, for the less experienced entrants, were held in one of several outdoor venues and were generally in the afternoon. Peg walked out on stage, shaking like a leaf, and thrilled by the crowd spread out on the grass between the stage and a row of trees. The sun was, fortunately, not at an angle to shine directly in her face.

Before she froze in place, she checked her guitar, played a note to check its tuning and began a simple country song that she had taught herself the previous week. Remembering some advice from Wayne Carson, when he had been teaching her and others at Meredan, she sang with her heart, while moving her head to be directed at all sections of the crowd.

A mental voice reminded her that, "You can look out above the heads of the crowd and it will seem like you are simply looking at people further back."

It had worked for her at Meredan, and it did again.

The applause was led by cheers and catcalls from her friends but it quickly spread. It gave her confidence and she began her second song. The crowd needed little encouragement that time, nor after the final song which was one of her own. It was a happier one than her first few, and well received by the audience.

She felt that she was floating as she moved off the stage. Back stage, she felt her back thumped several times and she was waylaid by a reporter for the festival magazine, and several people who she suspected were judging the acts. All asked if she had written that third song.

Peg heard Jack's whispered, "Well done", but refused his suggestion of heading away. She wanted to get a feel for the other acts and how good they were. Those before her turn were a blur, as she had been fighting off stage fright. She wasn't really a good judge of her own act versus theirs for she was all too aware of her lack of experience. For today, she settled for the thrill of actually performing.

At the end of the ten act competition, Peg slipped off with Jack who treated her to tea at the hotel. Once there, word had already spread to the on duty staff. All demanded to know when her next gig was. Some were still frustrated because they would not be free to go to it.

By the following week, with three gigs behind her, her confidence was soaring. Various people had written positive reviews about her act, and she had seen no negative ones.

Her next three gigs were in some of the town's smaller indoor venues. The last of them in the hotel where she worked. There was no way, short of confronting the management, to know if she was selected based on great reviews or because the hotel was supporting one of their own.

Jack was working tables in the hotel's function room on the Saturday evening when Peg was due to play. He had just slid a tray of used glasses through to the scullery and turned to get a clean empty tray when he almost walked into someone.

"Jack!" The amazed voice made Jack look at the speaker.

"Mike! Small world, huh! Why are you here?"

"Heard there were some interesting acts performing here tonight."

"Is Ian here too?"

"Yeah. He's been here since the start. He's covering the festival for a couple of Melbourne papers. I've just arrived. Where's Peg?"

"Shh! She's calling herself Megan Dawes."

"Right…so you two got hitched then?"

Jack grinned. "She is performing here tonight. This will be her sixth gig."

"I don't want to miss that. How good is she?"

"I am biased. However the reviews in the local rag have been positive."

"Ian mentioned the ones that he thought were the best up and comers, but I don't recall the name Dawes."

"She is using a stage name – Megan Arthur." Jack shrugged. "I don't want my uncle hearing the name Dawes. He is a damn nosy cop. Anyway, I am meant to be working, but if I get a moment, I will tell her you're here. We can meet later. I hope that your new found father doesn't recognise her."

Mike took the warning. "I will try to head him off if he starts to suspect." With a quick squeeze of his friend's arm, Jack moved off.

The program at the Tamworth Grand Hotel had six different acts. Peg was the first to arrive and was already dressed and made up when the others began to arrive. She had met three of them before and was chatting amiably when a minor furore erupted. A tall blond man entered, closely followed by two members of Festival security. A cadre of pleading girls were being firmly shooed away.

"Hey! Wayne Carson just walked in," one of the other female singers said excitedly.

Peg glanced at the man who was smiling as he approached them. Her first fear was that he would recognise her, but then she recalled that she looked totally different – hair colour, clothes, make up and all. When he introduced himself and shook hands, she simply gave her performing name and smiled back. He paid her no more attention than any of the others and she had no intention of putting herself forward.

It soon became apparent that he was the evening's star performer, although his name had not been on the flyer at the hotel entrance.

"Wow," the other girl whispered in Peg's ear. "This is totally awesome. We'll be performing with Wayne Carson."

"I didn't realise that he was in Tamworth," Peg murmured back. "Actually, I didn't think many of his songs could be considered country."

"Who cares? With him here, we'll get more people coming that will see us."

"Like that bunch of hopefuls crowding the door?" Peg grinned.

"Yeah. I bet they want our guts for being allowed in the same room with him." Those nearby heard that and laughed. The girl went on, "I think, while I have the chance, I will get his autograph. What about you?"

"Nah! I'll settle for the reflected glory," Peg told her. "Don't let me stop you though."

Peg found a seat and pretended to be tuning her guitar. She didn't want to push herself into Carson's company, although he didn't seem to mind chatting to the other performers. He was good like that – wanting to help up and coming artists. She knew that from Meredan, even though his work there was touted as a publicity exercise. Once he realised that she had some talent, he had gone out of his way to nurture it. That he was making a lot in royalties from her song meant that, in a way, she was repaying that kindness. It was just too bad that she couldn't sing that song tonight – not when he was on the same program.

Her thoughts were interrupted by the entrance of one of the waiters. It wasn't Jack, she realised with regret. From her position, she had a glimpse of the crowding teenyboppers, before the door shut again and silenced their cheers and calls.

Naturally, the waiter went to Carson first, asking if he wanted refreshment. In the break in the chatting, she wasn't surprised to hear him ask for ginger beer, even if everyone else was. In her turn, she asked for lemonade. It wasn't her favourite drink, but it was different to her Meredan preference of orange juice.

While she idly watched the waiter leave, to force his way through the girls, she caught movement in the corner of her eye. Wayne Carson was strolling her way.

"I don't bite," he greeted her. "You are welcome to join the rest of us."

She grinned. "I would be too fidgety with nerves," she told him.

Carson pulled up a chair and straddled the back. "Where have you hailed from? Around here?"

"Here and there," Peg parried. "Was down in Victoria for a bit, but will probably head back north after the festival. I must admit, I wasn't expecting you to feel at home here."

With a familiar chuckle, Carson said, "I have grown to like the style of music here. I might do a country style album next. My last single was much in that style." Peg felt herself blushing. "Yeah, that's true. I hadn't thought of that." She hoped that would explain her red face. "Did you plan on performing here or were you a fill in?"

Once again, Carson smiled. "That's putting me in my place! Actually, Harry Waters, who is a friend of mine, needed to get back to his family. He asked me if I was free, and since I am between contracts and on my way to Sydney – I didn't say no."

With relief, Peg saw the drink waiter balancing a tray through the door. Her face brightened. This time it was Jack. Carson glanced where she was looking and stood up as the tray approached.

"Your ginger beer, Mr Carson," Jack said politely. He had been directed to serve the star first. He moved to get Peg's drink, but the other three male performers hustled over to get their drinks. Carson passed the other girls their drinks, and would have done the same for Peg, except Jack beat him to it, then leant over and whispered, "Ian and Mike are here."

"In the audience?" she asked in a low voice. Jack nodded and moved off.

"It seems that I have competition," Carson murmured as if regretfully.

"Oh!" Peg didn't quite know what to say. Then she felt the imp of mischief and suggested, "Sorry, Jack is a friend. If you are feeling neglected, I could ask him to let in a few of the loiterers."

"Ah, no thanks. I prefer fellow performers."

"I suppose that it is a sign of success when you have that option," Peg countered, then took a gulp of her drink.

Carson copied her example, and then turned back to the others still grouped nearby. Peg allowed herself a breath of relief. Could Carson have found something familiar about her? She hoped not. At Meredan she had never been chatty with him, or dared to tease him, even though Carson had told her that he considered her a friend, criminal or not. On the other hand, they had spent a lot of time in each other's company during her music lessons. Her music style was based on his.

Even if she fooled Carson, there was still Ian Sinclair here as well. She had to fool him too, but at least, he had only met her once. Her most imperative worry was, what they might do if they did recognise her.

The crowd of fans had gone when Peg needed to leave the room to be ready to perform. Carson had opened the evening, but hadn't returned when the first and second of her fellow performers had gone on. She was next and when she stepped out into the spotlight, she saw that Carson had taken a place with the backing band. When her workmates began to applaud, she grinned at them, glanced around, and forgot everything but her intended performance. She gestured to the band, and began…eyes finding Jack at the rear and not trying to find anyone else. Her mind stepped up to another level. She felt herself freed.

As had become her habit in each of her gigs, she sang two well-known ballads or songs and then one of her own. The band leader knew that they didn't need to do more than strum a harmony. Carson didn't. After the first stanza he'd picked up the tune and from then on he alone accompanied her. It was not surprising perhaps, for the music to that song was not greatly different to that of her first song – his latest hit. The contrast of her playing with him at Meredan, and playing then, was the spur to surpass her best.

The applause was intense, and seemed to go on for a long time. Flushed with pleasure, Peg retreated, and found Carson beside her. "Well done, Miss Arthur."

She managed a blushing, "Thank you," before Jack reached her and gave his own appraisal.

"Incredible, girl!" He lifted her and spun her around.

Peg wriggled free. "Later, okay? What will Mr Carson think of me?"

Jack, with eyes only for Peg, suddenly turned. His fellow waiter, bringing Peg a drink, muttered, "That you are a couple of besotted newlyweds of course."

Carson was amused. "Congratulations." He shook Jack's hand and retreated, still smiling.

"Are you staying around?" Jack asked once he had gone.

"I want to. He mentioned doing a group number at the end."

"Just so you know, I have invited Mike to our room later."

"Great! What about Ian?"

"Mike says he'll have no trouble slipping away. Ian likes to revel in the ambience. Right now, he is chatting to the band. Likely he will catch you too, before the end of the show. He has spoken to the two blokes who were on before you."

"Timely warning," she murmured, glancing behind him.

"Miss Arthur, a word, if you have a moment?" Ian Sinclair announced with no trace of apology for interrupting. He introduced himself then, adding, "I was hoping for a brief interview for the Melbourne papers."

"Me?" Peg raised her brows, feigning surprise. "Or are you doing the same for all the wannabees?"

"Only the ones I believe have real talent," he said easily. "I saw how you impressed Wayne Carson."

"Me?" Peg repeated herself. "Oh, you mean because he acted as second guitar?"

"Unexpected, you have to admit," Sinclair said dryly.

"It did surprise me, though the melody was fairly simple."

"It is very like Carson's latest hit," Ian remarked.

"Too alike?" Peg queried as if concerned. "That song was kinda the inspiration for mine."

Ian shrugged. "If Carson didn't say anything, maybe it is not too obvious. Anyway, would you like to tell me a bit about yourself over another drink?"

"I'd like that, Mr Sinclair, but Jack here, who is my husband is on his break and we were going to have a very quick snack. So, maybe later?"

"Definitely," Ian agreed, backing off.

"Phew!" Peg watched Ian Sinclair disappear. "That man is too damn sharp. Now I have two of my songs that I don't dare perform."

"Which other one?" Jack asked, as he took her hand and urged her towards the lift.

"The one I call a sequel to Captive. Anyone who is a Carson fan will see the connection."

"As if your Freedom song isn't already a giveaway," Jack teased.

"I performed that once before, so I can't do too much about that. Anyway, no one can say I plagiarised Carson's song, since I wrote it anyway."

"If anyone did accuse you of that, you will have a hard time proving it without admitting who you really are," Jack warned.

"Were," Peg corrected. But Jack was right, and her guts clenched with worry. "I am really, Megan Blair Dawes."

"That is a technicality that the police may not accept."

"To hell with them. Do you think I should pull out of the comps and we leave here?"

They stopped talking in the lift, as there were other people inside. Two of them congratulated her on her act.

Alone in their room, Jack released a pent up sigh. "If you can convince both Carson and Sinclair that they don't know you….do you really want to?"

Peg didn't want to leave, but the idyll of the past two weeks had lost something.

"No I don't, but two people who know who I was, have found me. I shudder to think what they will do if they realise it. Rightly, they should tell the police. It's just not fair. Don't I deserve to try for the life I want?"

Jack didn't answer, just gave her half of the sandwiches that he had brought up from the kitchen.

Someone knocked at the door and called, "It's me, Mike Scott."

Jack told Peg, "Sit down and eat. You only have ten minutes before the rest of the show starts."

He looked through the peephole in the door before opening it. Mike edged in and thumped Jack on the shoulder. He went straight to the table and sat on the second chair.

"You were great, Peg," he said.

"Megan," she told him around a mouthful of ham sandwich. "Your new old man wanted an interview. Do you think he guesses? I met him at Jack Casey's one time."

"I can't tell," Mike admitted. "I'm really still getting to know him, and although he is making the effort, we are still more like strangers."

Jack interrupted. "What is so urgent that you had to see us now?"

Mike's smile faded. "Look, it's probably a bad time…"

Peg put her sandwich down. "What is it?"

Mike pulled out his wallet and took out a piece of folded newspaper. "Did you see this?"

Jack reached for it and read quickly. "No, nothing was in the papers up here. When was this from?"

"About a week ago."

"What is it?" Peg reached for the cutting. Jack ignored the tacit request.

"Oh, just that your police friends in Matlock identified that third body in the waterhole. Some heiress that went missing twenty years ago."

Peg studied Jack as he handed the paper back to Mike. Something about his careful neutrality bothered her, but she was distracted when he urged her to finish eating.

Mike took the implied hint and stood up. "I'll catch you guys later." He let himself out.

"So what was the urgency?" Peg asked.

"I'll explain later. The worst part is that your aunt was mentioned and they are stepping up the hunt for you."

"But why? How could I possibly know anything about a woman who died before I was born?"

"The article didn't say, but the police must have discovered something."

Peg cursed, and left the rest of her sandwich. "As soon as we can, we've got to hightail it out of here."

Chapter 15

Mike sat watching the rest of the acts with little enthusiasm. The other girl and the man were pleasant singers, but they didn't compare with the emotion Peg put into her singing.

Ian wasn't ignoring him, nor particularly studying the acts. He was drinking – more than he'd seen him doing since they'd found each other. For his own distraction, Mike took Ian's Melbourne Herald and began glancing through it.

"You've been drinking more than normal," Mike remarked. "Is something bothering you?"

"You're not my keeper, Mike. I will drink as much as I damn well please."

Mike didn't retort. Sometimes his grandparents' puritan teachings still reared up. "I know. I'm sorry. It's just that I want to be a good son to you, not an indifferent one."

Ian put his half-finished draught on the table. "I'm sorry too, but it is nothing that anyone can do anything about."

He took his paper back, flipped forward a few pages from where Mike had been reading, and stabbed an article with his finger.

With a shock, Mike realised that it was a follow up to the article that he had just shown Jack. This article had pictures, and the old photo of a young woman immediately held his attention. He had seen that picture before, in the album Peg's aunt had tried to burn.

"You knew her!" Mike guessed.

"Aye, I did that. Though she never told me her real name. Now I know why."

"Will the police know that you knew her?"

"Maybe. Probably. Her old man warned me off her, but she wouldn't let him stop her seeing me."

"They are not going to think you killed her?"

Ian's laugh was a sour one. "She was alive and well when the police arrested me on those trumped up charges. By the time I got out of prison, no one had seen her for over a year. It was more like eighteen years ago, not twenty."

The last act, with all the new talent as well as Wayne Carson was just beginning. Ian turned that way and added, "She called herself Megan Pearl. Megan – like that little starlet up there. She sang like an angel. I wanted her to join me as a singer for the 'Candles. I never had a chance to ask her."

Now, Mike noticed Ian staring at Peg. He went on, "If I had've known that old whore Ida Jessup knew her, I'd have confronted her long ago. Now, even her bastard niece is missing."

"The name is a coincidence," Mike said. "It is quite common at the moment."

Ian pushed his unfinished drink across to Mike. "You can finish that if you want. I'm going to bed."

Mike caught Jack looking his way, and gestured an invitation to approach. "Can you remove that?"

Jack was still on duty, so he simply asked, "Was there something else?"

"Yeah, is it possible to get a copy of today's Melbourne Herald? There's an article on page nine that you need to read."

"Okay, they have them in the lobby. What was your old man's problem?"

"He knew the missing heiress, and wished he had questioned Ida Jessup years ago."

Jack glanced towards the performers, but didn't tell his friend what he knew of Peg's real parents. "He seemed to be staring real hard at Peg."

"It's the name. Ian knew the missing girl as Megan, and she used to sing real well."

"I'll tell Peg to avoid Ian if she can," Jack decided. "Any other news?"

"Not that I have heard."

"Thanks, mate," Jack said, before departing with the half-filled glass.

Mike decided not to stay. He took Ian's paper and went to follow Ian back to their room at a local boarding house.

Jack waited for Peg to finish at the after gig party that Carson threw. He wasn't worried by Peg's insistence to stay at it. Having Carson as a friend could help her career take off. Trouble was, her career might end up wrecked before it began.

His shift finished before the late shift usually did because he had offered to work an extra shift to help cover the extra business. His boss had come over, once the crowd had dispersed, and said the regulars could cover the clean-up. It suited Jack who wanted to get Peg back to their room to tell her the rest of what Mike had found out. By luck, he had bought the last of the hotels supply of Melbourne Heralds.

Peg floated back to their room, still made up from her gig.

"What's got into you? Was Wayne Carson handing out illegal pills or something?"

"I am not drunk or anything. Wayne Carson just suggested, that next Saturday, here, he and I could do my Captive song as a duet."

"Hell! Did he recognise you?"

"I don't think so. He said he thought my voice and his would contrast quite well. He also gave me another two voice songs to learn if I could. I will have to practice a lot if I am to be any good."

"I guess that rules out any daytime debauchery for a bit," Jack teased her.

"Not the night times though," Peg grinned at him.

"I gather that Ian Sinclair, ace reporter, didn't join the party?"

"No, although I was expecting to see him."

"So did I. I was watching him and he seemed to be fixated on you."

"I don't look anything like I did when we met before."

"It isn't that. It is more the coincidence of your name being the same as that of someone he knew long ago."

"His missing second love?" Peg suggested.

"Could be. Anyway, it might be wise to avoid him if you can."

"It might be difficult, but I'll try." Peg felt herself want to yawn. "I think my manic energy has just fizzled. I think I will be asleep before I can fall into bed."

"Well, at least get that make up off, or I will think I am sleeping with a racoon."

He wondered if he should try to give her the promised more information. She hadn't asked about it, and might even have forgotten. He ought to, for the news article had been more important than he had let on to Mike, but she was almost asleep…maybe in the morning.

It was actually well into the night, when Peg stirred and woke, that she asked about the article.

"The third body, the woman, was identified as Margaret Blair," Jack said.

Peg went rigid. "Gee…zus!" That summed up the ideas now forcing themselves into her mind. "Just as well you didn't tell me that earlier. I would have clean lost all rational thought."

Jack thought Peg had gone back to sleep, but after a while she said, "I don't think that I should have been so shocked. It all makes too much sense. Aunt Ida had those old cases for that long. But that was my real mother, hidden in that hole all this time."

"There is something else," Jack decided to admit. "Mike's dad knew her. I think he must have been in love with her before he was arrested."

"Maybe he is my father," Peg blurted, twisting in Jack's arms to face him. She felt Jack shaking his head.

"I doubt it. But anyway, I don't think there is any hope of proving it – one way or the other."

"You are probably right, After all, my mother was another of Giannis whores. My father could be anyone, likely a criminal."

Peg's stomach lurched and she pulled out of Jack's arms, slipped from the bed and trotted to the ensuite. Jack followed when he heard her throwing up.

"What bought this on?"

Pale faced, Peg straightened, and ran water into a beaker to rinse her mouth.

"Aunt Ida assured me that I wasn't Gianni's get, or Harry Kings, but how can she be sure? I mean…"

"You mean that you can say you are not because you do not want to be. Besides, didn't you tell me that you don't look like any of your so called brothers?"

"That's no proof…"

"No, it isn't confirmation. I don't care who fathered you. He has had nothing to do with making you - the you I love - so do you feel like coming back to bed?"

Chapter 16

The final concert was a huge affair with already well-known artists rubbing shoulders with the newer performers – the twenty who had topped the voting and reviews. Peg had dreamed of winning, but in reality hadn't expected even to be good enough for this concert. She had been elated to discover that she was.

She would be doing two solos, but Wayne Carson had asked her to perform a duet version of his latest hit song – the song she had written. That was, to her, the pinnacle of the festival.

In the few days since she had met him again, Wayne Carson had been giving her voice lessons. Not once during that time, did she sense that he thought he may have met her before. Around him, she felt she could relax.

In that final concert, Peg wanted to be able to dedicate her performance to her dead mother. Only it would have to be a very private dedication, and she didn't even mention the idea to Jack – it was too private.

Jack had found her a new outfit – one that was more feminine than any she had worn before. She wanted to wear something special with it. Without thinking of the risk, she went to the bundle of things that she'd taken with her when she 'disappeared' and sought for the trinkets that had been in her mother's case. The first thing she considered was the gold necklace, but when her hand found the cameo, she knew that was what she wanted. The colour of the choker collar went so well with her outfit.

Jack frowned when he noticed it – mere moments before she was due to perform. "I guess I am paranoid. If it has been missing for twenty years – who is likely to recognise it here?"

"Exactly," Peg said, as she checked herself in a mirror one final time.

"Well, then, break a leg," Jack told her with a kiss on her nose. "I will be there to watch you when you are on."

"There's going to be a horde of people…"

"I have it covered. Ian gave me a backstage pass."

"Has he been bugging you about interviewing me?"

"I told him that after this you will settle down and not be battling stage fright. In other words, we'll have time to create a fancy fake background."

Jack watched Peg go off. He had traded shifts so that he could be free for the show. Peg had asked for a few days off leading up to this performance, and the hotel had been pleased to grant it. However, he had a lot to do before her gig. He went quickly back to their room and packed all their stuff into two ex-army duffle bags, and when he had done that and hidden them away from their room, he was going to wipe over every possible surface in that room.

It had to be paranoia, but for the last few days he had a very strong feeling of being watched – every time he had gone out with Peg. He had tried to find out who was watching, but if the person existed – they were good, and that was likely to mean that his uncle had found him and set someone to watch him. It didn't seem like they had recognised his companion as Peg, but…maybe they had.

He had decided to prepare, in case they had to flit. He had already recovered the stuff he had been keeping in the hotel safe. He had a new safe place in mind for it, but he wanted Peg, as Megan Dawes, to put it in the safe deposit box in the bank. He had already discussed the idea with the manager, and the man had also referred him to a discreet company of finance brokers who knew about share trading. For a little while it would be stuffed in his bag.

Getting their stuff away without being noticed was also thought out. It was useful being in the staff quarters, near to where deliveries were made. He would be taking them out in a huge laundry bag, and one of the drivers would deliver it to the boarding house where he had booked a room – that would come vacant when the festival guests left.

As far as the hotel was concerned, they were going to take a week's honeymoon, going north to Brisbane, and then planned to return. At the end of that week, he would tell them that they had decided to travel around Australia – working their way. Hopefully, the hotel people would still provide a good reference. They would need them to get work.

Many of the important townsfolk were present in the dressing area, congratulating the artists who had been invited to perform at this premiere event. With her closeness to Wayne Carson, Peg got to meet some of her country and western singing idols. The female artist that she was sure would win the top award, Suzanne Prentice, did not seem to be that much older than herself, but she'd been performing for years. Peg wanted to become at least that good, one day.

Peg had not mentioned to Jack about the cameo she had put on, she hadn't thought it more than an old fashioned trinket. When Wayne Carson commented on it, she said, "I was looking for something old fashioned. Jack found it in one of the op-shops we went to."

The conversation was overheard, and a stranger asked to look at it.

"I thought such things went out of vogue a generation ago," the man said. "That one might even be valuable."

His comment gave Peg a momentary quiver of apprehension, and her face must have betrayed it.

"I don't think he intends to steal it," Carson teased. "That's the district chief of police."

"Really? He doesn't look it," Peg tried to shrug off her fear, as she watched the man join the Mayor's group.

Jack arrived just as the Mayor and his group turned to go to their seats. He was watching from the edge of the stage and it only took a moments observation of the group to decide that one of the men was a high ranking cop. The body language was unmistakable, as was the way the man glanced back at the performers – at Peg.

He waited for the performers to assemble back stage before sidling up to Peg and whispering in her ear. She stiffened, then turned. "Idiot!" she told him, with a smile she didn't feel.

"Can I share the joke?" Carson asked casually.

Jack grinned. "Sorry. I guess I shouldn't proposition my wife in public. I just told her I had booked a bus ticket to places as yet unknown for when this fair is over."

"And missing the presentation dinner?" Carson asked with raised brows.

"I'm not going to win," Peg admitted. "And no one has even hinted at wanting to give me a recording contract."

"And I promised Megan we'd have a week in Queensland when we'd saved a bit of money. A proper honeymoon."

"Well…that does seem to trump a mere dinner."

Carson then gave Peg a thoughtful look. "Before you leave, I'd like to talk to Megan again, if you could give me that time?"

"Sure," Peg agreed. Jack held his tongue and mentally crossed his fingers.

Although disappointed not to have achieved the award for the most promising new performer, Peg was on a high and Jack didn't want to spoil the moment. He was glad that she didn't need to stay for the awards dinner. As the guests at the awards presentation began to leave the hall, Jack came up to Peg.

"We need to leave. NOW."

"But I promised Wayne I would talk to him first."

Jack wasn't listening, he was already half dragging her towards the rear door of the hall. "Take that cameo thing off!"

Peg stopped. "Why? What's up?"

"I don't know exactly, but I heard some bloke talking to the mayor about it. Something about it being stolen."

"What recently?"

"I don't know. Just that a picture of one has just been circulated."

"They are mistaken! Aunt must have had this since before I was born."

"Do you want to risk talking to the police? They are just out the front."

Peg's feet unfroze. "They can't know I am here…"

"At the moment, they are asking for you by your performing name. How long before they discover you are Mrs Jack Dawes? And how long after that before they talk to the Melbourne cops?"

"And your damn uncle adds one and one to get me?"

"Exactly."

"Megan, a moment!" Wayne Carson reached them just before they reached the back door. "I meant to see you sooner. Here is my manager's card. When you are back from your trip, give him a call. I would like to have you as part of my next gig in Sydney."

"Wow! Really?" Peg was instantly distracted. "I'd love that. Thank you."

"You have a real talent that I would like to see mature."

For just an instant, Peg's mind flashed back to Meredan, when Carson had first broached the idea of extra lessons. He had used the same words. Coincidence? Maybe. However, if he had any suspicions, he wasn't betraying them.

"Off you go. Have fun."

Jack nodded at Carson and yanked on Peg's arm, not turning to see if Carson's eyes followed their departure. There was a taxi waiting just down the road to take them to the railway station, and from there it was only a short walk to the boarding house. There they would be using the surname Blair. A risk, but it wasn't quite as uncommon as Dawes.

Chapter 17

"Stupid, stupid, BITCH!" Les Shaw swore as she looked around at the wreckage of the old farm house.

The bright police tape hadn't kept out looters it seemed. She continued her rant, not bothering to keep her voice down. "You promised me that you would be here. That we would take off together and start afresh. You promised, BITCH!"

There was nothing personal left in the house, only some old clothes and some tinned stuff left in the pantry. Since she had nowhere else to go, Les explored the rooms until she found the one that must have been Peg's. It was empty except for a bed frame and two mattresses.

When she wasn't talking, she could just hear the little rat dog – the one Peg had described to her that belonged to a neighbour. If it kept up that racket, somebody would surely come and see what the fuss was about. If they did, she would just say that she was Peg Jessup.

Les grinned sourly. That resemblance was part of her reason for renewing the bleach job on her hair, just before she was allowed out. With it, she and Peg could've been sisters. She'd never had a sister. When she'd first met the kid, she'd been a right nuisance, a tag along, but she wasn't so bad.

Self-pity was not a luxury that Les allowed herself. Peg was a deceitful bitch. Then a little voice in her head suggested that Peg was the only person who had liked her for herself. Not like Mick who had only wanted to flaunt her and shag her. To be honest, she'd be happy if she never saw him again. They still hadn't caught him though.

Making the decision to leave the house, Les grabbed an old shirt from the laundry, snagged some cans from the pantry, along with an opener and a spoon from a drawer, and made it all into a bundle. Outside once again, she strode around to the road at the front of the house and headed for town. Someone must know where Peg Jessup had gone. On a glance back, a flash of red caught her eye – up near where the yapping rat lived. She turned and made a rude gesture before continuing on.

The memory of the town's layout returned, and she headed for the town centre. All the way keeping to the edge of the road. She wasn't worried by the occasional car that went past. Most seemed to be weekend drivers, out for an adventure in the hills. In the distance, a red sports car came into view, giving her an excuse to vent more anger by denigrating the rich driver. As it approached, she considered trying to hitch a lift. It seemed as the car drew near that the driver was considering stopping, but then, unbelievably, the car accelerated right at her.

It never hit her. In spite of being locked up for two years, Les had kept fit. Before the car could reverse out of the ditch, she was at the car and dragging the stupid bitch of a driver out of the car, by holding onto her abbreviated crop top.

With her own face within an inch of the other girl's face, she used the rudest words she had ever learnt to describe her. Then she modified her tone, but increased the menace.

"You tried to kill me, bitch. That was a very stupid thing to do. Now, I don't know who you are but I am going to find out and sue you and your pampering parents for everything they've got."

Libby Falconer almost fell back on her bottom when she was shoved by the woman. She had made a very bad mistake, but still thought she could take control.

"It was an accident. You weren't hurt."

Without warning, Les grabbed Libby again and shoved her into the ditch. Then, very deliberately, she slammed the car door against her hip. Exaggerating a limp, Les stood over the now terrified Libby Falconer. "I am going to report you to the police. I am going to insist that you be charged. I hope you'll be sent to the hell hole where I have been for the last two years. Your kind gets eaten alive."

When she turned to leave, Les kicked the door shut, leaving a noticeable dent. "I am sure you are going to be a lying little bitch, but even if your rich parents get you off, I will get even with you."

Libby Falconer waited until the woman was a little way down the road before standing up. She resisted the urge to take her anger at herself out on the car. It was going to be hard enough to explain this new dent – just when her old man had lifted his banishment and restrictions. How was she to know that the bleached haired bimbo wasn't Peg Jessup?

This situation was her own fault. The town all thought Peg Jessup a murderer. If she had damaged her it would only have been just. She would be unable to run from the police again. Well, it wasn't like she had intended to kill her.

"Bitch! Whoever you are. They'll pick you up in town. I'll get there first and tell my story first!"

Libby made for the nearest house and asked to use their phone. She called her mother and claimed that she had just seen Peg Jessup up along Ridge Road. She smiled maliciously as she hung up. Her mother, still against Peg Jessup, would be calling the cops. They'd be sure to be along in jig time. In the meantime, she would try to get her car back on the road. If the police came, she'd blame the accident on seeing Peg Jessup unexpectedly, and claim the bitch had threatened her. Even if the police realised that mad woman was someone else, it would work for her.

Then a niggling doubt surfaced. The woman wasn't Peg Jessup. Wasn't a mouse she could threaten with impunity.

Les recognised the approaching car as a police car and began to exaggerate her fake limp. When it pulled up level with her, she glanced at the driver and continued on. No use pretending she liked cops. The car stopped and both occupants got out.

"You've had some trouble," the driver commented. He had senior cop impressed on his whole manner.

"Yeah. Some silly bitch in a red convertible hit me – deliberately drove at me. I am going to have a huge bruise on my hip."

"Do you want to make a report?"

"Too damn right I do."

"We can give you a lift. We were just on our way to check on an incident up this way."

The car radio squawked, and the younger cop went to answer it.

"Where have you come from?"

Les considered lying to the man, as she usually would have – just on principle. However, she decided that the truth…almost all of it…would serve her better.

"Peg Jessup's place. She invited me here once I'd got out of Meredan."

Senior cop nodded. So, he already knew who she was then.

"You went inside?"

"Yeah. So what? Your fancy tape hadn't stopped anyone else. The inside is a mess. Damn looters. I just took some cans of food. Peg promised to help me make a new start."

"Where did you encounter the car?"

"Near this end of Ridge Road. I think the dumb bitch thought I was Peg. If she is like the rest of the town, I sure know why the kid was desperate to get away."

The younger cop gestured to the car. "We will take you to a doctor and get your statement."

For a moment, she wanted to refuse – but she was innocent. The other bitch had run at her and deserved to be yelled at. So she accepted the lift, but sat right back in the rear seat, trying not to be seen if these cops spoke to the red car's driver.

Les could hear every lying word the bitch claimed and wondered who the police would believe.

"Miss Falconer, your mother told us that you had seen Peg Jessup up here," older cop asked.

"I did see her. She kicked my car door."

"Was that after you tried to run her down…again?"

"What do you mean? I didn't try to run anyone down. I was threatened."

"Now, now Miss Falconer. I can see you are distraught. How were you threatened?" That was younger cop, being placating.

Libby described the encounter, her voice rising to near hysterical.

"How did your car end up in the ditch?" The older cop wasn't stupid.

"Because I saw Peg Jessup!"

Les laughed silently. "That's for my friend, bitch. Keep it up. You are talking yourself into a stint in Meredan, or somewhere worse." Some of the poor bitches in there had done less than attempted murder to be called 'uncontrolled'. These cops were sharp. She would have to keep that in mind, but perhaps, if she asked nicely, they might tell her where Peg went.

Les allowed the doctor to look at her 'injury'. She pretended it hurt like hell when he pressed on it. He prescribed something for the pain, and suggested rest and to put ice on it. He even provided a bag of ice and a cloth to put around it. Les decided that she could keep pretending. The young cop was being quite civil, and really, he wasn't bad looking.

When she was allowed to go, he even asked if she was up to making a statement. Of course she would be driven to their station for that.

The older cop was at his desk when Les was escorted upstairs to the detective office. He said nothing, just allowed the younger one, York, to ask the questions after he had settled her in a chair.

"Okay, tell me what happened?"

"You know who I am, don't ya?" Les challenged. "Are you going to give me a fair hearing?"

York nodded. "I guessed it might be you when Mrs Bernstein rang report seeing Peg at her place. I also spoke to the governor at Meredan. He said that you had calmed down a lot since you arrived."

"Guess I did. Wasn't so much fun lording it over the others once Peg got out. She and I were going to start afresh somewhere. She promised to help me. I don't have any other friends. I thought she would be here. Do you know where she went?"

When York began to rub his chin, and then glanced at the other cop, Les decided that she wasn't going to like the answer. "She's not dead, is she?"

"It is seeming less likely that she is," York told her.

"What does that mean?"

"You haven't stopped in town then?"

"No. I went straight to Peg's. So what's the deal?"

"We haven't seen Peg since her Aunt was murdered."

"Shit! If you think Peg did that you're nuts. The kid doesn't have the guts for that."

York merely shrugged. Les guessed he wasn't going to tell all he knew.

"We also found clothing and blood near a local waterhole. The clothing was Peg's and the blood matched her type."

"You reckon she killed herself then? Found a body?"

York shook his head.

"Sounds like she is well rid of this place. I thought the kid was whining about trifles. Never really reckoned the town was out to kill her…until today. I want that bitch in the red car charged with attempted murder."

One thing that Les had learnt from Peg was how the truth could sometimes be used as a weapon, and this time, Les was enjoying herself. She had little doubt that the girl's family would extricate her somehow, but she had definitely heard the cop say 'again' along with running into someone. So, maybe they wouldn't.

"So I left Peg's place, gave the nosy neighbour the finger, and headed here to see if anyone knew where Peg was. Several Sunday drivers passed me, and then I saw this fancy red car approaching. I was having fun running down the rich bastard that had it when it came right at me. I didn't quite avoid it…"

Les stared at York, daring him to think she had lied. Who would believe that she had deliberately hurt herself like she had? She would have a bruise, but at that, it wouldn't be as bad as some that Mick had given her.

In answer to a prompt from York, Les continued, "Yeah, I yelled at her. She could have killed me and I wanted to put the fear of hell into her. I mean, she can't just drive at people and I wanted her to think twice before pulling that stunt on me again."

"She said you had threatened to come after her."

"Yeah, well, I was angry and that was part of the scare. Real thing is, the bitch isn't worth the trouble and I don't want to go back inside. I guessed she thought I was Peg and all, but really, that's a pretty sick minded reason."

"Will you be staying in town for when this goes before the judge?" York asked.

Les realised that staying in Matlock now hadn't been her plan. "Hadn't planned past meeting up with Peg. Can I camp out at her place?"

For a moment, York considered, he glanced at Maddern who had been silent throughout the conversation. He now said, "It should be fine."

York went on, "What then though? Where will you go? Back to your family?"

The crow-like laugh was out of her before she even considered how to answer. "My Ma is dead and my old man ain't coming out of Long Bay until he is dead. No. Me and Peg were going to travel and find jobs as we went. Dunno what I will do now."

Les knew the cops wouldn't like that. They would assume that she would go back to stealing, so she used the truth again. "Suppose I will have to go back to Melbourne and check out a few places the Chaplain mentioned where I could stay. I learnt typing in Meredan, so I can try for a job doing that."

Lie though it was, as far as the doing went, the cop relaxed.

"I will type up your statement for you to sign. If you like, I will get a sandwich sent up for you."

"Yeah, thanks. I would like." Les would have liked both cops to vanish so she could look through their file drawers for info about Peg, but that didn't look like happening, so she studied the office and considered ways to sneak in later. Mick had taught her all sorts of ways to get into places.

While Les was eating the sandwiches, the older cop, Maddern, had a call and went downstairs. She tried to hear the talking from down there, but could only here the general tone. The screeching that started, she decided was the bitch from the red car, and it sounded like the girl was hysterical. That wouldn't work in her favour. She sounded crazy.

No, the bitch was crazy if she risked her pampered life because of some petty grievance – like one of her persecution victims coming back at her. From the odd words that she caught, it suggested that the kid had actually grown a spine after all. This girl must have been one of those who had bullied Peg for years. Still, Peg shouldn't have let her off last time. That girl didn't deserve a second chance, didn't appreciate the advantages she had.

"Okay, Les, sign and date the last page and initial each of the others."

Les broke from her reverie and read the formal version of her statement as she finished the last sandwich. After signing, she asked, "What next?"

"I'll be going to collect the medical report from the doctor."

"Uh, I meant to ask. Am I going to have to pay that doctor? I don't have much money."

"No, that was official business."

Later, after York had found a blanket for her to use on the beds at Peg's place, and driven her there, Les felt at a loss for what to do. The police had requested the hearing for the following day, probably at the insistence of the girl's parents. That suited her. She wanted to be rid of this place as soon as possible.

Chapter 18

Mike Scott returned from Tamworth accompanied by his father, who he had told should talk to the police about knowing the woman whose body had been found in the waterhole. Ian had mentioned that he had recognised a piece of jewellery that he had seen on one of the new artists. He had tried to get to talk to the girl, but she had kept avoiding him.

It wasn't just because of that cameo, the avoiding had started well before he had seen that.

Ian had been around when the Tamworth police had turned up asking to talk to Megan Arthur. Mike had heard of it later, and assumed that by now, they knew her everyday name was Megan Dawes. Luckily, Jack had been ahead of the game, and with more luck, his friends were well away from Tamworth by now. Trouble was, their disappearance was going to look mighty suspicious, and the police would likely up the hunt for Peg.

As far as Mike was concerned, Peg wasn't guilty of anything except trying to stay alive. Yet, the only way that Peg could have got that cameo was from her Aunt's stuff. Her dead aunt!

Obviously, there was more to the whole affair than he knew. Like, how come everyone was looking out for that cameo now, when it must have vanished two decades ago? It should have been long forgotten.

The question was, how much did Peg and Jack know that they hadn't told him? Probably a lot, but he didn't hold that against them. Neither of them would want him in trouble for being involved with them. But he already was involved. He had taken stuff to be hidden in Melbourne.

While Ian went to the hotel where he had stayed on his last visit, Mike went home to the boarding house. He had had more than enough of his father's morose drinking. At least deciding to come here seemed to be bringing him closer to some closure about losing the love of his life. He was going to talk to Maddern in the morning, but had rejected Mike's offer to go with him. Not surprising, since it wasn't his business. It was just disappointing as Mike admitted to himself, he had hoped to learn something useful to Peg. After all, Ian had known Ida Jessup when she had been Adelaide Swan,

Too bad. Maybe though, once Ian had talked to the police, he might be encouraged to talk about things to him later.

With Ian likely to be busy most of the day, Mike went back to work. He was greeted with, "Glad you're back. Can you take over out here? I have some book work to do."

During the day, in the brief periods of quiet, Mike decided that he and Ian should visit Jack Casey. That might be the best way to get Ian talking. He was still considering that idea when some of the town girls his age came in and took over two tables.

"I hear they caught Peg Jessup the other day," one of the girls spoke in what Mike guessed was a deliberately loud voice. Since he knew Peg was in New South Wales, he didn't react, even when a second voice added, "Yeah, fancy that dumb bitch just going home as innocent as you please. She will be in more trouble for kicking Libby's car, too."

Mike went over. "What do you young ladies want today?" For some reason, his smile annoyed the girls. He took their orders, ignoring further snide remarks aimed at himself. He took the order to Eva, the boss's younger girl. She set about making the drinks and gave him a different story.

"Those girls want to think it was Peg, and half the town is convinced," Eva said, knowing he had liked Peg.

"So, if it wasn't her, who was it?" Mike asked quietly.

Eva glanced at the girls before answering. "Some friend of hers from wherever they had her locked up."

Only one person came into Mike's mind – Les Shaw.

"Those girls aren't too happy," Eva went on. "Their Mama's have told them to keep away from Libby Falconer."

Eva's malicious grin suggested that some juicy gossip was going around. "Oh?"

"Yes, Libby reckons she saw Peg Jessup up on Ridge Road and Peg threatened her. Her car has a huge dent in one door. I saw it. Not only that, the police say it wasn't Peg Jessup and the woman she tried to hit with the car has had her charged with assault and intending to kill her. Libby had to go to court and all. Heard later that she had to go off and see a forensic psychiatrist."

"I should think so," Mike muttered. "That's the second time she has done something like that. Did they revoke her driver's licence?" He started to prepare the tray for the drinks, and placed a plate of cakes on it.

Eva had one final comment. "I heard that she might even get sent away for being uncontrollable."

That, Mike decided, would serve Libby Falconer right. "Maybe it will be a lesson for her friends," he told Eva, just before taking the tray over to the group.

Now he had new thoughts to consider. Like would the rumours that Peg had come back reach Harry King and bring him back? Surely that bastard had figured out that Peg must have got away…hadn't died…

"How'd it go?" Mike asked Ian when he came to visit that evening.

"As I expected. They started off thinking me a suspect," Ian grimaced. "They only have an approximate date of death on those bones. Twenty years ago. That would have been before I was shopped for possession and trafficking – but she was fine before I was sent away. It was when I was inside that she vanished. Her parents have always blamed me for getting her hooked on drugs, but it wasn't me. I never touched drugs. It might have been one of the band, or roadies, but not me. The whole thing was a set up."

"But why?" Mike was confused.

"I think I can guess. Megan, I mean Margaret Blair, had a chunk of shares in her old man's company. I think whoever was Adelaide Swan's pimp, wanted them, so he got her hooked on heroin and made her a whore. The same guy that the task force has been after for twenty years. I was in the way. I might have…no, would have taken her away."

Ian was silent for a long time. Mike poured him a beer and waited to see if he would volunteer more.

"Maddern asked me if I knew she was pregnant."

"What?"

"Apparently, according to the autopsy, she had given birth shortly before she died. The bones hadn't gone back to normal or something."

"Was she? When you last saw her?"

"She'd not said anything, but we'd had sex a few times."

Now Mike began to understand the weeks of drinking. "You think it might have been your kid? And you are blaming yourself for what? Not knowing?"

"I know. It's stupid. If she had known, she would have told me."

"More likely, it's some other Joe's doing." Mike intended to sound harsh. "You were in jail for two years."

"Are you trying to tell me to be thankful to have found you?" Ian faced his son.

"Well…yeah!"

"I am, truly," Ian admitted. "I am lucky to have found you again."

"Don't get greedy then," Mike muttered. "Any others you lost on the way might have been real ratbags." He realised that he had spoilt the moment and added hurriedly, "Why don't we go up and visit with Jack Casey? See if he knows anything more about things."

Once Peg and Jack were in the boarding house, using a room that had been vacated only two hours before, they relaxed. Officially, they were not taking the room until the following day – so anyone who thought to check for new arrivals, wouldn't know of them yet.

"How long did you book this room for?" Peg asked, as she pulled out some clean clothes to change into.

"A week for now. Any fuss should have died down by next week. "

"Then what?"

"We need to plan what we do."

"Go to Sydney?" Peg suggested. "I still can't believe Wayne Carson wants me for a backup act."

"Yes, and as soon as you appear…" Jack began.

"Whoever wants me will come out of the air. Are we going to have to run forever?"

"As long as it takes," Jack promised. "Until we work out exactly what is going on."

"You mean about those shares?"

"That and everything else," Jack agreed. "It has to be more than just a takeover bid. Surely companies don't send out bullies to extort shares from people."

"Unless those who want to control the company are crooks," Peg suggested. "I know Harry King works for Gianni Costa."

"I know that too. That's what I mean. I haven't had much time to find out about this Costigan mob and how they might be related to Costa."

"And don't forget that shareholder's meeting. I sent off the RSVP."

"You are not still thinking of walking into that meeting as the lost heiress?"

"I want to go, but not with all the bells and whistles blowing. I'd prefer to be a mouse in a hole. But if I went, I wouldn't understand anything, and I don't want my alleged grandfather putting me under the spotlight."

"You want to know more about your mother's family?" Jack asked.

"Pretty much. I may decide I want nothing to do with him, but I already know that I don't want Gianni getting my shares."

"We need a broker then, or a financial advisor. You have a lot of money in an account we don't dare access at the moment. So we need someone who we can trust, who will let your whereabouts remain anonymous, and will give you good advice."

Peg flopped onto the bed and asked, "You have someone in mind?"

"No. I figured on going to a bank, not one we are using, and get them to recommend someone."

"If they do that," Peg said morosely. Then she made an admission. "Do you know what I would like to do"

"About what?"

"The money. I think it would be amusing if I could buy the horse farm where Mr Owens lives. Not to toss him off it, because he gave me a chance, but so he doesn't have to bow and scrape to the Falconers any more."

"It would be an investment," Jack agreed.

"And, I could have a slight hold over him so that when Ned and Jasper are released, and Stan, finally gets out, I can ask Owens to give them a go."

"You're incredible," Jack told her, going to lie on the bed next to her. "What if the old girl won't sell?"

"Hmmm. I will see if the old Lomax place is up for sale."

"That might be a better place to start. You said that was derelict, didn't you?"

Peg nodded. "Forever, it seems like."

"Let's keep that as an option. Do we want to look for an advisor in this town?"

"What do you think?"

"We could do a quick trip somewhere else, where no one will expect us to be. Somewhere between here and Sydney. Newcastle, Goulburn, or maybe Port Macquarie."

"There!" Peg decided. "I have never been to the coast."

"Port Macquarie it is then."

Peg dressed carefully for the appointment, wanting to appear as a polite, middle class woman. Jack, coming with her, was wearing a suit that he had found in an op-shop. They both agreed that if their selected advisor made them uneasy in any way, they would decline his services.

However, they decided they had chosen well. The man, Albert Stuart, was young, savvy and knowledgeable.

"Mr Stuart," Peg began, once they had been seated in his private office. "I have inherited a number of shares and I need guidance. Up until recently, my mother looked after these shares. Her advisor, however, has retired, and passed his file onto me. I was assured that it was up to date at that time, and all information that another advisor would need was included."

Stuart made no move to reach for the file resting on the edge of his desk, just waited for Peg to continue.

"However, I have since discovered that the company, whose shares I hold, is being subjected to a takeover bid."

"May I look at the file?" Stuart asked.

Peg slid it to within his reach. And studied the man's reactions as he read through the initial pages.

"Blair holdings. Yes, I'd heard of their situation. Have you decided what you want to do?"

Peg wasn't ready to say more, but decided to warn the man about her experience of unfriendly interest. She summarised that briefly, and went on to add, "So, you see, I don't know which group approached me. I do know that my mother was cast out by her father. I doubt I would be particularly welcome by him. I have no idea of my father, you see."

"Let me get my secretary to look up some information, while I look through this file."

Stuart made a phone call, and a short time later, a girl about Jack's age came in with two thick files in ring binders. He asked her then to find out the current value of shares in a number of companies that included Costigan Consolidated and Blair Holdings.

"You would make a hefty profit if you sold your shares now – if these latest figures are still accurate."

"I know that," Peg admitted. "I just don't know if I want to. There was a notice of a shareholders meeting on the fourteenth of February. I sent off the RSVP, but I am not sure if I would be wise to go in person and I don't simply want to give them my proxy vote. Not without finding out more about them."

They spent several hours talking and learning about shares and takeovers and how best to receive and invest the dividends. Stuart seemed to understand their desire for anonymity. He agreed to attend the Blair Holdings shareholder meeting and sound out his welcome. They promised to provide a contact number and be available by phone on the day.

"One thing," Stuart asked. "Where are the actual share certificates?"

With mental fingers crossed, Peg told him, "In a storage facility in Melbourne. For safety. Do you need them?"

"I may," he proposed. "I will let you know. For now though, have you any objection to my having a copy made of each of these documents?"

"For your use?" Peg asked. "I am wary of having the originals out of my possession."

"We have a very secure safe and the company has a reputation for the highest integrity."

Jack, who had said very little during the meeting, murmured, "They would be better away from us…"

Peg nodded, that she had heard him, and did trust his instincts. "Could you do two copies? One for you, and one for me. I will put the originals in a bank deposit box."

While the secretary was doing the copying, Stuart asked, "Was there anything else?"

Jack murmured, "Bank account?"

"Yes, maybe," Peg said. "Until I was eighteen, the dividends from the shares had been accumulating in trust for me. I have been considering what you said about investing them. If I wanted to purchase some property, could you act for me?"

"Certainly. Do you have a property in mind?"

"Not yet," Peg hedged. "Jack and I will need to decide where we want to settle. I am more interested in sorting out these shares at the moment."

"Fair enough. Where will I be able to contact you?"

Jack leant forward. "If you will allow us time to find lodgings here, we will be able to let you know. We were working in Tamworth during the festival, and need to go back to finalise our contracts. So for the next few days you can leave a message at the Tamworth Grand Hotel."

"I am glad all that's dealt with," Peg admitted as they headed for the bus terminal. "I hope he is as straight as he seems."

"I think he is. What I hope is that he doesn't tell us to take our business elsewhere. He is sure to have us checked out and that might alert the wrong people."

"He shouldn't be able to find out anything about Megan Blair," Peg pointed out.

"It is not you that I am worried about. One hint of my whereabouts will probably bring my uncle's unwelcome interest."

Even if his uncle was honest, as he wanted to believe, he didn't want to be questioned by him. He also hoped that Stuart didn't learn that Margaret Blair had died twenty years ago.

Albert Stuart arrived at the shareholder's meeting and was immediately aware of the hired security men ringing the conference room. When he presented the document, signed by Megan Blair and appointing him as her proxy, the greeter looked startled and when he checked the share numbers on the document, he gestured to someone. Two of the security men moved up behind him.

"Mr Blair would like to meet you, Sir."

The welcome hadn't surprised him, given the situation that Megan had confided to him. It was one reason why he had arrived early. He saw a big man separate from a group and head towards him. After cordial introductions, Blair invited him into a small side room.

The tone then changed to one of challenge.

"I am told you are acting on behalf of a Megan Blair. Tell me about her."

"I have only met the young woman on one occasion, although we have spoken by phone more often. She seems to me to be a serious sort of person." Albert watched the big man and saw anger, although it was quickly controlled.

"Mr Stuart, I don't know who that young woman might be, but I do know that the shares you claim to represent belonged to my daughter. I have recently discovered that she died twenty years ago. So, whoever has held these shares since then, stole them from my daughter. They do not belong to your client, and I insist that you surrender them immediately."

"You have no authority to take them, Mr Blair. I have all the paperwork from the time your daughter took control of them, and it is all in perfect order."

A growl came from Blair as he held onto his temper. Stuart took the opportunity to make a bid for top position in the confrontation.

"The important consideration for you is that I came here in good faith to hear what you have to say. I am instructed to act as I see fit. So far, my welcome is not cordial. If you wish, I can leave now and approach Costigan

Consolidated. I would advise against trying to block those shares as I believe that you require their voting power to prevent the takeover."

Blair had to keep his mouth tightly shut until he was able to say, "Very well, I'd like you to arrange a meeting between myself and your client."

"I will ask my client if she is willing," Stuart promised.

"I want a binding agreement to have sole voting rights for those shares."

"I will wait to hear what you have to say at the meeting, Mr Blair, before I make any recommendations to my client."

"Did your paperwork also include the information that those shares may have been given to my daughter, but they are held on the constraint that she couldn't sell them outside of the family?"

"Yes," Stuart confirmed. "However, the wording of that document does not state that a subsequent family recipient cannot sell them on."

Blair's face grew redder. "Are you trying to say that the current alleged owner of these shares is some illegitimate by blow from who knows what criminal scum?"

Stuart had the passing thought that the condition had been imposed so that if his daughter wanted money from them, she would have to come to her father to get it.

The old man now had a point, but, "I am not privy to my client's origins, but yes, I have seen proof that my client is indeed the daughter of Margaret Blair."

As he spoke, Stuart was aware of a younger man entering the room. Blair noticed as well and demanded, "What is it?"

"Everyone has arrived, Father," We are ready to start."

"I'll be out in a moment." To Stuart, he said, "I want a further word with you before you leave."

"Oh God, we're screwed," Peg wailed. "I didn't want my so called grandfather knowing about me!"

"Calm down! What did Stuart say?"

"Blair grandpa, wants to meet me. He told Stuart that my mother died twenty years ago."

"And…?"

"He wants to see the Power of Attorney that my mother did for Aunt Ida."

"That's not a problem. Will he keep it confidential?" Jack asked.

"I think so, but either I will have to tell him more than we want to admit or he is going to start investigating things on his own. That is sure to get to the police. If he finds out that the police want me – he will probably feel it is his duty to tell them where I am. And what if Gianni hears about it?"

"Stuart doesn't have this address, only the phone number and we are not using Dawes as our name here."

"Not the point! Your uncle could easily get that number traced, and you can't be sure to be around the phone when Stuart rings next. What if our landlady says there is no Mr and Mrs Dawes here?"

"Point. But we don't dare leave here yet. There is still a greater police presence here than there was during the festival."

"Like I said, we're screwed. They only have to do a building to building search and they might think it justified if they get a hint that we haven't left Tamworth. We can't keep wasting money on bus tickets we aren't going to use or weeks of accommodation fees that we don't use."

"Let me think," Jack asked. "We need a diversion."

"Why don't you ring Mike Scott?" Peg suggested. "Maybe he can start a rumour that I have gone back there. Then maybe they will think we used this number as a message service."

"That's not a bad idea, the message service. Mike might be in that. I will go and see if I can catch him at work."

When he returned, he found that Peg had repacked their kit bags.

"Just in case," was her reason. Then demanded, "What's so amusing," when she saw Jack's mouth twitch.

He shut the door and gave her a hug. "It seems that providence provided a diversion just as you ordered...."

"What? Out with it!"

"Mike told me that your friend, Les Shaw, turned up in Matlock yesterday and went to your Aunt's place."

"Yikes, I totally forgot when she was due out. Damn. I promised that I would help her get a fresh start. I wonder if Mike can get a message to her?"

"Do you trust her to keep a secret?"

"Totally. Anyway, go on..."

"Well, according to Mike, half the town knows she isn't you but the rest are convinced that she is."

"I assume the police know it is Les?"

"Probably, but the most amusing part , I think you will agree, is that little Miss Falconer, recently reunited with her fancy red car and allowed back home, is now in police custody for an unprovoked attack on your friend. She apparently tried to run Les down."

"Les is okay, though?"

"She claims to have a huge bruise on her hip and a limp, but Mike heard part of Libby's claim that Les slammed the door on her own hip and put a dent in it by kicking it. No one believes her it seems."

Peg knew it was wrong to laugh at Libby Falconers misfortune but she had brought that on herself. "Well, that makes it the second time she has used that car as a weapon. But as for Les, I can well believe that she did exactly what you said. She probably put the fear of hell into Libby as well. I suppose they will get shrinks to evaluate her?"

Jack shrugged. "Mike didn't say – but I reckon you might have your distraction."

"I need to talk to Les, can you see if Mike can give her this number?"

"What are you going to suggest?"

"Nothing specific, but if Les knows why I had to run, she'll be on our side. I need to explain. I will make her promise not to do anything illegal, and maybe I can send her some money. I suspect she will enjoy impersonating me. And causing confusion."

"I wouldn't want her to get hurt," Jack warned.

"You don't know her like I do. She taught me how to stand up for myself, and she can take care of herself."

"Okay, I will get onto that. Let's hope word filters up here quickly."

Two days later, Jack and Peg departed Tamworth with a refund for part of their originally intended stay. Their land lady had accepted Jack's claim that he was needed back home, since his brother had been hurt. He asked her if she would take messages if anyone called for them, and she readily agreed to pass messages on to the number Jack gave her for where they intended to stay in Port Macquarie.

The following afternoon, they presented themselves at Albert Stuart's office.

"I understand your concern, Mr Stuart," Peg assured him. "And there is information that I do not feel comfortable passing on. To do so would put me in danger."

"What can you tell me? You have a power of attorney authorising a Miss Annie Simmons to act for Margaret Blair. Who is this woman?"

"I was raised by her, only she had been using the name Adelaide Swan for many years. I believe she was presenting herself to your predecessor – the man who prepared that file – as Margaret Blair. No doubt it was simpler, avoided questions and reduced the chance of Mr Blair finding her."

Jack inserted a question. "Did Mr Blair give you any indication as to why he lost contact with his daughter some years before her death?"

"No. Is that relevant?"

"I think so," Peg gave her opinion. "If he had found her earlier, he might have taken her endowment from her. However, that's only one aspect. I believe that someone else had the idea of trying to get those shares from her."

"How can you possibly know that if your real mother died just after you were born?"

"Because Annie Simmons was killed recently," Peg said, trying to keep her voice even. "The men wanted those shares."

Before Stuart could take that in and comment, Jack added, "And if my wife had not been extremely fortunate, she'd have died too."

"So all that matters, is that I do have the right to have those shares," Peg told him. "And I have no interest in meeting David Blair, or claiming kinship with him. I reckon that his treatment of his daughter led to some other group seeing a chance to use her to get them. As I told you before, I am willing to use those shares to block that takeover, and thwart that other group. David Blair, can otherwise go and sit in the hell he created for himself."

"And you, Mr Stuart, would be wise not to try and confirm this for yourself," Jack added.

"I see…" Stuart wanted to sound calm. "Will you be staying in Port Macquarie for a few more days?"

Jack shook his head. "We've already made arrangements to leave. Our new number for messages is…" he slipped a piece of paper across the man's desk. "We will check it regularly."

Peg spoke then. "I would appreciate it if you could arrange transfer of the accumulated dividends to a new account in my married name."

"You were talking of investing in property," Stuart reminded her.

"Yes, but I think that will need to wait."

"And I think you should organise to make a will," was the next suggestion.

"We will be in touch, Mr Stuart," Jack promised, nudging Peg to stand and leave. "We will see ourselves out."

Peg was starting to recognise when Jack was feeling danger, so she took the hint and let him walk her back to reception. Before they left, he asked the girl if there were toilets they could use. The girl, was in the middle of connecting an incoming call, and merely gestured down a different passage.

Jack pulled Peg along, glancing back to check they were out of the girl's sight before stopping at a door marked 'switch room'. It was locked but Jack quickly had it open, pushed her in and closed the door after them.

"Don't touch anything," he warned in a quiet voice.

It wasn't quite dark in there, since there were a number of glowing red and green point lights.

"Was someone coming?" Peg asked quietly, keeping close to Jack.

"Hope not, but I had the feeling that Stuart was trying to keep us there."

"We are still here," Peg pointed out.

"Shh. If we're quiet, they won't look in here. We can leave after dark. Meanwhile, there should be room for us to sit."

They did, keeping close still. Peg put her mouth to Jack's ear. "What spooked you?"

"That call that Stuart got, just after we sat down. Whoever was at the other end said something about 'half an hour'."

"Who do you reckon it was?"

"Take your pick – Blair, Gianni, the police, my uncle…"

"Do you think we can still trust him?" Peg asked.

"For now. My guess is that he had started making enquiries, or Blair set someone on him."

"So we need to leave here," Peg said. "And I really like it here."

"We can always come back, but shh. If they come this way looking, I might be able to hear a voice I recognise."

Put that way, she might too. Jack was probably listening for his uncle's booming voice.

Their play of being newlyweds was continuing to give them excuse for keeping to their rented room and to appear infrequently. On the day after their night departure from Stuart's office building, their land lord brought a message from him. Just a request to ring. They went to a phone booth that was well away from their lodgings. While Peg did the talking, Jack kept watching around them. They looked like a pair of young men, and hoped to confuse chance observers.

"What did you want, Mr Stuart? To apologise for trying to get me killed again?"

"That's a bit paranoid, isn't it? Who did you think was coming when you fled like that?"

"Who was it that wanted to see us?" Peg asked.

There was silence on the line for long enough for Peg to be considering hanging up. Jack's paranoia was getting to her.

"The person who arrived was not who I expected," Stuart finally admitted. "He gave his name as Thomas Mason, and said he was a representative from David Blair. He was trying to purchase the shares for three times their inflated value. However, he did not seem to realise that I had talked to Blair two days ago. He wasn't happy when I told him that I didn't have the actual certificates, and needed to discuss it with you."

"What did he look like?" Peg asked.

Stuart described a tall solid blond man and Peg shivered. It had to be Harry King.

"Mr Stuart, be very careful. That sounds like the man who threatened my former guardian. I suggest that you mention him to Mr Blair and suggest he takes it to the police."

"I have already contacted the police. Our offices were broken into early this morning. The copy of your file was missing."

Peg swore a vile curse that caused Stuart to stutter, "Really!"

"What about the details for the bank account? My mother's and my birth certificates?" Peg demanded.

"They were with me, at home. They are safe. It was just the copies of the shares information. I had the originals."

"Can anyone use the copies to get control of them?"

"No – they may be hoping to find you. I now understand that you were not being paranoid and why you were being cagey and secretive."

Peg thought, as an aside to herself, that he didn't know all the reasons.

"Do whatever you can to help the police get that info back, Mr Stuart, but don't try to call us again. We'll call you."

She hung up abruptly, exited the box and dragged Jack into a nearby shop – one that sold fishing stuff.

"This place arranges fishing trips," Jack told her. "Shall I see if one is going out this arvo?"

"Yeah. Then I will tell you what he said."

Out on the water, with ten others who were all keen fishermen, Peg was able to relax. She didn't care about fishing – and those who were ignored her. Jack made a pretence of fishing, while Peg told him about the call.

"I wonder if this will be over, if the takeover fails," Jack mused.

Peg considered that, but not for long. "No, because Gianni will be livid. There must be a reason why he is trying to get control of Blair Holdings. Whatever it is, won't have changed. He will keep trying. As for Blair, I very much doubt that he will suddenly like his slut of a daughter's illegitimate issue."

"You are insisting that Gianni is behind the takeover, so what connection does he have to Costigan?"

"Damned if I know," Peg sighed. "And I am damned if I know why Gianni suddenly took an interest in Stan. She then had to explain to Jack what her eldest foster brother had told her.

"I might try to contact some friends of mine in Melbourne," Jack decided. "Other than that, let's just enjoy ourselves for a bit."

All was quiet when they returned to their lodgings with several decent sized ocean bass to present to their hosts.

"Well cook these up tomorrow," was the promise, and since the woman made no mention of any messages for them, they slipped up to their room with relief.

Although the combination of wind, sun and fresh air had tired them, neither were ready to sleep. While Peg went for a wash, Jack found a channel on the TV covering motor sport and settled in a chair to watch it. He took his turn in the shower when she had finished, and returned to find her paying rapt attention to an interview with a V8 driver.

He listened for a while, saw the caption that identified the driver as Reg Costigan and guessed what had caught her attention. However, she surprised him by pointing to the driver. "I've seen someone like him before."

Jack studied the light haired man. He was tall, solidly built, and a striking figure in his racing suit. He knew Costigan by sight, since he liked to watch V8 racing.

"Seen when…?"

Peg's comment had been more of a delaying tactic, because she was still trying to convince herself of something she'd seen – just for an instant. All of a sudden, she pointed a finger at a figure in the hovering crowd. "There! Look! That fat man."

Now Jack realised that he had been mistaken in who he had thought she was pointing to. "What about him?" Jack found it hard to recall details from that glimpse.

"Did you have this on for any reason?" Peg asked. "I was ignoring the show until Reg Costigan was mentioned. "Who does Reg Costigan remind you of? Someone you met recently."

They had met lots of people recently.

"Just before we left Matlock," Peg hinted. She saw by the look on his face that Jack had made the connection.

"Stan," he murmured. "But this guy has blond hair…"

"Bleached," Peg determined.

"He's clean shaven, well fed, but yeah, I think I can see a likeness."

"Stan is Gianni's bastard son. If he is like Reg Costigan, there has to be a connection. And that fat man I pointed out, grey haired and clean shaven? He has a figure like Gianni Costa."

"Why hasn't anyone seen this before?" Jack stared at Peg.

"It isn't that obvious I suppose, unless you know the people. I had never seen Reg Costigan so clearly before, so I never connected it. And it is pure fluke I even saw Gianni with Aunt Ida, and heard his name."

"We have to tell your Jack Casey about this," Jack told Peg. "The police have been after Gianni for twenty years, or so my uncle says. All he is, is a name, no one is even sure he is real."

"Except for me," Peg said carefully. "Although I hope Aunt Ida never told him that I had spied on him once when he came to visit. And I know what she was to him. Undoubtedly he has got an alter ego that is perfectly respectable. I need to remember some stuff Aunt Ida was saying once… something she said. But I do remember that she was scared because….well, I think she recognised Gianni somewhere, before hearing him called something else. I think she did discover his second identity."

"You're saying that he is John Costigan," Jack summarised, shaking his head. "It can't be, my uncle is friends with him."

Peg twisted to face him and merely said, "He has got to be exceedingly clever. Your uncle, if he is honest, can't be the only person he has fooled."

"My uncle is…"

"Never mind, I don't want to argue about him."

"So…you don't want to tell the police either."

"I don't have any proof."

"Okay, the idea needs investigating. What say we mention the idea to Mike, who can casually mention a likeness to his dad…"

"Hang on, how will Mike explain meeting Stan?"

"Okay, he can mention it to Jack Casey instead. It will keep your disposition a mystery."

"Might work…"

"Okay. I will call him from a phone box tomorrow."

Jack turned the TV off and said, "How about bed?"

Peg squeezed into the phone booth with Jack after he had spoken to Mike. He had agreed to propose the idea, but had a request of his own.

"Is Peg there? I have somebody here who doesn't believe a word I say."

Peg took the phone Jack handed to her and said a cautions "Hi," into the mouth piece.

"Is that really you, effing little bitch?"

"None other, Captain Shaw," Peg confirmed her identity by using some cant from Meredan. In the back ground, she heard Les tell Mike to "Nick off."

"What's this about you being dead? Who's the bastard who tried it?"

"Long story, Les. Where are you staying?"

"With that cute guy you just called. Why?"

"We can call you there and talk longer."

"You'd better be a good little bitch. You promised to be here. Where are you?"

"North, but we will be moving soon. Have to."

"You serious? Some bastard still wants you dead?"

"I'm hoping he thinks he succeeded, but at the moment, he wants something that I know where is, and he might stumble onto my new name and stuff."

"You need my help, kid. Again."

"I wouldn't argue, but I have no idea what you can do without getting thrown back into the like of where you just left."

"You tell me all – tomorrow – and let me decide. Have you heard any more about where Mick is?"

"In hell, I hope. He talked Stan into escaping, but Stan is back in custody. You aren't going to try to get back with him?"

"Nah! He was losing interest anyway, but if he is still free he has found himself a nice crooked hideout and his protectors might know things useful to you."

Peg did not say that she agreed, but Les had a point.

"If you do that, be careful."

"Always am, kid."

Les hung up abruptly, and Peg eased out of the box to let Jack hang up the phone.

"Silly bitch is going to find out who is hiding Mick Devlin and work her way in with whoever is protecting him."

Jack rolled his eyes and refrained from comment. He just set about making another call, to one of his less than legal friends. Peg took over the role of watching out for anyone that might be taking an interest in them.

"So, that's it. My uncle must have lost our trail if he's pulling in my old mates to question them about me," Jack told Peg as they took a back route back to their lodgings.

"He might have, but King is still well onto the trail of those damn shares." She didn't need to remind him. "As soon as Stuart comes through with that bank account and I get the passbook, we can leave."

"I wonder if Harry King knows that name you are using." Jack wondered aloud. "Next time we speak to Stuart, we need to ask him if he mentioned it. If King is still looking for someone posing as Margaret Blair then he doesn't know too much."

"Or he is being cagey. David Blair only knows me as Megan Blair and the shares are now held in that name."

"But my uncle knows that we intended to get married, but may not have learnt the Blair name."

"I wonder - would your uncle recognise me now? Could you convince him that I am just another female you picked up since Peg Jessup is supposedly dead?"

"If we use all those names, we might confuse everyone who's looking for us," Jack said quietly. He started to grin. "What if we make another account and keep moving your money around – so all accounts seem active."

"So, when I go to Sydney, I'll go back to being Megan Arthur and get paid in that name. Cash I hope. At least my guitar should be safe with Carson's manager. It's one less thing to worry about.

When Jack turned up to collect the new bank book, he claimed to have come by bus and only had an hour before returning. He told Stuart, "We are still travelling around. I will contact you if we decide to settle for a bit."

"Fair enough," Stuart decided, the proposed something he had mentioned before. "I don't know if you heard my advice to your wife about making a will."

He gave his reasons and Jack saw the importance, and also a way to further confound the worst of those looking for Peg. "How do we do that?"

"We have people here who are experienced…"

"No."

"Well, you can find a solicitor somewhere or use one of those simple will forms. They tell you what you need to do."

"That will do for now," Jack decided. "Do you have two copies?"

Stuart took a second folded sheet from a drawer.

"Now, you told my wife that the thief only got the file related to the shares. Please be honest. Did you mention us by name when that man was here?"

"No, the man was simply referring to Margaret Blair. I did not choose to correct him. I assure you, client confidentiality is very important to me."

"Then how do you think this man Mason discovered you were dealing with Blair shares?" Jack demanded.

"There is a certain amount of due diligence that I needed to do," Stuart explained. "I mentioned no names, when I made the enquiries."

"Who did you contact?"

"The central share registry and I followed up on the RSVP to the shareholder meeting. At the share registry, I was attempting to understand the reason why Costigan Consolidated wanted Blair Holdings. All I could come up with was that they want to expand further into road transport."

In Jack's mind was the idea that Costigan's had an agent in the share registry. Stuart had contacted Blair and he had no reason to send anyone. It was just more evidence that Costigan's was involved with King or Costa.

"Right. If it wouldn't contravene your principles, could you not mention my wife's surname? Ideally, just refer to her as Margaret Blair?"

Stuart forced a smile of agreement, and Jack left.

Chapter 19

Jack heard a polite knock and expected to see their landlady at the door. When he had come in earlier, she had mentioned that she'd be bringing fresh towels and linen up for them.

He did not expect to see his uncle and his moment of hesitation was all Taylor needed to push his way in. Even if he hadn't, slamming the door in his uncle's face would not have made him go away.

"What do you want?" Jack demanded, keeping his voice low. His hosts did not need to hear an argument.

Taylor went and sat in one of the two easy chairs in the suite. "Sit down, Jack."

"No thanks. You won't be staying long."

"I am glad that you intend to cooperate." Taylor took a searching look around. "Are you still shacked up with that floosie from Tamworth?"

"That's none of your business."

"It might be," Taylor commented.

"Get to the point, uncle, or leave."

"Very well. I want to know what kind of scam you are trying to pull."

"Scam? What are you trying to pin on me now?"

"You know very well. Shares in Blair Holdings. You've got your floosie pretending to be the daughter of a dead woman."

Jack was about to protest, but if his uncle didn't think he was with Peg, he shouldn't refute it. Before he could think of a comeback, his uncle went on, "Did that Jessup trash tell you about them before she took herself off?"

Jack knew his uncle would take silence as guilt, but he didn't know what to say. Peg didn't trust him, had made accusations about him.

"No."

"Don't lie to me! The owner of those shares died twenty years ago. Her remains were found in a dam in the very district where the Jessup girl lived."

"That's a damn flimsy connection," Jack said, beginning to feel on safer ground. The feeling didn't last long.

"Is it? Margaret Blair was a whore, just like Ida Jessup, who moved to Matlock a year or two before the Blair girl died."

"It's nothing but conjecture!"

"Is it? Yet here you are, at the number your gullible advisor gave me to leave a message for you. He seemed to think that you had already left here."

"But, we told him it was a message drop." It was out before Jack could censor it.

"Yes, and I knew if I called it, you wouldn't answer it - since you have been avoiding me since your girlfriend killed herself. So, I had the number traced and waited outside. Saw you come in. I had a chance to glance at the register when I came in. If you are so squeaky clean, why use a false name? Obviously, the Mr and Mrs is so you don't advertise your adultery."

Jack still hadn't thought of a story that wouldn't sound contrived.

"How did you know to rush up to Matlock?" Taylor demanded.

"A friend."

"What did you know when you left to go?"

"Peg was in trouble."

"She'd killed her aunt? Did she say that? No, of course she wouldn't. So what happened?"

Jack shrugged. "I got there and heard about her aunt. I sat in town a while, hoping she would come. Then I heard about her clothes and the blood and how they thought she had jumped in the dam."

Jack recalled his desperation at that time and hoped some was revealed in his body language.

"So you went to her house?"

Jack nodded, rather than state the lie.

"When was that?"

"After all the forensic guys had gone."

"Where did you find the shares?"

"I didn't."

"Don't lie!"

"I'm not," he protested. He wanted his uncle to believe him. "I went there, but there was police tape all around. And I heard a car coming. When it stopped in Peg's drive, I hid under the house. I found a box of stuff under there."

"What else was there?"

Jack shrugged again. "Old letters, some photographs, nothing of value to me. Except there was one from a solicitor, and a birth certificate."

Now it seemed like his Uncle believed him, and that gave Jack amusement. His uncle wasn't as sharp as he thought.

"So you picked up a floosie, and taught her to be the dead woman's daughter?"

This time Jack said nothing.

"Have you got the actual share certificates?"

"No."

"The truth, now!"

"I said, no."

"Do you know where they are?"

"Truthfully, no."

"Who made up the fake birth certificate for the so called daughter?"

"Honestly, the certificate isn't a fake."

Taylor glared at his nephew. "It has to be. Margaret Blair didn't have any children. She was a whore."

"All the more chance she could have. Peg's aunt had Stan, Ned and Jasper. Anyway, how come you know so much about her? Did you visit her for sex?"

Colour suffused Taylor's face.

"Ok, Uncle. Back to the shares. Who told you how to find that advisor guy?"

The penetrating glare, a sign that his uncle was still really angered, did not relent.

"David Blair and I have known each other for many years. He asked me to check out the imposter who was trying to con him. I have already ordered the bank to freeze that new account that future dividends were going to go into."

Jack didn't react, even though he was sure his uncle expected him to. He forced himself to stroll, towards the window. He wanted his uncle gone before Peg returned, and he expected her soon. He had an idea occur to him that should further unsettle his uncle.

"So, did you send that guy, Thomas Mason to visit Stuart?"

"What are you talking about?"

Jack explained, and added a description of the man and the fact that Stuart's office had been burgled. He was watching his uncle's face and saw the livid flush suddenly fade to white.

Just then, Jack heard the door being unlocked. Peg came in, but her different appearance only confused him for a moment. She gave him a quick wink as she took in the scene.

"Didn't know you had visitors coming, Honey." Peg was imitating a particularly fluff headed wannabee from Tamworth. Jack hurried over, digging into his pocket.

"Here, Honey. Go and get yourself a drink at the pub. I'll join you there later." He passed over some coins and made a shooing motion with his hand. He mouthed the word, "Hide."

When Taylor looked her way, she pouted. "You don't be long, ya hear, Honey," and sashayed from the room.

Taylor spoke again. "If I were you, I'd leave here before you get hurt, and forget about your little scam."

"Or what?"

"I don't think I need to spell it out. The Blair girl is dead. Ida Jessup who looked after those shares and lived off the dividends, is dead. Your criminal girlfriend is dead."

"How can you be sure?" Jack blurted.

His uncle gave a laugh that wasn't mirthful. "How are you? I let you go before, because I figured as soon as I did, you'd go looking for her or she would get in touch with you. Now I find you shacked up with the first girl foolish enough to agree with you. I had my doubts before, but not now. Pack your bags, boy. You are coming back with me. Now."

"No."

"Are you daft, boy? If I could find out about your scam, others can. Probably already have since you say that the advisor was burgled. They will be after you next. Might even grab your floosie to force you to tell what they think you know. Even if you could tell them where those shares are, they will kill you. Leaving now, is safer for you and for that silly fluff head."

"Go to hell. When have you ever had my best interests at heart?" Jack was thinking back to when he'd been arrested for joyriding. His uncle hadn't even given him a personal reference or offered to keep him out of trouble.

"You are family, Jack. I do what I think best."

"Like putting me in jail!"

"I can make this request formal if that is how you want it? Charge you with criminal conspiracy and use handcuffs. Drag you out of here…"

The bastard would, Jack knew, even if he wasn't in uniform. He tried one last ploy. "You never read me my rights. Nothing I've said, or you've tried to get me to agree to, is admissible in court."

"Is that how you want it? You've been watching too much American TV."

"What about Megan? I just can't walk out on her."

"Fine. I will pick her up too. Charge her with being an accessory."

Jack's jaw dropped, and his mind capitulated.

"No, she doesn't know anything." His admission made him sound guilty, but he didn't want Peg taken too. She would guess what his uncle had done.

"Alright, damn you. I'll come, but under protest, you bastard."

"You'll thank me for this, Jack," Taylor insisted implacably. "Get your stuff. You can leave a note for your floosie if you must."

Jack didn't have much to pack – most of his spare clothes were already in the kitbag – thanks to Peg's 'just in case' feeling. He didn't have anything to leave a message on, so he used the back of an information brochure.

In the blank section for putting an address, he wrote, "Gone with my uncle. Use the $200 for accommodation and food until you get a job."

He wrapped all his spare cash in the paper and put it on his pillow. If he'd had paper and more time to write, he would have explained more and left the letter with his landlady. It would have been more private that way. His uncle wasn't a patient man.

Even as he thought that, Taylor came into the room, saw the note, and without apology, read it.

"Very gallant of you. Are you ready?"

To try and make it seem less like he was being arrested, because his uncle may have said he'd come on official business, Jack gave his land lady a wave as he walked from the stairs, through their parlour. He had removed the irritated look from his face, thanked them for their hospitality and mentioned that he had left a message for his wife upstairs.

"Nothing is wrong, is it?" his landlady called to him.

"Just some family business I need to deal with urgently," he told her as casually as he could. "I am hoping it won't take too much time and I can get back soon. My wife knows where I will be, and I have left money for her to follow."

Outside, still mutinous, Jack dumped his bag on the backseat of his uncle's car and sat in the front passenger seat.

After a period of silence, as Taylor turned to drive back towards Victoria, he remarked, "You're a twisty tongued type, aren't you?"

"Learnt it from you," Jack retorted. "So why aren't you out finding who killed all those others instead of hounding me?"

"I want to know everything that Jessup girl might have told you."

"When you threatened to arrest me for consorting if I ever went near her again?"

"Didn't stop you, did it?"

Jack shut up. His uncle was fishing for information and he was beginning to wonder if Peg's accusations were accurate. He wanted to challenge his uncle about being in Peg's house just before her aunt's murder, but if he did, he would betray the fact that he'd seen Peg after she had run from the place, when she had obviously been taken and tortured right after. He shuddered at the thought of how Peg had been when Stan had taken her up to the old miner.

"Peg hasn't contacted me," Jack said, toning down his answer as if he were going to cooperate.

His uncle concentrated on the road, and didn't urge him to continue.

"But I'd hoped she'd got away. I saw a news item about her stuff and the blood by that water hole and how everyone assumed she was in it. Either she had been dumped there or had drowned herself. You said they dredged the hole."

"They did," Taylor said tersely.

"Did they… find her?"

"No."

"You mentioned they found a woman, but I read she'd been there a long time," Jack prompted. He wanted to hear what his uncle knew.

"The two males were identified as bikers, who may have been the ones who terrorised Ida Jessup. The woman had been in there twenty years. The very Margaret Blair whose shares you imply you have. So how can you claim that your floosie is her daughter? That birth certificate you showed your advisor, has to be a fake."

Jack fell silent, wondering if it could be a fake, and Peg wasn't the woman's daughter. Finally, he decided that no, Ida Jessup had promised the dead woman to look after her affairs…for her child. How could he use that to rattle his uncle?

"It wasn't a fake. I checked the details on it with the registry of BDM."

He didn't expect the reaction he got. For several minutes, his Uncle accelerated to way over the speed limit, but then braked and pulled over to the side of the road.

"You checked it?"

"Yes. Didn't you?"

"I haven't seen the original."

Jack told him the dates, adding, "So even though the birthdate is in 1954, it wasn't registered until the following year."

By the rigidity of his uncle's posture, there were a lot of thoughts passing through his mind. Then suddenly, Taylor relaxed.

"That's after she ran off with that itinerant muso…"

Jack didn't know if his uncle realised that he had spoken aloud. "You did know Margaret Blair!" he blurted.

His uncle jerked and looked at him.

"We were engaged to be married until that rockstar wannabe bewitched her, introduced her to drugs and who knows what."

"You thought that kid might have been yours," Jack realised.

"It wasn't or you might have been intending to marry your first cousin!" Taylor said harshly.

Jack's gut clenched for a moment. He was appalled. Yet his uncle had said the kid couldn't have been his. Rather than think on that, Jack said, "So that's how come you knew David Blair. Isn't this a case of personal involvement?"

With a repeat of his mirthless laugh, Taylor said, "That was twenty years ago, near enough."

Jack subsided. It might have been, but his uncle had never married.

Peg had been on her way back from the shops when she had seen a figure she recognised going into the guest house. She stopped at the nearby bus stop and considered what she could do. Jack's uncle might possibly recognise her.

This wasn't the time to consider how he had found them, he could have had his police colleagues looking. The question was, what did he know and what did he intend?

Since this visit was hard on the heels of the break in at Albert Stuart's office, and he knew them as Mr and Mrs Dawes, she had the sinking feeling that she knew part of the story. At least now, if Jack's uncle was going to drag him off again, she didn't need to worry about money. Stuart had come through and transferred the accumulated dividends into the new account, and she'd just moved most of it on into a new account that Stuart didn't know about. She hadn't touched the new account that her advisor had created. Future dividends would go into that one.

Her delight in the two new performance dresses, bought with what was now her money, had soured. To herself, she murmured, "What to do…?"

She only needed to see Jack for a moment to let him know that she knew something was up. He would give her a hint of what to do.

She saw a bus approaching, so she moved herself and her bags away from the stop. Then she caught sight of the public conveniences and an idea crystallised.

Jack's uncle had seen her as a thin, just released felon with short bleached hair. Her natural shade was brown, but she had been maintaining it as black coloured and it was now shoulder length. She would not look like he expected, and she could play the part of a singing wannabe again.

Only a short time later, she had changed into her country style new dress, with her other clothes in the bags, and was walking fast back to the house. The sight of the car outside the house reassured her that they hadn't gone anywhere yet.

Inside, at the reception desk, their landlady greeted her and admired the dress. Peg swirled around, grinning.

"Mrs Dawes, your husband has a visitor….um… a policeman. Visiting."

"Really? I had better go and see what's up." She betrayed no sign of worry, just trotted upstairs.

Before she went in, she listened at the door. Only the tone of the conversation was audible, not the words. She took a deep breath, recalled all the hopefuls at Tamworth and went in.

Jack came over as soon as he saw her. He was reaching into his pocket. She winked at him, since his uncle had not yet looked around.

"Didn't know you had visitors coming, Honey."

She took the money Jack pushed into her hand, ignored the go and get a drink suggestion, which was misdirection, and took in the real message. His hand moved in a shooing motion, and he mouthed the word "hide".

Now Jack's uncle was studying her, so she pouted. "You don't be long, ya hear, Honey," and sashayed from the room.

Leaving as if obediently, she let Jack shut the door behind her. Her extra bags had been stashed in the bathroom and now she needed to confirm

Jack's misdirection.

As she returned past the desk, she was asked, "There's no trouble?" by her landlady. She sounded genuinely concerned, but it could have been that she didn't want a criminal in the house.

"Oh yes, and no," she answered. "Family business. Jack and his uncle are discussing it. I'll wait in the pub for them to finish."

The lady seemed satisfied, and Peg continued outside, but not to the hotel. Instead, she went around to the back door of the house, and slipped back upstairs to the bathroom. Once back in ordinary clothes, she waited there until Jack, carrying his kitbag, left with his uncle. She went to their room as soon as he was out of sight.

A quick glance around showed no sign of a note, so she went into the bedroom and spotted the paper on the pillow. She read it quickly.

"Why give me money?" was her first thought. "He knows I can use mine now…or is he saying that I shouldn't?" That was possible, if the police could get to hear of any transactions. Use for accommodation? Did he think that she should stay here? They had been planning to leave for Sydney next day – had their tickets booked already.

Staying in Port Macquarie wasn't safe, if both King and Jack's uncle had come there. Besides, she had a gig to go to. She may need a place to stay until she met up with Wayne Carson and his manager. Maybe that was what Jack meant. Then, when he could, he would find her in Sydney. If that was the case, she should finalise things here so she could leave early next morning. Perhaps she should book her bags in that evening, so if she felt the need to skip out during the night, she could. Paranoia, was a safety line. So would be cashing in Jack's ticket for one to Melbourne, implying she was now heading there.

Chapter 20

"What are you doing here?" Mick Devlin challenged when he saw Les Shaw about to strut past him in the dim smoky room, where a lot of people were at tables, gambling, or playing pool. He was leaning against a wooden bar servery, keeping his eyes on all the guests.

"Not looking for you, that's for sure."

"Well, you found me, or are you auditioning to be one of Gianni's new whores?"

"No more than you'd be one of his paid gigolos," Les Shaw retorted.

"How'd you find your way here?" Devlin challenged.

"How did you? I'm surprised that you knew where to come?"

"I was invited, bitch."

"Well, good for you for getting here."

"At least I did. That moron Jessup got himself caught again."

Les Shaw shrugged, "His lookout! At least they let me out. Buy me a drink for old times' sake?"

Devlin gestured to the barman, and within moments, a double scotch was slid his way. He passed it to Les and waited for her reaction.

She tasted it, drank half and grinned. "You must be doing well, you were never this generous before."

"You won't get anything more from me."

"Don't need anything from you."

"So, why are you here?"

"Heard this was a place to try my hand at the tricks you taught me playing cards. I plan to make myself a stake and get lost up north."

"I thought you'd be off after the kid. You two were getting pretty chummy together. Like a couple of lesbos. Gone to see her yet?"

"Didn't bother. Read she'd bumped herself off, the stupid twit."

"Who's this, Mick? Friend of yours?" The new voice only caused Les to twist around long enough to give the man a raking head to toe, dismissive glance.

"Bugger off," Les retorted.

"You look familiar," the newcomer insisted, coming closer and putting an arm around her.

"Remove your arm if you want to keep it," Les threatened.

"She's not worth it, Harry," Mick said, before he laughed. "This is one of my ex's. From before my recent holiday. Reckons she wants a stake to get her away, but not from lying horizontal."

Now Harry laughed too, but he removed his arm. "Now I know why you look familiar. What's your name?"

"Les."

"Well, maybe we can make use of you. What can you do?"

"I leave the gun stuff to Mick, and I only whore with those I choose, but I'm game for just about anything else."

"So, where are you staying?" King asked.

"Haven't got a place yet."

King pulled out a wad of dollars and peeled off five twenties. "Around the corner in River St is a boarding house. Tell the lady I sent you."

"And you are?" Les sneered.

"Harry."

"Old Harry, great."

Les saw the man straighten, and then grin. "I like your attitude. More life than your little country mate."

"Her? She'd have been eaten alive if I hadn't decided to protect her."

"Well, why don't you go see about a bed? Come back at 8 tonight. That's when the marks come in to play cards."

"Great! See ya."

Harry King watched the girl leave and then turned to Devlin. "Do you trust her?"

"She's out for herself, but if you make it worth her while, she's game."

"You've had enough of her?" Harry suggested, not that he cared if he poached another man's woman.

Mick shrugged. "If she comes on to me at the right time, I'll give her what she wants, but I don't care if she goes elsewhere."

"Reckon she'd help us spring your mate Jessup?"

"If she gets paid more than a man's attention."

Harry chuckled. "I might just try her on some other jobs first. Just to see what affect the Bitch training centre had on her."

Mick shrugged again, "Whatever. When are those blokes coming in?"

Les Shaw was happy enough to get a place to stay off the streets. What really fed her ego right then was how she had found Devlin so quickly. He probably didn't know that she'd made a habit of going through his private stuff back when they were a couple. He had thought he controlled her, but she was using him for protection. Had her old man come after her, Mick would have been his match. And she enjoyed sex with Mick, much more than the mauling and molesting her father had treated her to.

Since leaving Matlock, it had only taken her two weeks to pick up Mick's trail. He'd lived in Melbourne once, until he'd killed some bloke and had to flit interstate. He kept in touch with his mates, though, and Les recalled their names. She'd just had to go down into his old stamping grounds around Flemington and ask around. Once they knew they'd been separated by the legal system, and how she wanted back with him, a couple of the mates' girls had given her a couple of places to try.

That she was going to have to prove herself was a given. That she was going to have to do more illegal things equally so, and that didn't bother her. The police had no clue of all the bad things she had done, and got away with.

As for her recent stint in the training centre – she blamed Mick for that. He'd got himself blind drunk the night before the job. That and the fact that he was making it clear to her that she was losing appeal – still made her angry. However, the time out since then now let her approach revenge in a cool, calm and indifferent way.

She had also decided to include Harry King in her vendetta. Peg had told her what he'd done to her before as a kid and before she was even old enough to want it. That had made a bond between them. It was good fortune that the creep had been there when she'd found Mick. Now she knew what he looked like.

Chapter 21

Jack didn't know why his uncle had brought him to such a seedy looking pub in North Melbourne. He had come into the archive basement where he had been going through land transfer data on microfilm, and simply said he was shouting him a meal.

In no way loathe to leave the boring task, Jack agreed. However, apart from that command, his uncle had been uncommunicative. That indicated that CI Taylor was worried, but asking questions as to why, was no use. His uncle would never tell his reluctant assistant.

So, Jack worked his way through a surprisingly decent schnitzel and chips, and the beer that was on the house, and waited. It was only after they had both pushed away their plates and the detritus had been removed that the tall blond man approached, and gestured to his uncle.

"This shouldn't take long," Taylor told Jack. It was the first thing he had said since giving his meal order.

Jack began to rise, some instinct urging him to follow and see who else wanted his uncle.

"No need to poke into their business," a female voice drew his attention. He turned around.

The first sight of the short bleached hair, stopped him in mid-movement. The woman who continued closer, slipped past him and into the bench seat opposite. It would still be warm from his uncle's body heat. That she reminded him so strongly of Peg, brought with it the realisation of who she was.

"What do you want?" he asked rudely.

"To keep you out of trouble."

"Did my uncle send you?"

"No. Harry did. They didn't want ears on their talk."

Taking a moment, as if thinking, Jack waited a while before asking, "Harry King?"

The woman merely smiled. "Thinks he is. Do you know who I am?"

The answer was beating its way around his mind, but he didn't answer in the way the girl would have expected. "So, you got tired of settling Peg's scores in Matlock?"

The laugh was genuine. "That rich bitch had it coming."

"So, why are you here, Les?" Jack asked, studying the woman that Peg called her closest female friend.

"I like you, Jack. Didn't think I would since Peg ran off with you without waiting for me."

"Shhh," Jack hissed, just audibly.

Les's grin didn't change. "I came here to see if I could find Mick. And, to work up a stake to leave and go north. The little bitch promised to help me. I didn't expect her to go ditch herself."

Very quietly, Jack asked, "Is Mick Devlin here?"

A slight headshake and a low, "No, he's where the Docker's union hang out. But don't go blabbing that to your uncle. He knows already."

That news rocked Jack. "Is he on the take?"

Again, a slight headshake. "Nothing so obvious, but they are using him. It might be blackmail. I don't actually know. I've only been here a short while, and neither Mick nor Harry ever say anything straight. Buy me a beer, will you?"

Jack gestured the waiter, to cover his unease. For, despite Peg's words to the contrary, he still wanted to believe his uncle was honest.

The two tankards that were delivered were still on the house. Les took hers and slurped readily. Then she stood and slipped around to sit next to Jack.

"I am supposed to be trying to keep your mind off your uncle's business and you would be wise not to mention what I told you to him or anyone else. If you do, they will blame him for turning them in." The words were mere whispers in Jack's ear. A little louder, Les suggested, "What say we slip away somewhere? They have some card games going on upstairs."

"No thanks. I am glad to have met you, Les, but…no thanks."

"Mike said you were straight one," Les sighed. "I wish I had met you first. That Peg is a lucky little bitch."

"Don't let on that she is alive," Jack insisted, trying to disentangle himself from her abrupt embrace. She had seen King and Taylor returning, as Jack himself had.

"No way," Les promised as a whisper in his ear. "Does he know?"

She shrugged at Taylor, still several tables away.

"No, and the bastard scares off any girl I try to get close to." Jack pitched his voice to carry to his uncle. "He thinks they are all brainless whores."

"You're finished here, Jack," Taylor said stonily.

"See what I mean, darling," Jack smirked. "Another time, then?"

"If you are game, boyo," Les smirked back.

Taylor watched until Jack began to follow, and then started to push his way through a standing crowd of punters watching a trotting race. Jack was aware that King was studying him, and so he never glanced that way.

When they reached Taylor's car, and he was unlocking the passenger door, Jack wrenched the keys from his uncle. "I'll drive."

"You impertinent bastard," Taylor swore.

"Yes," Jack agreed calmly. "Something has you in a temper, and when you are like that, you are not fit to drive."

He continued around to the driver's seat and was still surprised at his easy victory. Then he wondered if he would have any luck trying to find the problem.

He waited until he had pulled up outside his uncle's house before saying, "I didn't expect you to be so chummy with that bastard King."

Taylor's fist flew out without warning, but Jack had moved, just ahead of it.

"What do you know about him?" Taylor's fierce gaze was fixed on Jack. "Tell me!"

Jack glared back, making him wait. "For one, he's Gianni Costa's hitman, and for another…he's a paedophile."

"Tell me how you know that?"

"You tell me what horrendous thing they are trying to make you do," Jack countered. "Maybe I can help."

"Keep out of this, Jack. Better that you keep hating me."

"Oh, I do. I assure you. But I hate King more, and I know he was hanging around Matlock. I know he raped Peg twice – with no thanks to you."

Taylor's face drained of all colour, and sweat formed on his brow. "Did the Jessup girl tell you this?"

"About King raping her? And her aunt letting him?" Jack asked, then went on, "Yes. She was only 15 the first time, and it was the real reason why she wanted to leave Matlock."

Some colour came back into Taylor's face. "When was the second time?"

"You're the clever cop, uncle. You figure it."

"What about the rest?" Taylor asked instead.

Jack took the change in topic to be confirmation that he already knew. "Peg told me that she'd heard Stan say what King used to do to him. Not to Ned or Jasper, they were his, just Stan who is Gianni Costa's son."

Taylor said nothing,

Jack asked again, "So what do they want you to do?" His uncle stayed mute.

"Oh, go to hell!" Jack said, tossing the car keys onto his uncle's lap. He was out of the car and shutting the door when he heard, "Jack!" He ignored the plea and strode off.

Jack didn't go home, for if his uncle stopped worrying about his own predicament, he'd go straight there to demand to know what his nephew had as good as admitted. Instead, he went to the bowling alley and worked off some anger of his own. Even after that, he didn't hurry home, and when he did finally get there, he was so tired that he didn't notice the car parked outside. When he reached his front door, he heard, "Jack Dawes? Police."

He turned, seeing two strangers, one of whom was holding up a police badge.

"Who are you?" Jack asked.

"Sergeant Banner. With me is Detective Peters."

"So, what is this about?"

"We want you to come with us," Banner told him, unhelpfully.

"Why?"

"Are you going to come quietly?"

"You haven't told me why, and as far as I know, I haven't done anything to be arrested for."

"How about compounding a felony?" Banner suggested.

"What felony? You sound just like my uncle – making up charges because he could. What if I don't want to come?"

"It would not help you," the other one, Peters, offered.

"Who told you to come and get me?" Jack decided to ask. He thought he had a damn good idea.

"Chief Superintendent Halford of the Organised Crime Task force," Banner finally admitted.

That wasn't the name he had been expecting to hear, but if it was them, not his uncle…

"Very well," Jack finally agreed, taking a step back towards the detectives. They didn't bring out the handcuffs, so he wasn't being arrested.

He only recognised the big house as the car was gestured through the gate. It wasn't CI Taylor's modest house, but that of ex-Chief Superintendent Taylor - his uncle's father.

Jack shrank into the seat. The old man was no blood relative, and was as caustic as acid. After their first and last encounter, he had never wanted to see the man again.

His escort opened the car door to let him out, and then escorted him to a man who had come out from the front door. That man thanked the detectives, who returned to their car and drove off.

Jack turned from watching them leave when the greeter spoke. "Jack, thank you for coming. My name's Halford."

The senior policeman didn't offer to shake hands, but then, Jack didn't want to be say the meeting was a pleasure.

"I hope someone has some coffee."

Halford didn't comment, just led the way through to what Jack knew to be his adoptive grandfather's study.

The room seemed full of people. Most noticeable was his uncle, now looking unkempt with no tie, and his collar unbuttoned. Jack ignored him, walking past to go and greet his Grandfather, Eugene Taylor.

"I'm glad to see you looking well, Sir."

"Thank you, Jack. I think you probably know almost everyone here. Halford, you just met, and the other is the task force legal officer, Wilson Harlow.

Jack glanced around, saw Mike Scott hiding in a corner, Ian Sinclair sitting in a chair next to him. Jack Casey, the old miner from Matlock, rose to greet him.

"Good to see you again, young man." Casey did shake hands. "We need your help."

"Perhaps someone will tell me what is going on, first. I don't like being picked up by police for no reason."

Halford invited him to sit. "I know you have heard about the organised crime taskforce."

"Of course I have," Jack agreed, turning to stare at his uncle and wondering why he was in the room. "Are you sure that things we say here won't get back to the crooks?"

Justin Taylor spoke up. "I've asked to step down from my position."

"So why am I here? To give them more reasons to suspend you?"

"If you want," his uncle agreed. "However, they already know everything."

"That you were with Ida Jessup just before she died – taking orders from Harry King?"

"I made it possible for your girlfriend to get free," Taylor told him.

"Yeah, right into the hands of another of King's flunkeys. Did you see King kill Peg's aunt?"

"No!" Taylor denied with force. "King sent me out after your girlfriend. I didn't find her."

"In my mind, that still makes you guilty of accessory to murder. You could have told the police in Matlock that she hadn't killed her aunt. They might have found her before King got at her again."

"Jack!" Eugene Taylor called him to order. "There is more going on here than you are aware of. Justin has been, well, not exactly undercover, but liaising with King for many years, trying to pin down Gianni Costa."

Jack felt an insane desire to laugh. "I'm not sure that the association has not sullied him beyond the hope of absolution. I reckon they have simply been laughing up their sleeves all this time. What have they been doing? Dobbing in their rivals? People they want out of the way?"

"It served a purpose," Eugene Taylor told him.

"Got the shit off the street so the big crook could get richer," Jack sneered. "The crooks have been using the whole damn police force for twenty years."

"You see!" Justin Taylor growled. "There's no reasoning with the wretch. I tried to keep you out of this, Jack."

"As a reasoning adult, I'd like to know why? You never cared for Peg. Nobody ever did but me, Mike and Mr Casey."

"Perhaps some coffee," Jack Casey broke in before Justin Taylor could counter the accusation. "I can see that you are tired, lad."

The tension in the room eased and Mike came over and squatted by Jack's chair. Their gazes met and Mike said, "I was dragged here because I had made friends with Peg in Matlock. They think she was in a position to learn things that might help the investigation. We are the only links to that info."

"So what could you tell them?" Jack asked. He was really asking if Mike had kept all her secrets.

"I doubt if I have been much use," Mike said. "All I said that interested them was the message I gave Peg…just before…"

Jack squeezed Mike's hand, silently passing on his thanks. When he was sure of the point of this gathering, he might tell them more.

Casey took the cup of coffee from one of Eugene Taylor's servants, and passed it to Jack.

"I was worried about you when you didn't get to my friend's house."

Jack asked Casey, "You told them that she didn't die, did you?"

"They needed to know. Your uncle…thought he had helped kill her. He was…"

"Never mind the excuses," Jack told the old man. "Did you tell them that King raped her again?"

Casey nodded. "When your uncle heard what I knew, he asked to step down. What happened after you left?"

Jack didn't want to tell it all yet, so he mixed truth with misdirection.

"We had to stop. Peg had a raging fever. I was awake all night, trying to get it down. Near morning, the fever broke. She fell into a quiet sleep, and I dozed off too. When I woke, she'd gone. She had found a scrap of paper to write on, and wrote that we were safer off apart, since my uncle would be sure to come after me and charge us with consorting."

"Did you try to find her?" Casey asked gently.

"Of course I did. I even rang the nearest hospital. You saw her Jack. I hoped she'd go there and report the assault and get help."

"You wouldn't stay away…" Justin Taylor began.

"Shut up, Uncle."

Halford stood up and said, "It's late. We are all tired. Jack, I would like to talk to you in the morning. Anything your friend might have told you about her aunt, and any of her friends may help us."

"I doubt that I know much," Jack told him. "But okay."

Eugene Taylor levered himself from his chair with the help of a walking stick. "You can stay here tonight. My son will also be staying."

The senior policemen left the room. Casey spoke once again when the door had shut.

"Your uncle mentioned that you had been talking to Peg's friend, Les Shaw. Did you learn anything?"

Jack shrugged. "I couldn't tell what she was at. She said she was distracting me from interfering in the conversation Uncle was having. Then she seemed to be coming on to me."

Mike spoke up. "After she rang you that time, she said she was going off to find Devlin."

"She did," Jack told them. "And said I would endanger uncle if I said where."

"Telling me isn't like telling the police," Casey suggested. "We can make it seem that someone else gave us the tip."

After a moment's thought, Jack said, "The pub where the Dockers' Union hang out. In addition to that, I got the impression that Devlin and King have become very buddy buddy."

By the time Jack finished his coffee, he felt less tense. The remaining person in the room chose then to come over.

"Remember me?" Ian Sinclair asked. "We met in Tamworth."

"Yes. How are you?"

"Fine." Ian looked like he wanted to say something more. He finally went on, "You may not think that it's my place to say anything, but…Don't be too hard on your uncle."

It wasn't at all what Jack expected to hear, but suddenly several snippets of information fell together. "Was it you who stole his fiancée?"

"I didn't exactly steal her." Ian gave his version. "I met her at a number of gigs. She loved music and sang really well. I did love her, truly. For many years, I blamed your uncle for setting me up on fake charges. He was the one who arrested me. I know now that it was a coincidence, and if any set up went on, it wasn't his doing. We've…agreed to start afresh."

Jack's mind went elsewhere as more pieces of information jumped into a mental line.

"Is my purpose here anything to do with those damned shares?"

"That's part of it," Casey told him. "It's what Halford told you. We need to know what Peg might have known. You and Mike are all we have available."

"I suppose."

"Your uncle said you had a birth certificate in the name of Blair," Casey suggested.

"Yeah, and another for the woman's kid."

"You used it to action some shares," Casey prompted.

"So?"

"They will ask about that tomorrow," Casey warned him. "I was asking, because no one knew that girl had birthed a child until her bones were found."

Jack didn't want to say more about the birth certificates. Peg had said, if the girl had known her aunt, she had to have been a whore too. Her kid could have been anyone's. The only point that mattered was that it was Blair's grandkid and the father might well be dead now.

Mike decided enough was enough. "I'm staying here tonight too. You can share my room, Jack."

Once in the privacy of the borrowed room, Jack admitted, "At least you are a friend. Why are you here anyway, apart from what they said? Have they drafted you to the taskforce?"

"Me? Don't be daft. Ian has been though. Casey's been with it for years. He is David Blair's brother in law, or so I discovered earlier this evening. They will brief you tomorrow I expect. Your grandfather said this was a think tank to come up with new avenues of investigation."

Jack snorted softly. He was making up a bed on the trundle that pulled out from under Mike's bed.

"It's too late at night for this."

"I agree. My head is so full of stuff and I can't even think on it."

They were both awake early, and Mike asked, "Did you get the postcard sent from Sydney?"

"Yes, I did. Thanks. At least Peg had somewhere to go. I called, and all is well. She's met up with that bloke she met at the training centre."

Mike knew he was referring to Wayne Carson and that he was being cryptic on purpose.

Jack changed topics. "So what were you all discussing before I got dragged here last night?"

"I am hardly in the know," Mike clarified. "Most of the others were referring to things they all knew and I didn't. All I figured was that your uncle got orders to do something outright illegal and 'they' have something on him that they think will make him do it."

"I wonder if the task force really do know all my uncle did?"

"Maybe the question ought to be - how much does he know that the crooks don't, or how much he knows that they don't realise he knows."

"Are you trying to make out my uncle is a saint?"

"Wouldn't dream of it," Mike grinned. "What I do want is to know why events of twenty years ago have suddenly gained in importance."

"You mean apart from Gianni Costa coming on the scene about then,"

Jack asked, and then stopped to gather ideas. "Uncle has had me going through old microfiche records – newspapers, electoral rolls, land transfers, BDM, and one thing I found was that Costa's father, who migrated here, was known to be a black marketeer during the war."

"Ah…interesting. I didn't hear that mentioned yesterday."

"Probably because all those police types already know," Jack said sourly.

"Find anything else of interest?"

"No, that lead petered out into a dead end. Haven't found anything for Gianni Costa. So we have to assume he is still alive somewhere. There were one or two photos in old newspapers before his father died, but nothing after that. Anyway I know Gianni is still alive. Peg saw him and King when they visited her aunt one time."

"Do they," Mike gestured beyond the bedroom door, "know about that?"

"Casey does, but Peg only gave a verbal description. If my uncle had ever met him, they wouldn't, in theory, still be looking for him."

"They seem pretty certain that Costa is still in charge of various rackets." Mike considered. "And no one sees him these days."

"Well, I reckon Harry King is his front man. Too bad they didn't try to question Peg's aunt, years ago," Jack said sourly.

"The new question is – where does Costa hang out these days."

When Jack didn't make a comment, Mike turned to stare at his friend. "What? Did I say something?"

"Mike, they want new ideas, try this one. Costa has given himself a new identity. One in which no one would suspect him of being a crook. He can strut around in public like a saint."

"Do you have someone in mind?" Mike asked.

"I do, but we'd need proof. What if I mentioned a few facts? One, Costigan Consolidated is trying to take over Blair Industries. Two, the missing Blair shares were in Ida Jessup's possession. Three, Ida Jessup was killed for something, after I heard mention of dividends being traced to her. Uncle was investigating the shares for Blair, but someone, King I think, went to the bloke Peg and I took the shares to and stole a copy of the file."

"Not the shares?" Mike queried.

"No, they were not in the file. They may be with that stuff in Melbourne. Where was I? Oh yeah, before uncle dragged me back here, Peg saw – on the TV – a man in the background of an interview with Reg Costigan, the V8 driver. She reckoned that the man was Costa, but clean shaven."

Mike whistled, "And did I hear right, that Stan Jessup is actually Costa's son?"

"Yes. Peg couldn't see the likeness, because when she saw Stan last he was undernourished and untidy. However, Peg did say that his beard, if trimmed, was like Costa's."

"If Costa and Costigan are the same person," Mike mused aloud, "He must have all the bases covered, or he would have been caught out years ago. Maybe that is why they are now interested in people who knew of him back then. When might he have changed his name?"

Jack shrugged.

"I would definitely mention that idea. The police sketch artists might have a good enough eye to pick resemblances."

Eugene Taylor called Jack into his study as soon   as he had finished his breakfast. This time it was just the two of them.

His first question was, "How did you meet the Jessup girl?"

"Uncle knows that!"

"Tell, me, Jack."

Sighing and settling back in his chair, Jack did. He realised then that this grandfather figure was not being judgemental or suspicious, simply asking for facts.

"So, no one introduced you, it was just you were both in a mutual place."

"Yes, sir. We just hit it off."

"I can understand my son being jaundiced, and perhaps you will too when I explain that Gianni Costa began his empire with a string of brothels and illegal gambling dens."

"I guess. Can I ask a question?"

"Certainly."

"How long has the task force been interested in Ida Jessup?"

Eugene Taylor tapped the arm of his chair as he thought back. "Probably ten or so years. What made you ask?"

"Just that Peg was asked whether she knew of certain people – this was just after she got out. That was all. Did you ever question Ida Jessup?"

"Once or twice, but she kept saying that she didn't know where Costa was these days. We only discovered where she had disappeared to, a few years ago."

"Jack Casey did was it?"

Taylor nodded. "Tell me how you got hold of the information relating to some shares in Blair Holdings?"

"Peg had the stuff," Jack summarised. "I rang Mike Scott when I heard

Uncle Justin on the phone telling someone that dividends had been traced to Ida Jessup."

"Yes, your friend did mention Peg Jessup grabbing stuff to take with her. Why do you think that was?"

"Because her aunt had been acting strange, pretty much since Peg got back there. She finally got her aunt to admit that Gianni Costa was mad at her because of some shares he thought she had."

"The Jessup girl told you this?"

Jack nodded.

"What else do you know about them?"

"That Ida was pretending to be Margaret Blair, and the real Margaret Blair had willed them to her daughter."

"And you decided that it was logical to assume that Peg Jessup was that daughter."

Jack answered that challenge with, "Ida finally admitted that Peg was not a blood relation."

Taylor considered things for a while. "That fits with what Stan Jessup said. He recalls his mother bringing the girl home with her as a squalling brat. So, did the birth certificate you had for the child, give the name of the father?"

"No sir. The birth wasn't registered until several months later. I think by Ida. Maybe the mother had died already."

"Do you remember the relevant information?"

"Yes, sir."

Taylor pushed a writing pad across his desk. "Write it down."

Jack did and pushed the pad back.

For a while, Taylor studied his youngest son's stepson.

"You are no doubt aware that Costigan Consolidated is trying to take over Blair Industries. The move can only be described as hostile. The production of the valid proxy for Margaret Blair's shares, effectively blocked the move. Prior to that, many of the Blair Holdings shareholders were being bullied into selling. Blair was forced to buy back shares at an inflated price, from loyal shareholders, to protect them. As you might realise, that is likely to have had an extremely ill effect on the company's cash flow."

"Have you looked for a connection between Costigan and Gianni Costa?" Jack blurted.

Taylor held up his hand, and continued. "Yesterday, Justin received a message to talk to King. The instruction he received was to make sure that his friend Blair, paid up or else."

"Huh? Pay up for what?"

"Late yesterday, David Blair's son, Richard, was abducted whilst on his way home from a meeting. We are expecting a ransom demand – one that will be so huge that Blair will have to sacrifice his company or liquidate a lot of his properties."

"That sounds like revenge for some major disagreement," Jack said, feeling ill.

"I agree, but Blair can't say for what, only that the two companies have clashed in the past. We have the company squad looking into that."

"Sir, I had a really crazy idea about a possible link between Costa and Costigan."

"Why don't you tell me?"

Jack did, following the same logic he had outlined to Mike.

"It's worth looking into," Taylor said, rubbing his chin. "But John Costigan…."

"He is rich enough to be able to throw his money around to buy a reputation."

"He was at school with Justin's older brother," Taylor commented, still thinking. "And Blair's wife, Megane, was on committees with Costigan's late wife."

Taylor continued to think and finally decided, "I am going to sit on this idea for a time." He forestalled Jack's protest. "Justin told me of events after you approached that NSW solicitor. It does add force to what you suggested. Your friend doesn't happen to know where the actual share certificates are? That would solve part of David's problem."

Jack could only stare.

"Son, I am quite in favour of her seeming to be dead. Can you contact her?"

Slowly, Jack nodded. "She didn't bring them with her, and didn't say she knew where they were. I have only two ideas. One, in a lock box somewhere. Peg was given a key by Ida. Or two, with a pile of other stuff she stashed."

"Can you get that key, or a picture of it?"

Again, Jack nodded. "I think so."

"Can she get to her stash?"

"I'll ask."

"We had Ida Jessup's house emptied of everything portable and had builders looking for hidden places. We found nothing, but there was a hiding place under some boards in Ida Jessup's front room. We can't be sure the shares weren't there."

"I don't recall Peg mentioning that place."

Taylor suddenly sat up, as if he had made a decision.

"I want you to drop everything you are doing for Justin, and check for those shares. That is most urgent. Will you?"

"Yes, Sir."

"Right! Then I am going to give you a list of other things to look for in the records."

"Okay," Jack's sigh was resigned. "Is this voluntary or paid?"

Taylor chuckled. "I will match what Justin is paying you. I asked him to put you to work, and I am very pleased with your determination."

"Most of what I was doing seemed pointless, though after you told me a few things, it's making more sense. Still, I haven't found anything much of use."

"We haven't been asking the right questions. We have been trying to find the activities of Costa, and while searching for the things on the list I will give you, keep an eye out for his name, still."

"Okay, sir," Jack agreed. "I'll get started when I get your list."

"Take young Mike with you. He can help as well, if he has time."

"Paid?"

"Of course. However, you are not to discuss anything you find with anyone but Mike, if he is helping, and myself. Understood?"

Jack nodded.

"We are going for a drive," Jack told Mike a short while later. "I want to make a call, but not from around here."

"How did your meeting go?" Mike asked, thinking he was changing the subject.

"Not as bad as I thought," Jack admitted. "Our previous meeting was poisonous. This time, the old man is just consigning me deeper into old records' archives. He said you could help out. He's paying."

"Might. How do you read it?"

"Huh? I reckon it's his way of keeping young hot heads out of trouble. Do you want a coffee before we start?"

They stood outside a café, several car lengths away from where Jack had parked his car. "I need to go through the stuff you stashed for Peg," Jack said quietly as he pretended to sip his hot drink.

"You could have told me that in the car."

"Call me paranoid, but uncle took me with him yesterday and King seemed to be memorising my face."

"So?"

"So, maybe someone bugged my car."

"More likely he'd bug your uncle's car, but I'll play along. What do we need to find?"

"Those bedamned shares. The actual things. There is a chance they were with the stuff Peg took, since they weren't in the folder with all the records, transactions and correspondence."

"And the call?"

"Peg has a key her aunt gave her. We don't know what it's for. The old man wants a photo of it. So while you drive us to the storage place, I will look for a phone box nearby."

Mike, who had arranged the storage cubicle, arranged for Jack to have access as well. They decided to leave the key with the manager, since only one key was ever given out, and Jack didn't want to have it on him.

Once inside the four foot square room, with the door shut, they set to work. They each took a pack and systematically took everything out of them and spread the contents into close piles on the concrete floor. Obviously irrelevant items were immediately put back.

Jack took up the deed box that they didn't have a key for, and tried to pick the lock. He soon gave up. Mike was looking through a pile of letters he had taken from a hand bag.

"What have you got," Jack asked.

"Letter to someone called Megan Pearl. I think some might be from Ian, others are from Ida Jessup. Did your uncle ever write to her, do you think? What's his name, Justin? There are some from other people."

"Justin, yeah. I don't reckon he is the letter writing type though."

Mike went back to taking letters from envelopes and glancing at contents and writer. "Most of these are nothing, but I think someone should read them all, just in case."

Jack had taken up a shoe box that had been tied closed with a ribbon. It too contained envelopes, like cards in a filing system. He took out one, and found it to contain negatives and a sheet of paper, the latter having names, date, place and time. He held one of the negatives up to the light coming from the bare hanging bulb. He whistled softly, and then wordlessly handed the negative to Mike.

Mike moved his arm down and handed the negative back. "Are they all like that?"

Jack checked several more envelopes and nodded. "I'd say so."

The two diaries that had also been in the box, turned out to contain a day to day list of names with the same information as on the slips of paper.

"I think, I will ask Peg about this stuff before I give it to the old man. I may just keep the two diaries too, and make a copy of the information – particularly the names. Not sure what to do about the deed box. I'd like to see what was in it first, before giving it to the old man."

"What do you reckon about these letters?" Mike indicated the ones from the bag. "Do you reckon to hand them over?"

"I think Peg should have a chance to go through them first. Did they seem important?"

"Not that I saw at a glance. Seems like private stuff."

"They can stay here for now. We can come back and go through them when we have time. We'll just bring the deed box."

After leaving the storage place, Jack drove to where he had noticed a phone booth. By then, it was after eleven and Peg should be well and truly awake. He just hoped he had enough coins for an interstate call. Mike lounged around outside, watching the people and cars going by.

He wondered how Peg was affording to stay at the hotel that the number went through to. They had agreed that she should be careful using her Blair account and there wasn't much in her Megan Dawes one.

"Hi," he said when Peg answered.

"Jack! I've missed you."

"Ditto, you sound well."

"This is so exciting, Jack! I'm going to be lead in Wayne's backup band and do several solos. We're going to be here at the Illawarra Club for two weeks and then somewhere else. What about you?"

"Been doing boring stuff. Delving into archives." He wasn't going to mention the previous day, but risked being explicit about what he needed. "Peg, I can't explain why, but have you any idea where the actual share certificates are?"

Peg didn't answer right away. "Aunt Ida implied they were thick paper with stamps to make them official. I never saw anything like that. What about in that box I couldn't open?"

"That was one thought, but I'll have to get a locksmith to open it. Or just give it to the old man, my uncle's father."

"Have you heard any more about the take over?"

"Your proxy enabled them to block it, but it's most definitely a hostile action. There is more I can't mention."

"Gut feeling, Jack? Should I give over that locked box?"

"I think so."

"Alright, but tell me what's in there."

"If I can. That shoe box had envelopes, with negatives of a porno nature and details of who, where and when."

"That bitch!" Peg exclaimed. "She swore she didn't have any more negatives. If she wasn't already dead, I'd kill her myself."

"Peg, she did look after you…"

"Yeah, well, I don't want to think about her. I reckon those negatives were Bertie Jessup's insurance. Not that they helped him. I think Aunt Ida was meant to give them to some reporter. Ian Stone or something."

"Ian? Might that be Ian Sinclair? Mike's re-found dad?"

"Dunno. Maybe you can find out if it is likely?"

"Yeah, I will. And one last thing. Can you send me photos of that key your aunt gave you? I think we need to find out what it is for. If the shares aren't in the deed box. They might be in where ever that key fits."

"Yeah, look, I'll arrange for that photo, have you got somewhere I can fax it to?"

"I will get a number and call back. I am about out of coins. Oh, another thing. You'd better make a will and fax that to me as well. Mention those damn shares in it. OK?"

"Yeah okay. I'll fax you my mother's will too and mine and her birth certificates."

Just then the connection dropped out, so Jack hung up the phone and emerged.

"No one was paying us any attention," Mike reported. "Now what?"

"I want to make notes or copy the diaries. I might get access to them again if I hand them over, and I might not. And I'd really like to know what's in that box too."

"My suggestion," Mike offered, "is to hand it over as it is. That way, no one can say we interfered with the contents, and we can honestly say we don't know what's in it."

"You're probably right, although Peg does want to know what's in there.

Where do you reckon to go to do the copying?"

"Let's drive further out of town and find a library," was Mike's idea.

"And a newsagent to get some paper and pens," Jack added.

While Jack got started making a list of names and dates from the diaries, Mike went off to find if he library had a copy of Who's Who in the reference section. They did, and he took it to the table they were using. He took the second diary, and began looking up the names in there.

After an hour of solid writing, they both paused for a break.

"So," Jack asked, indicating Mike's notes.

"So…a lot of those people," Mike pointed to the diary, and continued, "Are well known and rich now. Ten or twenty years ago, more of them might have been. Can't tell if all of them are still alive."

"Have you looked up John Costigan?" Jack asked.

Mike smacked his head. "I was going to start with him and Blair."

He flicked through pages, stopped, read for a bit and whistled. "Listen to this. John Costigan born 1922, his father was Louis Costigan mother Maria. There's stuff about his schooling. He married an Alida Andrews in 1938. Has a son Reginald, born in 1939. He enlisted in the air force before the war, but left it before the war began. They also have his net worth at about eleven million."

Jack's expression had gone blank, so Mike stayed quiet to let him think.

"Something about some of those dates are nagging me," he finally admitted. "However, one thing I am sure of is that Stan Jessup is older than Reg Costigan, by a year or two. That means, Peg's aunt knew Costa 34 years ago, and quite some years before. She moved up here after that with her boys, then Peg came along."

Mike continued the train of thought. "Is there a way to find out when she moved to Matlock?"

"I think she owned that house she was in," Jack considered. "I might be able to find a record in the land transfer archives. Keep checking that book, even though I doubt Costa will be in it."

A quick flick through pages confirmed Jack's prediction. "How long to you want to keep at this?"

"Let's give this another hour, then see if this place has a fax machine Peg can send to."

"Will that be enough time? Photos take a while to get developed."

"She will have her mother's will and stuff and if the photo isn't ready, I'll find another place to send it."

"Why did you tell Peg to make a will?" Mike asked.

"Insurance – like getting her mother's will. So there is a written record of ownership. For the shares, mostly, but now that she has assets, it is a good idea. I don't want Blair getting his hands on those shares, and arbitrarily claiming them back. This way, if he tries it, I will call him a thief."

Chapter 22

"What's that noise?" Jack had to speak loudly, as Peg's voice had been drowned out by a babble of background noises.

Peg, with the hotel's public phone hard at one ear, had a finger in her other ear. "Just some school group come for the music comps. They just arrived."

In fact, the people in charge were trying to impose order. She was relieved when the noise abated.

"What were you saying about this club?" Peg asked.

"I said I didn't know about that one. I just said Blair Holdings have a lot of clubs on its list of properties."

"And you said that Costigan's control a lot of road houses?" Peg checked.

"Yes. Do you have one near you?"

"Um, yeah. Just before you come into town, on the highway. Actually, it isn't that far from here. That shouldn't be a problem."

"Probably not," Jack agreed."

"So what else have you been finding out?"

Jack groaned, then heard his last coin drop. He searched his pocket unsuccessfully for another. "Nothing obvious. I have been tracing ownership of properties on Blair's list, and those we know of Costigan's. Found a few that both had at some stage."

"Jack, if you can, see if you can find a property that used to be owned by somebody Simmons."

"Why?"

"It's something I think I remember HK saying. About my aunt. It's possible her birth name was Annie Simmons."

"Okay. When roughly?"

"Not sure. My aunt mentioned something about GC helping her when her parents died. Selling her house and getting her a more modest one."

"I'll check that name," Jack promised, just as his money ran out.

Peg sighed when the connection dropped out, but she was used to it. Hearing from Jack at random times was better than no contact. He had also said he was using random phone boxes to call her, and for her not to call him. He never seemed to have many coins though, and this time she had not asked him if they had opened that locked box, or if they had identified what the key was for. Next time, she promised herself.

As she considered what to do next, she spotted Wayne Carson emerging from upstairs. She thought for a moment to join him, but even as she thought it, half the school uniformed group spotted him. His timing was off this time, she grinned to herself. Regardless, his performance persona switched right on as he approached the group.

Over the past month, she'd figured out that Carson was really a private person, even though he knew he had to be more flamboyant as a performer to keep up his record sales and fill his performance venues. Then again, he did like to help young musicians, and the swarming girls were that. And since she wasn't dressed up as his co-singer just then, she couldn't exactly go and help him. The poor tour leader could do that.

Carson looked at her, but she just grinned and moved back near the phones again. In her off time, she usually looked, as then, more like a boy. Even some of the boys were gravitating towards him now.

One of the phones on the reception desk rang just then, and the name called was barely audible over the new babble. One of the baggage guys came over to the tour leader, spoke quietly, and pointed towards the house phones where Peg was standing.

Carson was doing his usual magic, and the teenagers were quietening down to hear him asking them questions. A woman joined the group, dressed like the man who had gone to the phone. She was not in a school uniform, but wore the blazer common to the whole group. She soon had the attention of her charges and began handing out room assignments.

Peg knew Carson had an appointment somewhere. Their manager had mentioned it earlier. She wasn't needed. Her own intention that morning had been to go looking for a souvenir of the town, to add to her 'tour' collection.

While waiting for the crowd of students to disperse, and without intending to eavesdrop, Peg's attention was caught by the comments the school tour leader was speaking into the phone. They were cryptic, but the man had become tense, and his voice serious. When he turned towards the group, he seemed to be looking for a particular student amongst them.

"Will they want him to go home?" A pause. "No, I'll tell him and make him understand that he needs to stay with the group." A longer pause, then, "Such a watch would need to be discreet."

The teenagers and their instruments in travel cases, were now heading upstairs in a neat two by two parade. When a short dark haired boy began the ascent, the teacher quickly ended his call. Peg wondered if that boy had been the subject of the phone call. Then she noticed something being passed along the moving queue, from the back. It reached the boy she had spotted, and he stopped abruptly.

"Keep moving," the woman teacher called, from somewhere above. The man strode to the end of the group and asked the older boys at the back a sharp question.

Peg walked over to the newspaper stand and scanned the headlines. One jumped immediately to her attention, and with a glance at the disappearing students, wondered if that was the article that had meaning for that boy.

It seemed that news of Richard Blair's abduction had finally made the papers. Peg had known about it for two days, as Jack had told her. The article, which she read after buying the paper, told her little that she didn't already know. The police were asking for any witnesses to the abduction to come forward. There had been no mention of a ransom in the article, though Jack had been certain that one would come.

Well, she couldn't do anything about things, even though the missing guy was her uncle. She had never met the man, and his father, her maternal grandfather, was a right tyrant. He was lucky that he had got her proxy vote, or that her suspicions about Costigan's made her like that side even less. But, what if one of these students was related to Blair? If it was that boy, he would be her cousin. A real cousin, quite a different prospect to having just foster brothers.

Reality slapped her mind. What could she do? They didn't know her, and she didn't want her connection to the Blair family made public. Ah, but she could keep her eyes open. If Gianni Costa was behind the abduction, and had eyes on the man's kids as well, he would likely send his front man, Harry King. She would phone the police without hesitation if she saw that bastard.

How could she find out if her guess was correct? Could she get Wayne

Carson, who was now talking to the tour leader, to find out? No! She was still ambiguous about whether Carson knew that she was once called Peg Jessup. He had never even alluded to her past, except relating to Tamworth. If he knew, he was keeping it to himself. If she started meddling in things, based in Melbourne, her manager Alec MacMasters would start asking questions.

"Megan," Peg turned and found Carson approaching.

"I'm going to invite some of that school group to play a segment tonight. They need some performance practice. What do you think?"

"Classical or country?" Peg queried, eyes raised in mischief. "Have you told Mr Mac about this?"

Carson grinned. "They are not all doing classical pieces in the comps. It might be an interesting mix."

Peg shrugged. "I'm game. Let me know the toned down answer. When do you expect to be back?"

"Before lunch. We may need to rehearse this scheme of mine. What are you off to do?"

"Keepsake hunting," Peg told him. She didn't need to be told to be back in time. She knew she had to attend rehearsals.

Wayne Carson's spur of the moment suggestion of allowing some of the students staying at the hotel to be part of his show, gave Peg the chance to speak to the selected few and find out more about them. When she had appeared, her reception was a more subdued version of her mentor's. She wasn't that well known yet – but when they reached Sydney, she was going to cut her first record album. Then, she hoped, her career would take off.

The group, from a notable private school in Melbourne, one of six coming up from Victoria, were part of two dozen schools Australia wide that were competing.

The students chosen for inclusion, were those whose instruments blended best with guitar, piano and drum.

Acting as if she had just heard of the planned collaboration, Peg used the opportunity ask each of the six their name and what they played. Some, she discovered, also sang. Amongst the six, was the dark haired boy. He was not acting like his friends and asking questions, instead he was quiet, just listening. He was James Blair.

Peg was only a few years older than most of the kids, but she was pretending to me 20, not 18. McMasters was running the rehearsal. His quick business mind was already planning how to get the most publicity out of the event. He had already lined up a film crew and photographer to record the event. Some of the filming was being done during rehearsal.

The segment with the students was to include a medley of three songs that they all knew, none of which was their performance songs for the comp. She and Wayne Carson would alternate, playing duet with each of the musicians – or accompany them as singers.

The rehearsal was exhilarating. Peg found these students so very different to her own school fellows. It might have been that she was young, and Wayne Carson's backup singer, or simply because these kids had no preconceived notions about her.

Young James Blair was noticeably quiet. He was intent on his playing, but it lacked passion. Peg made a point of casually chatting to him, trying to be encouraging.

"The mob that come in here for the show aren't that sophisticated. They just like good music," she told him, but knew others were listening.

Then she had to answer questions about the Tamworth Festival, her own unremarkable music instruction, and the luck that had attracted Carson to her.

She was more than relieved when the male tour leader/teacher, called the group away.

"This stunt is not likely to be a one off," McMasters was telling Carson. "Somehow, word has spread. I have had three other schools contact me. Naturally, I agreed. We can hardly show favouritism."

"Is that my karma for suggesting it?" Carson laughed. "The comps are on Wednesday, aren't they?"

"No, the heats and trials start tomorrow. The finals are on Wednesday. I also suggested that the winners could perform with you, but I am told that most of the students leave Thursday morning."

McMasters gestured Peg over. "What did you think of this? Or need I ask? You look like you enjoyed yourself."

"I did!" Peg admitted readily. "Where will they be in the act?"

"In the first bracket. They have a 9pm curfew. What songs are you planning as solos?"

Peg told him. Some of her songs they did each show, the others varied.

"Okay, go get something to eat and have some rest."

Generally, she would go and rest in MacMaster's suite, and keep his wife Claire company. This time, she felt too keyed up and said she wanted to go out and get a feel for the evening's crowd in her anonymous persona. Claire merely nodded that she had heard, and went back to her tapestry work.

The Club was adjacent to the hotel, and intended for a higher class of patron. Most nights it had a show for the diners. The hotel had a bar and pub meals, more aimed at the local working folk. This was where Peg went, not to drink or socialise, but to check out the patrons while she played on one of the arcade game machines. That night, she only stayed fifteen minutes. She needed to get back to prepare for the show.

Walking back, she glanced along the road. In this part of town, the highway was divided, and she saw on the far side, one of the big double trucks had parked. It hadn't been there when she had come out, and apparently they weren't meant to park there. Many did though, just while the driver had a tea break or toilet stop.

Seeing a vaguely familiar logo on the van, she ambled down level with it. As soon as she read the name of the trucking company on the cab door, she had an urgent desire to go back into the club. The logo had been that of Costigan Transport. Better that she didn't court trouble.

All the way back to MacMasters's suite, she glanced around, assessing people entering the club or the restaurant or the pokies room.

Peg had almost finished doing her make up when the extension pinged, indicating a call for her. She answered with her standard, "Hello" and heard, "Megan, I'm glad I caught you."

It was Claire McMasters. "Can I let the three girls come up and you can help them with their make up? I'm needed to help with the boys."

"Sure, just give me five minutes."

She used that time to finish her makeup and add the long, dark wig that was part of her stage persona. She had quickly become proficient at those tasks, although her first attempts had been disasters. At least now she was confident enough to help the girls.

From then until the last set, Peg was, as usual, too busy to worry about anything but her performance. That didn't mean she didn't notice the people in the audience, and the backstage helpers. That night, there were two new ones that she had decided were policemen. She had spotted four more in the audience, two near the front door, and two near the kitchen doors. She wondered, deep in her mind, whether the police actually expected an attempt to be made to snatch James Blair. She hoped not, the kid was sensitive and gently reared. Not at all like her.

Once the school performers had finished, leaving the stage to considerable applause, she forgot him. She and Carson returned to their normal style, finishing as usual with a duet. Their final exit, before the curtain closed to thunderous applause, was into a back stage that was unusually agitated.

"What's up?" Carson demanded.

Peg realised that she was expecting the news. "One of the school kids is missing."

There was a thorough, but low key search going on. Most people were probably thinking abduction, and that could be right, but she had her own reasons for wondering if the boy had his own reasons for hiding.

As soon as she was in her 'boy's' clothes, she went outside. Her first interest was to see if the Costigan truck was still illegally parked. It wasn't, which might be significant, or irrelevant, depending on when it left. It was more than an hour since the schoolkids had left the stage, and well past their 9pm curfew. Had the men she had tagged as police got slack and expected the kid to stay in bed?

What would she do in similar circumstances? Difficult question. She'd never had a father, and her aunt an indifferent guardian at best. She wondered how much the teacher had told him, or did he only know what had been in the paper? Would he try to go home? Or ring home? Surely, if he had asked, they would let him contact his home. The kid was only 14, or 15.

Peg recalled, all too well, being 15. It was when she had done the most stupid thing in her life, even if she had learnt a great deal from the experience. Without planning, she walked towards where she knew a phone box to be. She passed guests from the restaurant, still idling back to their cars, and some less than perfectly sober patrons of the hotel, heading home on foot.

The phone booth was empty, and she only then realised that she was heading towards the roadhouse. There was another phone there, which she might just as well check before giving up on what she knew was a useless search. And there was the chance, if he had seen this place on the way into town, that he might come here hoping to find a Melbourne bound truck.

As far as trucks went, there were enough of them parked in the truck bays. She counted a dozen before entering the narrow space between two that seemed to be locked up and deserted. The drivers might be sleeping in their cabs, she knew. It was what Mick Devlin had relied on in their ill-fated robbery attempt. As she was about to emerge from between the trucks, and cross to the road house, she saw several men talking and smoking. Instantly, she pulled back, but not before one of the men saw her. She ducked under the right hand truck, and crawled to its other side and took off at a run. She had ducked behind a waste skip before the man had run around the truck. From the shadows, Peg saw the man clearly in the ambient lighting.

Damn! What was Mick Devlin doing there, when he was meant to be on the run and hiding?

Admittedly, he had grown a moustache, and his hair was shaggier, but it was him. If she had needed any more proof, it was the low growled curse, "I'm going to get you, you little gutter rat."

He had lost sight of her, for he began to scan the shadows. He began to walk her way, when he saw the blue strobe lights of a police car. He abruptly turned and strode back to the trucks. Peg had an insane desire to attract police attention to Devlin, but stifled it. Better to get to the phone in the road house and report sighting him.

She slipped from behind the skip and moved towards a pile of left over building materials. Then she heard a muffled whimpering. The source, a curled up ball of human misery.

"Jimmy?" she spoke softly, crouching down nearby. "It's Megan, we met this afternoon."

The boy raised his head from his clasped knees. "Why are you here?"

"Maybe, because I'm not that much older than you and know it is possible to do really stupid stuff. And I didn't want you to have to deal with the consequences."

"What will you do?" Jimmy asked softly. "There is a really nasty man after me."

"Hopefully, he will keep out of the way. Some police just arrived. We can either go to them, or slip back to the hotel."

"I'll be in so much trouble."

"If it is only with your teachers, consider yourself lucky," Peg told him. "How do you want to play it?"

"Hotel?"

"Okay, come on. This way."

"But the road is that way," Jimmy protested.

"Too open, don't you think?"

"Oh. Okay."

Old habits of learning her way around had caused Peg to wander in the area around the club in the week and a half they had been there. She had also studied the town map, so even though the road she took was not one she'd travelled, she knew it went the way they wanted to go. She was quite agreeable with the boy's choice. She had personal reasons not to want to go into a roadhouse owned by Costigan's, particularly if Mick Devlin was around. In her current guise, he might well recognise her.

When they came to an area of deeper shadow, well away from the roadhouse, she pulled the boy down in a driveway and peered around a hedge, back along the road. Jimmy was smart enough to ask no questions.

Seeing a shadowy figure, coming past the last streetlight, Peg whispered, "Change of route. Come on, quiet as you can."

They trotted another fifty yards and turned into a cross street. It took them longer, but they arrived at the back of the hotel without spotting anyone else. Several regular reflected blue flashes told them that police cars were still out the front.

"How did you get out past the minders they had on you?" Peg asked in a whisper.

"Who? The teachers? I just went to the toilet and crept out."

If that was true, the police were slack. Or they believed that he was an obedient boy who would calmly go to bed and sleep all night when his father had been abducted. Idiots. There were limits, even for obedient boys.

"What were you trying to do, anyway?"

"Ring my mum, but Mr Wright was near the phone, so I went out to find a phone box."

"You're worried about your father, huh?"

He was close enough to her that she felt him nod. "No one would tell me anything after Peter showed me the paper."

"They may not know much more. However, if you want to be sure your mum is okay, why don't you ask your teacher to help you phone home?"

Jimmy stiffened.

Bingo, Peg thought.

"Listen, Jimmy. I have been around a lot more than you and I damn well know this world isn't perfect. I guess you have ideas of wanting to help find your dad, but the fact is, no one will let you, okay?"

"My mum will need me…"

"She will have your relatives, and do you have any brothers or sisters?"

"A brother."

"Okay. She'll have him. And the best thing you can do is keep yourself safe so she doesn't have any extra worry, okay?"

"Ye….es, I guess."

"An even better thing, would be to do your damnedest in these comps. So, maybe, you can give them some cheerful news. Then, when your dad is found, he will be so proud of you."

"I don't think I can concentrate."

"Bulldust, Jimmy. You're good. Way better than me on that recorder of yours. And if you would take some cousinly advice, play that thing like it was the answer to your prayers. Put your heart, soul and all your anguish into it."

"I'll try."

"Good. Then let's get you inside and back where you belong. And you should tell your teacher everything that happened, and don't run off again."

"Yes, mummy," Jimmy finally managed a faint jest.

"Idiot. The best I could ever be is a distant cousin and that is unlikely."

As soon as she said it, Peg regretted the impulse. Oh well, I can talk around it….

The police pounced on them as soon as Peg led Jimmy into the deserted restaurant, being used as an operations centre.

Once the initial fuss was over, and a much verbally chastised Jimmy was led upstairs by the more sympathetic female teacher, Peg found herself under scrutiny.

"Now, do you have some ID, Megan?" the senior police officer demanded.

"Not on me, no." It was a bit of a lie. She had told them her stage name, and her ID was as Megan Dawes. "But I work here. I'm Wayne Carson's back-up singer. Either he or Alec McMasters can confirm who I am."

The man had been about to make a sceptical remark when she mentioned Carson, probably thinking she was using this as a chance to see him, but his face changed when she mentioned her manager.

Still suspicious, he challenged, "Megan Arthur had long black hair."

"So I did, and now I look like me and I don't attract hordes of wannabees, who'd scratch my eyes out for being lucky enough to have this gig."

"Okay, settle down, Miss Arthur. What can you add to what Jimmy told us?"

While explaining that she liked to walk around for a bit to calm down enough to sleep, she mentioned the illegally parked Costigan's truck, her own lucky escape from the trucker, who had started to follow her, or might have thought she was the boy he had lost.

Then, when asked if she'd had a good look at the trucker, she thought for a moment, and gave an excellent description of Mick Devlin, added the moustache, and ended with, "I am sure I have seem that man's face recently – somewhere. Maybe in the papers."

She couldn't please them when she told them she didn't have a home address, so she suggested he got one of McMasters's business cards.

Finally, they allowed her to go upstairs, but she was not feeling like sleeping. Lying awake until almost three o'clock. It meant that she slept late, to nearly noon. It meant that the school kids had gone off to the comp venue, and her manager was up to speed with her activities of the previous night.

It was her turn for a lecture, and McMasters was good at them. Didn't tone down his language, even for her.

When she was able to defend her actions, she began with, "I didn't exactly go out looking for the kid. I knew he was missing, so I just kept my eyes open when I was out walking. I knew what he looked like, because he was one of the kids that performed with us."

Wayne Carson had been discreetly looking out of the window of McMasters's suite during the harangue. He added a snippet of information. "Young Jimmy Blair reckoned that his cousin helped him."

The guy was teasing her, but Peg groaned. Why had the kid mentioned that? "I gave him some cousinly advice, or that's what I called it. I'm not that much older than the kid, and I caught myself sounding like his teacher sounded when we got back. I thought if I toned it down that way he'd listen."

McMasters had the last word. "Well, the local police want you to keep off the streets after dark. It seems that there were some nasty types about. And if one had tried to snatch the boy, on purpose not just opportunity, they might have tried it on an unwary girl."

"Alright, alright, I took that in the first time. I know I was lucky, but I have been around a bit…"

"I have told the police to keep your name out of the media. That sort of publicity, is not the sort you need."

"You mean, 'Singing sensation saves silly schoolkid?'"

"More like, 'Silly Singer Risks Retribution'," McMasters retorted immediately. "From what I hear, this business with the boy's father is a nasty one."

"Yeah, alright," Peg finally decided to stop stirring her manager. She hoped though, that the police found Mick Devlin.

Feeling sure Peg was through being the rebel, he changed topics onto the other reason for the meeting. "Okay, I have lined up two more venues…."

It wasn't the last unpleasant scene she had to endure in Bathurst. David Blair, having heard about the attack on his grandson, had come to talk to those mentioned as helping to recover him. Carson, being prominent in the reports was one of his targets. He'd had to wait until the show was over, and the two artists were mingling with guests in the lounge bar. By then, he'd had time to link the name Megan Arthur to the girl in Tamworth who had been seen wearing a cameo that had belonged to his daughter, and likely was also the one who was pretending to be his daughter and actioning his dead daughter's shares. That had taken precedence in his mind and he wanted the girl charged with fraud and receiving stolen goods.

His friend, Chief Inspector Taylor, had told him that the girl had been living in sin with his nephew - the guy who'd been friends with the Jessup girl in Matlock. The same place as where his daughter had been found. The kid of the whore, Ida Jessup, who had been hiding the shares all these years.

When Peg had felt her arm being grabbed, she had projected her voice as Carson had been training her, and demanded to be released. This had brought over the hotel security who were always nearby, and alert Carson.

"I have an appointment with Carson," Blair had stated. "Speak to the manager, of this place."

He was asked to release the woman, and to wait while his claim was checked. Meanwhile, Carson shepherded her out through the staff section and back upstairs.

"Did you know him?" Carson asked on the way up.

Although she had a thought on the subject, it was the truth when she said, "No."

When they reached their suite, Carson called down to the hotel manager and checked the man's claim.

"He is David Blair," Carson told her.

"What does he want with me?" Peg asked.

"We should, perhaps, allow him to talk to us."

"He wanted to see you," Peg pointed out. "I wasn't mentioned in relation to the kid, who I assume was his grand kid."

"True. I'll hear what he wants to say." Carson gave permission for the man to come up.

Peg went to remove her makeup, intending to stay out of Blair's way. That didn't mean, in this case, that she wasn't doing her best to overhear the conversation.

Blair was asking if Carson had more information about how his grandson was taken and returned. He didn't seem satisfied that the Good Samaritan had been a local kid.

"How would a local kid know all the stuff my grandson told me? He said his cousin helped him."

Carson saw Peg was listening and called her out.

"Our manager did not wish Megan's name to be mentioned," Carson told their visitor.

"And I gave the kid some cousinly advice," Peg told Blair. "I thought that would be a way he might listen. He wanted to go home and help his mum. I am just glad he is safe."

Blair was staring at her. She looked different without the stage make up. "I know about you!"

Peg glanced at Carson, and he spoke up.

"You should thank Megan for helping young Jimmy. At least you do not have to worry about him as well."

Peg was sure that Blair wanted to accuse her of being involved with the attempted abduction too. "He's a great kid. Very musical. He was one of the group that performed with us."

Behind that comment, she wondered what he had found out and who had told him.

"You may have tricked Taylor into thinking that you are some floosie his nephew picked up in Tamworth, but you are not, are you?"

Peg simply stared back as if ignorant of his meaning. "You have me confused with someone else."

"No I don't."

"Blair, I think you have said all you need to," Carson warned.

"Do you even know who this woman is?" Blair demanded, turning to stare Carson directly in the face.

"Miss Arthur is my protégé. Why does it matter to you?"

"That woman is a con artist and I do not believe that is her real name!"

Even though she wanted to shrink into the nearest crack, Peg stood her ground. At least Carson had taken the confrontation out of the eyes of the public. It meant that the media would have to guess what caused it. Would Blair keep his mouth shut?

"No, Megan uses Arthur as her performing name. I ask you again, what business do you have coming here and making accusations?"

"Don't you care that this woman is a criminal?"

"Where is your evidence?"

Blair's face had gone a dark red and his fists were clenching. He didn't care if he maligned her in public, but he wasn't wanting to blurt his own sins out.

"This woman has been in prison for abetting her brothers in an armed robbery."

Peg felt her face go cold, as if all the blood had run from it. Her legs felt like jelly. Carson didn't even glance her way to see her reaction. Fortunately, Blair didn't either.

Carson spoke mildly, in contrast to Blair's loud accusation. "Some people believe that being loyal to one's family is a crime. I see that you are one of them."

"The police thought her guilty! The court put her away."

Peg felt anger beginning to replace the panic. Who was he to accuse her of being a criminal? She had paid for choosing to try to warn her brothers. Carson had called that being loyal to her family, and that had been true. She hadn't wanted them caught. Hadn't wanted them involved with Devlin's plan, but then, Mick had them all in his thrall. They hadn't wanted her involved – being lookout had been her idea and Mick had promised her a small cut too. And Blair couldn't talk. He'd kicked his own daughter out onto the streets.

Before she could blurt any of that out, Carson spoke again. "I am aware of Megan's past, Mr Blair, and it is past. If you had done your research, you would be aware that she was sent to Meredan not so much that she had been an accessory to a crime, but because she was in grave moral danger were she to stay with a drunken slut of a guardian. Many other girls were sent there for the same reason, and not for any crime they had committed. In fact, some were sent there just for being a bit wild. And that could have happened even to girls of the highest breeding."

Until now, Peg hadn't been sure that Carson had recognized her from there. He had never asked about her past prior to meeting him again in Tamworth. He was helping her to get a fresh start; Blair was trying to ruin that. What was more, if he knew who she was, how long before Gianni

Costa sent his hit man King after her? The panic began to return.

"What do you mean by that remark, Carson?"

"I meant that everyone can make a mistake. I would like to think that you trying to drag Miss Arthur out of the club was a mistake."

At least, Blair had not blurted out her real name when he accosted her in the lounge bar. Well, to be perfectly truthful, Peg Jessup wasn't her real name, any more than Megan Arthur was. Did he suspect that she was his grand-daughter?

"Well?" Carson prompted.

Blair turned to glare at the woman Carson was protecting. Peg hoped he was having doubts.

"This woman is a thief. She has something that belongs to me."

Those shares are mine you beast! You only think they should be yours.

Before she could censor her words, Peg blurted, "Well, it sure isn't gratitude for saving your precious grandson from a dangerous predator!"

Blair, who had begun to move towards her, stopped and rocked in place.

"And if you make public any unfounded accusations against me, I will have you sued for libel!"

"Slander," Carson corrected softly. "Defamation, anyway."

"So, you deny that your real name is Peg Jessup? And you deny impersonating a member of my family to gain benefit from shares stolen from my daughter?"

"Yes. I deny both those statements. I do have shares that are legally mine and had been held in trust until I was eighteen. They have nothing to do with you."

"Shares in what company?"

"That is my business, not yours."

"Give me an answer and I will go," Blair insisted.

"The Commonwealth Bank." Peg said the first thing that came into her mind.

"You little liar!"

"That is enough, Blair! I must insist that you leave," Carson stated. "Hotel security guards are on their way. If you leave now, you will not make a media sensation of yourself by being man-handled out."

That jolted Blair back into a semblance of sense. "You haven't heard the last of me, you lying little bitch. I will have my lawyers on you." Then he leant towards Peg and hissed, "I do know who you really are, and that your mother stole the shares from my daughter. I think she killed her and put her into that dam in Matlock. I also know that you have made everyone think you are dead."

Peg answered in a similarly low voice. "You need to be absolutely sure of your facts before you come back making more ridiculous accusations. I read about that woman they found. Your daughter, was it? Well, do you know why they found her? It wasn't some tip off. She would still be there, unsuspected, if they hadn't been trying to drag the dam to look for some other poor girl that had gone missing, that they thought had been raped and killed. So if you don't want another death on your conscience, besides your daughter's, you will keep your fat mouth shut and not spout your ridiculous theories to anyone."

At that moment, Blair was grabbed from behind, and two hefty security officers began to drag him away. He tried to shrug them off.

Carson closed the door behind the men, and glanced around. "Megan?"

She wasn't in sight. He checked each room of his suite and finally found her in the bathroom, sitting on the floor, arms hugging her knees, her whole body shaking.

"Come on out, Megan, Do you want to talk about this?"

Peg shook her head.

"Don't you trust me?" He didn't hear an answer so he went on, "How about some afternoon tea then? Hot chocolate and cakes? After that, we can work on your new song."

Peg looked up. "You don't need to be caught up in this. It would be better if I resigned that contract and disappeared."

"Perhaps. Is that what you really want?"

"No, but…"

"Megan, I knew who you were the moment I heard you sing in Tamworth. As far as I am concerned, you have great talent. Any mistakes you made in your past are over and forgotten."

"It's not that simple."

"Well, when you feel up to warning me about what dung is being readied to be flung in my face, I will be ready to listen."

"Dung! What an understatement!" Peg looked up. "If word gets out about all that, your name will be dragged through the mud too – particularly if you admit to knowing any of it."

"We'll see. How about washing your face and tidying yourself up while I order room service?"

Peg stood up. "Does Mr McMasters know who I am?"

"I haven't explicitly told him."

"What will he do if he finds out?"

"Well, I think that he will say very little. He was not against me teaching some of the girls at Meredan. And he is impressed with your talent."

Carson went back to the main room where the telephone was ringing. Peg could hear him answering. "No, Mac, everything's fine. A misunderstanding, that's all. Megan is a bit shaken up, but we are going to work on some new material." Then he was silent for so long that Peg thought he had hung up, but he spoke again. "Yes, I have all that and I will talk to you later."

"Did McMasters hear about Blair?" Peg asked as she returned to the main room.

"Yes, he did. There were a couple of journo's in the bar, and they tried to ask Blair questions as he was being escorted out. He was smart enough to keep quiet then, but they cornered McMasters."

"What did he say?"

"Him? He wasn't around to see the incident and said as much." Carson patted the table. "Take a seat. I just want to read through this score of yours." He took up the paper she had used to jot the tune down, and after a while, began to hum parts – making minor modifications until he seemed satisfied.

"What do you think?" Peg asked.

"It's better than the first two," Carson said. "You are a master of allusion – I wonder who knows you well enough to read beneath the words to the truth."

"Only Jack," Peg admitted. "But I am not the only person to have a rotten life and have to start over. That's the message I want to give out. I think I will title it, 'Picking up the pieces'."

"Is it finished?"

"I may decide to add to it," Peg admitted, for the recent events were already stirring words in her mind. "And I am no longer sure I like the ending it has at the moment."

Chapter 23

Mike had come down to Melbourne, mainly to get to know his father better, but he didn't mind being co-opted into helping Jack look through old records. He was finding the tedious task unexpectedly interesting.

He had offered to find basic personal data on the people who had been set up by Gianni Costa, and who had been in Bertie Jessup's ledger. He'd spent a lot of time looking in the registry of births, deaths and marriages while he had been looking for his own father, and was used to using the equipment. He often had to estimate ages for the people, though some of the data he obtained from Who's Who.

He set about things systematically, having some exercise books and keeping a page for each person. Where there were multiple possibilities for each name – he wrote them all down.

After talking to Peg last, Jack had added another name for him to check – Annie Simmons. He had said it might have been Ida Jessup's real name – from before she became Adelaide Swan. And he kept in mind the possibility of similar names – Symons, Simons, Seymon and so on.

He had made a start on her information, when he came to Luke Simmons in Jessup's list. He recognised the name and felt a surge of excitement. If Jack had not been off in the land registry archive, he would have spoken aloud.

Luke Simmons was born in 1875, married in 1917, died in 1935 as a result of an accident. His wife, Mathilda, also died in 1935, same cause. Annie, their child, had been born the same year they were married. He looked for other children that Luke and Mathilda might have had, and found none.

Having confirmed Annie's date of birth, he went back to the marriage records, to see if there was a marriage certificate for her under that name. When he had looked before, there had been a number of possibilities. There had been none under Adelaide Swan.

"Bingo!" Mike exclaimed softly. He started to copy the information he had just found. It was the registered marriage details of Annie Simmons to Gianni Costa. He already knew of Annie's parents, but apart from the fact of the marriage itself – in 1936 – he now knew that Gianni's father was Luigi. Gianni's birth place was given as Potenza. His mother was Maria. He made a mental note to have a look in the immigration records to check if she had arrived in Australia too. Jack had mentioned they arrived in 1920.

While he was in the marriage records, he went on to looking for marriages involving the men he had birth information on. While he was looking for a different name, he came across a marriage certificated for John Costigan. The details matched with what was in Who's Who.

He decided to go back further and look for details on Costigan's father, whose name was Louis. His mother was Mary. They married in 1921, in Australia.

Well, Gianni was older than John. So they had to be two different people….that wrecked Jack's theory.

Mike kept working until the registry closed, then went back to Jack's place.

Jack had preceded him, and was busy putting his notes in a logical order. He was happy to stop and hear what Mike had found.

"That's the first I've heard about Ida Jessup actually being married to Gianni," Jack said thoughtfully. "Peg was told that her marriage to Bertie Jessup was a sham, and the photo in the paper that I found, seems to confirm it. This proves it – unless they divorced?"

"I suppose I should check," Mike decided.

"Peg never hinted at the idea her aunt was married to Gianni. She couldn't have known," Jack wondered.

"Never told me that much anyway," Mike countered. "I might ask some questions of Ian. He was hanging around the fringes of the criminal scene back then."

"Ask him if he knew Bertie Jessup. That was something else Peg mentioned when I told her of Jessup's pictures. Bertie gave Ida that box of photos, to give to someone named Ian. A reporter, Peg said. Surname may've been Stone, or not."

"Yeah, I will. I think Stone was his nickname once. Anyway, that is not my best piece of information."

Mike told him the coincidences about the names of Gianni Costa's parents and those of John Costigan.

"Interesting, since Louis, Mary and John, could be anglicised versions of Luigi, Maria and Gianni," Jack mused.

"However, according to what I found, Gianni, is older than John by about two years. They must be two different people." Mike watched his friend's face as he gave the additional details.

"Seems so," Jack had to agree. "If those two were brothers…why have them both with pretty much the same name?"

Mike shrugged. "Anyone's guess. On my way back here I thought it might be worth checking school records. Gianni would have had to go to school, at least for a while."

"Might mention that to the old man. I don't know if we can access that stuff," Jack made a mental note. "Maybe the connection is a coincidence, since there wouldn't be two entries for the same person. Can you look for records of changes of name?"

"Maybe, but there are limits for some things. I can't get into the deaths that are more recent than thirty years."

"If you can't get at the data, tell my grandfather. He can get someone official to find out. Anyway, let me have the rest of what you found out."

"There's not much." Mike gave Jack his exercise books and decided, "I'll go and think of what we can eat without going out."

Jack went back to adding his day's meagre findings to his master report. He commented to Mike, "It is definitely much easier to find information about property transfers if you have the file designation of the property. So far, I have been working from a list of Blair's holdings, and those of Costigan's. Tracing each from previous owners. They won't let me at the cross reference index of current ownership."

"Ask you grandfather to arrange access," Mike suggested. "After all, he put you on the job."

"Probably only to keep me off the street," Jack retorted. "Nothing I have been told to do involves confidential information. As for you, checking BDMs – that sounds like make work too. Grandfather will have people interviewing anyone in those diaries that are around to be found. One of the task force is probably doing traces on them."

"True, since a lot of Bertie's subjects are well known. What about the others – those I didn't find in Who's Who?"

"Actually, that is a point. I really need to be able to find if Gianni was buying up properties. None of the transfers I have recorded are from before 1940. And like I said, I am working from a list of Costigan's. None of the names in Jessup's diaries has cropped up."

"I guess that this grunt work won't be wasted," Mike sighed.

"At least it keeps my mind busy," Jack admitted. "Otherwise, I'll find myself wanting to go north."

That reminded Mike of Peg, and he changed the subject. "I don't suppose you have heard if they got that box open."

"No, and I probably don't need to know. I just hope that if the damn shares are in there, that Peg doesn't lose them."

"Yeah," was all Mike could think to add. "How about baked beans on toast? Will that do you?"

"That'll do, and put the news on will you?"

"Mike, do you think that a place like Matlock would keep records of property transfers for local properties?" Jack asked out of the blue. He had just finished eating his tea.

"I reckon they would." Mike pushed his own plate away. "What are you thinking?"

"Not sure yet. I was wondering how to find out what happened to the property of Annie Simmons' parents. If Gianni actually married her, he would have control of it. Peg said something about her aunt claiming Gianni sold it and helped her find another place. Maybe it was the place in Matlock. Or maybe he helped her get that too. Not sure if it will mean anything. Would you be willing to go check?"

"If your grandfather okays it. When do we need to report to the think tank again?"

"Tomorrow. That's why I am trying to get all my stuff in order."

Mike reached for his exercise books. "I have it in mind to create a timeline – to compare what various people were doing and when."

Jack looked up and stared at him. "What do you mean?"

"All these dates are getting mixed up in my head. So, I will put down dates for the major figures in our researches. Starting with when they were born, married, had kids, and putting in any other details we find out, and when they happened. A visual cross reference. You never know –something might jump out at us."

"That's brilliant! Who will you include?"

Mike considered, he'd only just thought of the idea. "Okay, Blair, Costigan, Gianni, Ida Jessup, and anyone else who might be useful. Like my old man, Ian."

"How about including my uncle as well. He knows Blair, and Costigan, and Ian. Plus the bastard has been a dogsbody for Costa most of his working life."

"Okay, start with him. What can you tell me about him for a start?"

Mike opened up another page of his exercise book, and headed the page Justin Taylor.

"Well, he was born in 1930. He had his 40th birthday three years ago. Then, he became a member of the family tradition when he turned 18, so that would have been 1948 or 1949."

"Anything else?" Mike prompted.

"Well, he's never married. He was in love with David Blair's daughter. Met her because he was at school with her brother." Jack had refrained from referring to the woman as Peg's mother.

"I wonder if that was reciprocal," Mike mused. "After all, she ran off with my dad."

"Depends on if he was a rigid, arrogant, righteous jerk back then."

"You know, now that I have met your uncle, I reckon he is a lot like Blair. He was probably considered a better prospective son in law than an itinerant muso."

"That's probably why the girl ran off. Blair's a jerk."

"Yeah, but I still feel kind of sorry for him, having his son abducted and all," Mike said. "Did you hear on the news earlier that someone tried to snatch one of his grandsons? The kid was with a school group at a music comp."

"No, I missed that," Jack said, leaning towards Mike. "Up Sydney way was it?" He added the town where Peg was playing.

"You did hear!"

"No, but when I spoke to Peg last, some school group had just arrived where she was."

"I hope she is keeping a low profile! I also heard that there was a sighting of that Devlin guy up there."

Jack's face lost colour. "If anyone would recognise that bastard, it's Peg. I have this awful feeling she's put both feet in deep shit again."

"Her?" Mike laughed. "She has had practice shovelling manure. Besides, in case you are worried, if something happened to Wayne Carson's backup singer, it would be all over the news."

"True, but when she is not performing, she looks nothing like her stage persona. What else did you hear?"

"Only that some local kid found Jimmy Blair and took him back to where he should have stayed. Seems he ran off with a half-cocked idea of going home to his mother."

"Some local kid!" Jack shook his head. "How much do you want to bet that it wasn't?"

"I wouldn't win that one," Mike said.

"I just wish I knew what part of 'lie-low' that she doesn't understand. The last thing she needs is for the police to discover who she was. She is just starting to make her name as a singer. She deserves a fair go."

"Yeah, well, if she reported Devlin, I suspect it is her wanting to see certain other people go down. Are you keeping her up to date on what we know?"

"The little scraps, you mean. Yes. I find it sometimes jogs her memory about stuff her aunt mentioned. Like checking out Annie Simmons. Have you put Harry King on the list for your timeline?"

"Haven't anything on him yet," Mike said.

"Harry King may not even be his real name," Jack proposed. "And it occurs to me that he has taken on the role of Gianni's front man, and if Peg hadn't seen Gianni and Harry not that long ago, I'd wonder if Gianni Costa was dead. What gets me is where could that guy be hiding? I'd say that no one, but King, I assume, ever sees him."

"Have you given up on the idea that he and Costigan are the same?"

Jack considered, "Not completely. All we can prove is that there are two different people. They have to be related in some way, I reckon. Peg does have a good eye for faces."

"Well, we will keep an open mind. Is that meeting in the morning or evening?"

"Evening. Why?"

"I had a thought." Mike flopped into one of the two battered old arm chairs. "You found when Gianni and his parents came here, so I decided to look for where all those Italian immigrants settled. That would be where I would start looking for schools that Gianni might have gone to."

"It would be a logical starting place, but I think it will only confirm that Gianni and John are two different people."

"I thought maybe we could get names of classmates and if they are still around, ask them what they remember about Gianni. Like if he had a brother."

"A brother? What makes you say that?"

"It's possible."

"Yeah," Jack agreed with the last statement, but was thinking. "I'd say nix to the finding classmates. One, its fifty years ago, and two, if any of them are keeping in touch with Gianni for some reason, word might get back to him."

"Well, it was just an idea."

"The records yes, it may be worth seeing if they still exist. Did you find anything on Louis Costigan?"

"Marriage and death certificate. Not a birth one. Maybe he immigrated too?"

"Did you find a death certificate for Luigi Costa?" Jack asked.

"No, come to think of it," Mike admitted. "I will look for that next visit. And at the immigration records."

"Yes, do that, but then I think you should work on that timeline of yours and drop checking on Jessup's list of victims for a bit. I have the names, and can look for them in the land records."

"Do you have something special in mind?"

"Yeah a break from the land archives. Trying to find where Annie Simmons parents lived. I am going to start with the newspaper archives, to see if any covered the car accident they were killed in. Then, if they mention a suburb where they were from, go onto the electoral roles for back them to get the address. Maybe the local council has more accessible land records. Right now, though, I am going out to prod the memory of a mutual friend of ours."

Chapter 24

"Hi Casey," Peg greeted when she recognised Jack as her caller. He was using Casey Jackman as an alias when he rang. Peg knew that Wayne Carson knew who he was, but McMasters and his wife did not know that he was her husband, they assumed it was a boyfriend.

"How are things at the farm?" Peg asked, using that as a message to tell Jack she wasn't alone, when he said, "I need to talk to you."

McMasters stood and helped his wife up and then gave her a terse goodnight. It was nearly midnight.

When she was alone, Peg curled up in an armchair that was near the phone and spoke quietly, "What's up?"

"I've a couple of questions. First, did you know that your aunt had actually married GC?"

Peg's instant reaction was, "Really?" Then she went silent, thinking. "She never told me she was, but it might explain why she tarted herself up when he came. How do you know she was?"

"We found a record of the marriage. Him and Annie Simmons."

"Okay…she was in a particularly maudlin mood one day and mentioned something. Let me try to think back. She was supposedly married to Bertie Jessup, but she couldn't have been if she was married to GC."

"You said that she said that marriage to Bertie was a sham."

"I know, but when GC was coming that time I spied on her guest, she had said her expected visitor was married."

"Who to?"

"She didn't say. She just said that she and Gianni were in love, back when he was getting started in business. Later, she said she didn't see as much of him because he was often away on business. Then he told her he was married, and the wife had found out about her and was making a fuss. He didn't want to leave her because he had a legitimate heir on the way. He was going to buy her a place, so they had somewhere to be together."

"Was that when she moved to Matlock?"

"No, she moved there later."

"When would that have been?" Jack asked Peg.

"I don't know. Stan was maybe eight, the other two were still little if I remember right – but I really don't know."

"I will see if I can find anything on all that," Jack thought aloud.

"I'm sure that if she knew she was married to him, she'd have said," Peg gave her opinion.

"I will keep an open mind. Anyway next question. Do you know anything about her parents?"

Peg thought back. "I think they'd been well off, but when they died, there wasn't as much money as everyone thought. She met Gianni about then and he supposedly helped her invest what there was, so she could keep her parent's house, and appearances."

"Interesting." Ideas were coming into Jack's mind. "And you have no idea where the properties were?"

"None, sorry. Was what I said helpful?"

"I don't know yet. Did she say if Gianni ever sold her parent's house? Or if it is still hers?"

"I seem to recall her mention that when she moved the first time, that he'd sold the house to get something more modest," Peg told him, "But I don't know if it was true, and if it was what happened to that place when she moved to Matlock. She'd been there twenty years or so. GC was sending clients who paid her."

"The creep is kindness itself," Jack said derisively. "I will have to think on what you said. It raises more questions than I had before."

"Anymore word on the absent father?" Peg asked.

"Not that I have heard. How's the kid?"

"I think I convinced him to stay with his friends. I haven't been able to get near him since. We had another of the school groups performing with us tonight. Some of those kids are better musicians than I am."

"Only on different instruments and they probably don't sing as well," Jack countered. "One last thing. Did your aunt's will leave her house to you?"

"No. To the boys. Probably because I had all the other stuff. Why?"

"I wondered if it mentioned the actual details of the property. I want to look it up. Confirm the ownership, previous owners etc. The copy you faxed of the will, I gave to my grandfather."

"What details do you need?"

Jack told her.

"I'll have a better look at it. The legal jargon was hard to follow. I need to find a way to probate it or whatever is needed. I am supposed to do it, but, well, I am pretending to be dead. When are you likely to call back?"

"Ah," Jack thought. "Got a meeting tomorrow night with my grandfather. So not then. What is your schedule like the following day?"

"Free in the morning."

"I'll try then," Jack promised. When he hung up after sending a few kisses to her, he had one coin drop out.

Mike was sitting in a chair and still awake when he returned. "Well?" he demanded as Jack closed and locked the door of his flat.

"Well what? She didn't try to avoid admitting that she talked to the Blair kid." Jack smirked. "If that is what you meant?"

"Okay, you were right on that, but I meant about the other questions."

Jack quickly repeated what Peg had said.

"I reckon that certificate you found, with Costa marrying Annie, is a fake."

"Why register a false marriage? Bribe a celebrant to sign it and all?"

"Why? To take over her inheritance. I mean, a bloke marries an heiress, he's the one to control the money."

"You are probably right, and I wonder if that was the first time he did it? And if he did it again?"

"If you are right and he is Costigan…."Mike suggested.

"Yeah." Jack flopped into the other chair and continued thinking aloud. "Since Annie had lost her parents – don't think there were any close relatives – he probably thought he could get away with it. Anyway, I wish I knew where her parents used to live. He might still own it."

"Do you think he might be living there?"

"Who knows?" Jack shrugged.

"Can we narrow down the area?" Mike suggested. "Annie/Adelaide's parents died when?"

Jack recalled the date.

"Okay, if her parents were rich, where might they live? Toorak? Sth Yarra, Malvern? Could we check census results for likely places?"

"I thought they destroyed the original data sheets," Jack told him.

"I don't know – but they probably do income versus area analysis."

"Well, if the newspapers don't mention a suburb, I might have to resort to that," Jack decided. "I do wonder if Adelaide, formerly Annie Simmons, hadn't been as destitute as she thought."

"Are you saying that he wanted to corrupt her?" Mike asked.

"Why not. He was probably trying to do that to Blair's daughter – seeing how he is still after those damn shares. Think about it. Annie was a nice girl who became a whore. Blair's daughter was wild, yes, but someone got her hooked on drugs, and turned her into a whore too. They may not have been the only ones."

"Maybe you should mention that to your Grandfather. Maybe other rich girls ran away, died, or became junkies back then. He can get one of the task force guys going through old police reports." Mike, thinking of it, paled. "If that idea is fact, I hate to think what other horrors we will find."

"Not us. For the police to find." Jack stressed. "We are mere civilians."

Jack presented himself at his grandfather's house, just after the household had finished breakfast. His uncle saw him, but didn't even have a snide remark or a reply to his polite greeting. That made him uneasy. Regardless, he continued through to his grandfather's study where the servant had said Eugene Taylor could be found.

"Come in," a voice called, still strong despite the speaker's advanced age.

"Ah, Jack. What is it that you want?"

"I have a request, Sir."

"Go on."

"Is it possible for me to have permission, or some formal mandate, to access current ownership records in the lands archive? At present, I can't use the cross-reference index to find out if a person owns other properties."

"Why do you want to do that?" The question was posed in a neutral voice, but Jack knew his grandfather was studying him.

"Sir, finding information on a particular property is easy if I have the registry number – which I do for the properties on Blair's list and Costigan's list. However, it doesn't tell us if either of those men have other properties, perhaps in their own name or that of a family member."

"We can't just search at random, to see if Mr and Mrs A have land or not. We need to have a reason," ex Superintendent Taylor explained.

"I understand that, Sir. But yesterday, I found a marriage certificate for Gianni Costa, and Annie Simmons. Annie, I am reasonably sure, changed her name to Adelaide Swan when she took up with Gianni Costa."

Eugene Taylor leant forward abruptly. "Simmons! Adelaide Swan was

Luke Simmons daughter?"

"That's what I believe."

"Go on with your report, Jack."

"I think the marriage was a fake, because later, Adelaide Swan married Bertie Jessup – supposedly, and there is no record of a divorce. Mike suggested that maybe he faked the marriage so he could get control of her inheritance. I have an informant who told me that Adelaide Swan, believed that she was almost destitute when her parents died, and that Gianni promised to invest the small amount that was left, sell her parents' house and buy a more modest one where she could keep up appearances. That same informant had the impression that Adelaide was not married to Gianni."

"I think I can see where this is going," Eugene Taylor said thoughtfully. "Continue, lad, I would like to see if our thoughts agree."

Jack shook his head. "That's as far as I got. I am thinking that he took over the house, as Annie's husband, then maybe sold it and kept the profit after buying a smaller place for Annie - or still has the property."

"And you think it will be still under the name of Gianni Costa," Taylor queried. "Why not just keep it in the girl's name?"

"I'm inclined to think the former, since it gives him control," Jack gave his opinion.

"So you want to check that out?" Taylor asked neutrally.

"Well, that's the thing. I don't know where Annie Simmons used to live, and I don't have the property registration details."

Then Taylor surprised Jack. "I think you have proved your discretion, son. Give me a few minutes."

That's the first time he has ever called me, son! Or even admitted we are related through his younger son. The astonishment escalated when he heard the requests his grandfather was making of whoever he called. Apart from requesting ID for him as a police aide, he asked for some old files to be delivered to him ASAP. Then he hung up and studied Jack again.

"Has it occurred to you that Costa might have done a similar thing before, or later?" Taylor asked.

"Yes, sir. If it was Costa, other rich girls might have been corrupted and fleeced of their inheritance. I reckon he tried it on Blair's daughter."

"Are you still convinced that Costa is related to Costigan? From your informant?"

Jack tried not to blush and merely nodded.

Justin Taylor entered with a cardboard filing box. He placed it on his father's desk and departed, still without a word. Jack's eyes followed him, and he wondered.

"There's no news of Richard Blair, then?" Maybe that was the reason for his uncle's reticence.

"No," was the short answer. "We have planted informants in the Waterman's Bar in Newport, where the docker's union hang out, but that has told us nothing."

"What about that sighting of Devlin, up north." The words were out before Jack thought to censor them.

"If it was him, he eluded us. How did you know of that? We didn't make the sighting public."

Jack wanted to say nothing, but could not even think of way to explain his knowledge.

Finally, Eugene Taylor waved the question aside. "The police up there will keep a watch out for him, and a guard on Blair's grandson. The boy was damn lucky."

Peg was damn lucky, Jack thought to himself.

Taylor reached for the record box, but needed to stand to look at the contents. "Going back to your report, Luke Simmons was in the brewing business. He ran a small brewery in Fitzroy. He and his wife died in a car accident. Allegedly, he had been drinking. The coroner recorded an open verdict. He could not rule out suicide, or the possibility someone tampered with the car, I do recall that he had lost heavily as his investments turned bad. Follow up the idea, lad. Let me know what you find."

Taylor wrote an address on a piece of paper, and passed it over.

"As I said earlier, Jack, the police are not allowed to idly look at information. In theory, you are only allowed to look for specific information on specified people. I believe you have a list of people?"

Jack, nodded, wondering what his grandfather was getting at.

"We do need to cross check all information, cover all bases," Taylor stressed. "Do a thorough job."

"Of course, Sir," Jack agreed. Is he actually giving me tacit permission to look everywhere? To poke around at random, or go off on sidelines?

"Report what you find to me, discreetly."

"Yes, Sir."

"Good. Go and get some more breakfast or something until that ID arrives. Will I see you this evening?"

"Probably, Sir."

Jack left half an hour later, with a letter of authority enabling him free access to all files in the land registry, to check on the list of people he had. He also had two identification folders, for whoever had arranged them had also done one for Mike as well. He wondered if that arbitrary decision had been his uncle's.

He detoured via his flat to pick Mike up, and then drove to near the MCG to park. At that time of day parking in the centre of town would be impossible. A train and tram would be quicker.

With two of them working on the files, they soon began to see a dark picture. They took a break for lunch and went to where they could talk without being heard by anyone else.

Mike summed it up, "If that bastard wasn't corrupting the children, he was blackmailing the parents."

Name after name on Bertie Jessup's list, turned up as the seller of land acquired by Gianni Costa. Some of the land was, in turn sold on to developers for a "handsome profit".

Jack had accessed the cross reference files, found Costa's name and checked out nearly two dozen properties. Of these, five were still held in Costa's name. One of those, had been the Simmons property.

They went back to work, and by earlier agreement didn't discuss the search, so there was no chance that other users of the archive could over hear.

In the late afternoon, Jack sat back and gestured Mike over. Speaking in a very soft voice, Jack said, "Something odd. After 1938, I have found no mention of Gianni Costa acquiring land. Can I have that list of names you have?"

Mike handed his notebook over and Jack went back to work – writing down land registry info for Mike to check further. At closing time, Jack handed it back in exchange for his own, that Mike had been using. They didn't discuss anything until they were back at Jack's flat. They had just enough time to freshen up, grab a snack, ready to go see Eugene Taylor.

While eating a cheese sandwich, Jack compared his notes and Mike's. He was particularly interested in properties that Costa had once owned.

"In 1938, Costa sold a lot of his land holdings to six different companies," Jack noted.

"Hiding his tracks," Mike suggested. "Maybe those companies should be checked?"

"That will be a proper police job," Jack guessed. "But that wasn't what I was getting at. Each of those six companies were acquiring land in a separate area, and I would need to check, but I think each of those areas was where a major development was later instigated."

"Smells a bit," Mike commented. "Particularly if the original land owners were forced to sell. The value of that land would multiply afterwards."

"It did. And if you come to think of it, Costigan's have been buying up land out Melton and Sunbury way, just recently."

Mike snickered, "What do you expect. The government announced these plans to build low cost housing out from Melbourne – satellite towns. Pakenham was another area suggested."

"Pakenham?" Jack queried.

"Yes, what has you so interested?"

Jack was flicking through his notes. "Blair Holdings has been buying up land out there."

"Well, that's interesting, but not what we were out to find. We were trying to see if the poor sods in Bertie's list, were blackmailed into selling."

"No, but I might mention it anyway," Jack decided. "Let's get this stuff to the old man."

A sharp discussion within Eugene Taylor's study was silenced when the manservant knocked to announce Jack and Mike. Moments later, a glowering Justin Taylor stalked out, ignoring the two younger men waiting just outside the door. Jack kept his face impassive, extremely glad that the old man wasn't raging at him. Once had been enough. He was surprised that his uncle was not exempt from his father's stringent views.

"Come in," Eugene Taylor called after a moment.

Jack went first, and saw the flush on his grandfather's face fading. He exhaled the breath he hadn't realised he was holding.

"Sit down lads, and tell me what you have found."

Jack began, but Mike and he alternated giving information so it came out in logical progressions. When they finished, Eugene Taylor considered.

"On the surface, most of that just indicates that someone was doing well speculating. Toorak, Caulfield, Hawthorn – there used to be more large mansion estates in those areas. In the 50s and 60s they were cleared for residential subdivisions. And the shopping centre at Chadstone was being built in the late 50s. I will have people check out those companies. I will also instigate a search of police records on those names – we may not find much if they didn't make a report. We might only find out if there was foul play or the death was thought suspicious."

Jack and Mike stayed quiet, letting Taylor continue to consider their findings.

"It is interesting that you only found mention of Costa until 1938. It could be taken that something happened to him at that time. That he died. We did do a search through the tax records and his last tax return was that year. He could be dead…."

"No!" Jack blurted. "Peg saw him with her aunt."

"Ah yes, the missing Jessup girl." Taylor didn't look that way when he said that. "Too bad we can't question her. That tip about her aunt being Annie Simmons has proved to be very interesting. You say that there has been no change of ownership on that property since Costa acquired it?"

"That and five others," Jack reminded him.

"I wonder if that is significant," Taylor mused. "I find it very interesting. Someone must be paying the rates, electricity, and other municipal fees – even if it is being rented out."

"Do you want us looking?" Jack asked.

"No…I'll get some of the task force to do that. Maybe we can take a leaf out of the American's book."

"Sir?" Mike queried.

Taylor smiled faintly. "They got Al Capone on tax evasion charges. Leave that with me. I will have to see if I can get the banks to reveal if he still has active bank accounts. We might be able to force him out of hiding if we officially have him declared dead, and the government seizes those properties."

Mike grinned at the thought, but Jack didn't. There was a risk of that idea backfiring and Peg being in trouble.

"If they did that," Jack thought aloud. "Would the government keep the properties?"

"It's only a notion at the moment," Taylor reminded him. "What are you thinking?"

"That Stan Jessup's birth certificate actually has Gianni Costa as his father. Also, we have the link from Ida Jessup to Adelaide Swan to Annie Simmons."

"Yes, indeed. You have a devious mind, Jack Dawes. I will think on all that too. Was there anything else of interest that you have found?"

"I think we covered everything," Mike said, glancing at Jack.

Taylor changed the topic. "We haven't had any luck finding this Harry King you mentioned. There are no police records, tax records, or bank accounts that relate to a man such as you have both described."

"Uncle Justin has seen him too," Jack reminded his grandfather.

"Yes, he provided a list of places where he has seen King, and these have been checked, but no luck so far."

"He's had a good look at me," Jack warned, not sure what he might be asked to do.

"And he might recognise me," Mike added.

"I don't want either of you to confront him, just look out for him."

"Sir, what are you suggesting, exactly?" Jack asked directly.

Taylor gave them both another searching look.

"Very well. You have both given me some very good ideas for new avenues of investigation. And in most instances, I have not mentioned where the ideas came from."

Jack let out a "phew" of relief.

"I haven't made it widely known that it was you who proposed a link between Costa and Costigan. The names are suggestive enough, but not proof. I do think that it is becoming more and more obvious. Your report today of not finding traces of Costa after 1938, made me recall you saying that Costa's father Luigi died that year. Again, I don't know how that fits, but I don't trust coincidences. What really points that way is the fact that King told Justin to give Blair a message, sort of 'pay up or else'. So far, we have made it seem that Justin is being held incommunicado and can't deliver the message. Earlier, he had another threatening call from King, ramping up the threat to Richard Blair. You might understand the pressure, when I tell you that Richard and Justin have been good friends since high school."

"Have they delivered a ransom demand?" Mike asked.

"We think they have, but Blair refuses to confirm it. So we still have to go full out with the investigations into where they might be holding him. Now, these five properties that you mention, still in Costa's name, are worth checking out."

"I had thought the Docker's union hangout," Jack blurted.

A faint smile preceded Taylor's reply. "That has been checked. We have several informants, well entrenched in that union, and they are sure that he is not being held there. Costa doesn't own everyone in that union. I also think, that Costa, if he is as rich now as we might find, wouldn't want to spend time in such a public place. His face may still be known there. No, I think, that if Blair is where he is, it will be somewhere more private."

"Okay, that's logical enough," Jack agreed. "But what do you want us to do?"

"I know you drive, Jack. What about you, Mike?"

"I've a licence, no car though."

"Hmm. Perhaps together is better. I had the idea to have you two drive by those five places and see if you notice anything odd or unusual. Of if people are living there or not."

"When?" Jack asked.

"Tonight, instead of being around for the meeting."

Mike noticed Jack staring at his Grandfather.

Taylor went on, "It is not that I don't think you can add value to the meeting. You already have. If you are not there however, no one is likely to think my information came from you. Not even Justin will know. He thinks I have only got you doing minor grunt work."

"Which it is," Jack pointed out.

"Yes, but you have exceeded any preconceived expectations that I had, and I don't want that to be implied anywhere, but between us, in this office."

"You want everyone to think we are unimportant?" Mike asked.

Taylor nodded. "I believe you can both guess why."

Neither listener reacted, but Taylor smiled at their reticence.

"There's not a great chance that we'd see anything," Mike told him. "Particularly if the place is set back off the road behind a fence."

"You'll be able to get some idea of the front of the property from the street."

"I am not sure that using my own car is a good idea," Jack said. "I think a hired one would be better."

"Fine. I will reimburse you. Now, scatter, before the others get here."

"Am I imagining it, or was he telling us to scout around those houses, without actually saying so?" Mike asked, once they were in Jack's car and away from the house.

"I think that is exactly what he was saying," Jack admitted. "The old bastard! He is using my old claims against me."

"How so?"

"Way back, before I spent time in detention, I was sometimes sneaking in and out of houses. My mates of the time were nicking cash, jewellery – small stuff. More often, I was look out and driver."

"You said you were sent up for joy riding," Mike recalled.

"I was, and probably the reason that neither he nor my uncle spoke for me was that they were sure I was as guilty as my mates were, of theft, but they couldn't prove it. I wasn't with the others when they were caught."

"So?"

"So, I claimed that I had only ever stayed in the street and looked at the places…"

Mike laughed. "How do you want to play this, since I don't think we will see anything from the street?"

"Like I said, I will hire a decent car that will be less out of place in those areas where the houses are. A Mercedes perhaps. If we can get a couple of bikes and have them in the boot, we can use them once we park in the area. It is easier to stop for bit, for a drink say, at a convenient gap in a hedge or fence, than peeking from the car. Perhaps our excuse will be we are looking for a runaway dog."

"Are you thinking of going off the road?" Mike asked, unsure of what he thought of the idea.

"Depends," Jack hedged. "Anyway, I want to go to that Kew one first. It is only two streets away from where David Blair lives."

"Okay. No one with expect Blair the younger to be there. Not even me. Then where?"

"Hawthorn," Jack decided. "That is the old Simmons place. I am more curious about that place than expecting anything."

"That leaves Toorak, Malvern and Brighton," Mike prompted.

"Maybe Malvern next. The other two I think will be less likely."

"Brighton is near the beach, and there will be lots of people. Same in Toorak where the yuppies go out a lot to restaurants and shows."

"Do you really think the guy might be being kept at one of these places?"

"It is worth checking, and two young fools on bikes are less likely to spook the kidnappers than police cars with lights flashing. Anyway, I know someone who might lend us bikes."

Not only did Jack manage to organise the bikes, but he had the promise of some binoculars too. Though, before going to pick them up, he went home so they could change into more comfortable, and darker, clothes. They also put on wool hats and coats, for there was a hint of rain in the air.

At the hire car place, Jack dealt with the paperwork. His story was that it was his sister's birthday and he was treating her and a friend to a fancy night out. He was able to leave his old car parked nearby, using the Mercedes to go to his friend's place for the bikes. Both were smaller than ideal for both him and Mike, but they did fit in the boot of the Mercedes. Jack promised his mate a dozen bottles of beer, and then he and Mike headed for Kew.

"I used to come this way at Christmas," Mike recalled. "The houses along the Boulevard would do their houses up with fancy coloured lights."

"The address we want isn't far from there," Jack said. "It backs onto the river. We may be lucky and find there is a track along the river to ride on, so we can check the back out too."

"How will we tell if what we see is significant?" Mike asked.

Jack said, with a touch of sarcasm, "If we see Harry King, anyone fitting Peg's description of Costa – we will hope to see cars or people that we can describe. First though, we will want to see if there are lights on in the house. The old man wasn't telling me everything, but I wouldn't be surprised if he also has these places staked out. We might truly be scouting for him – or a useful distraction."

"I am beginning to understand your less than buddy-buddy relationship with your uncle and grandfather. How did you get on with your step-father, was it?"

"While he was alive, well enough. He was good to my mother."

"Is she still alive?"

"Yeah, over in Adelaide. With my half-sister. They live near Mum's relatives. My sister, Kelly-Ann, is nearly 12."

They continued to talk of inconsequential things, until Jack parked in a side street, near their destination, and emerged to take out the bikes. By then it had begun to rain lightly, so no one was lingering on the street. Both studied the street directory so they would be able to find their way back to the car.

Jack led the way, and stopped outside the gates of one of the surviving large estates.

"Keep your eyes out for cars," Jack directed as he took the binoculars from the case on a strap around his neck. He began to search the darkness beyond the gate.

After a while, he said, "I can't see a damn thing. No cars, and trace of lights."

"Do we find the back?" Mike asked.

"Yeah, but..."

"What?"

"You game to hide the bikes in the bushes just inside and sneak in from here?"

"We are still looking for a black Labrador aren't we?" Mike said obliquely.

"That's it," Jack grinned. "We saw it run in here."

With no one around to see them, and the gate wide open, they were soon working their way around the grounds, close to the fence. From that vantage, they saw several windows at the side and the back where the curtains were not closed as well as those at the front. Light shone from several. Two were upstairs.

Out the back, two vehicles were parked – a recent model light coloured Mercedes, and an anonymous van. The van's number plate indicated that it was quite old. Jack memorised both number plates. Mike whistled softly from the back wire fence, and Jack joined him.

"There's a gate here."

Jack used the binoculars. "And a short dock at the river. Let's head back. We've seen enough."

"Do you think they might be here?" Mike asked as they eased their bikes out of the bushes. He checked the street.

"Someone is," Jack summarised, as the rain began in earnest. "Let's get back to the car."

They hadn't ridden far when blue flashes and the short wail of a siren from behind them.

A car slid alongside them as they stopped. A voice from the window asked, "Out for a night ride?"

Jack growled, as he stepped of his bike. "I should have guessed. Didn't I say it?" he said to Mike.

The two officers stepped from the car, and came around. Mike relaxed when he recognised one of them from the 'think tank'. Jack subsided when the first officer scrutinised his ID via torchlight and didn't immediately harass them.

"You picked a lousy night for a ride. Notice anything out of the ordinary on your way? Old Squizzy asked us to do a follow up."

"Squizzy?" Mike murmured.

"Grandfather," Jack explained tersely. He gave his attention to the officers and, in a low voice that didn't carry, reported all that he had been able to make out, not omitting the gate in the back fence and the car regos.

"We'll pass that on. Where are you headed next?"

"Hawthorn. Are we to expect another shakedown there?" He received a grin in reply.

"Off you go," they were told, and they didn't need more encouragement to get on their way, back to the car to get out of the rain.

Jack drove past the Hawthorn address before parking a street away.

"Well, I guess that place is not where Blair will be," Jack remarked. The house had been well lit up, and cars had lined both sides of the street. The resident was having a party.

"Not unless they are celebrating getting the ransom, or the guy's discomfort," Mike agreed. "Not all of the cars are expensive."

"However, I doubt that we are dressed well enough to gate crash the party," Jack observed. "But, we could work our way into one of the neighbouring places and look over the fence."

Having had proof that their forays were sanctioned, Mike agreed. In a way, the nights work was exciting. They still didn't want to be seen or in any way noticed. He followed Jack's example until they were in the furthermost corner of the back yard of the neighbouring property. He could understand that Jack may have done this more than a few times.

"Keep watch," Jack whispered. This time he didn't use binoculars, in case the light in the back yard reflected off the glass. He carefully climbed onto the cross bracing of the wooden side fence, watched for a time, and slid down.

"There are quite a few people under cover on the patio. Mostly younger than us. Party clothes."

"Another down. Do you think they will raid the other place?"

"Dunno. Let's get out and find the police patrol."

The Toorak destination turned out to be a block of flats. "Don't know how I missed finding this out," Jack muttered. "They don't look all that new. What can we do here? We can't check every flat."

"Sit and watch who comes in and out?" Mike suggested. "See what kind of people live here. I doubt our quarry will be here."

"So do I," Jack agreed, but he was reluctant to just leave. "Did you hear how Blair was abducted?"

"Someone got him on the way home. His car was found at Spencer Street Station," Mike was able to tell him. "No witnesses as far as I know."

"They could have made him come here at gunpoint," Jack considered. "But I think this place has too many people for Gianni to come here himself."

"King might," Mike countered. "But only minor flunkeys would guard a prisoner day to day."

"I am going to call the old man," Jack said suddenly. "He might be able to get the names of the tenants and run them through the police records. I might ask if he thinks it worth hanging around here, and skip the other places."

The rain was still falling steadily, as Jack strode back along the road to where he had seen a phone box. Mike moved into the driver's seat, so he could move the ignition key to get the radio playing. He glanced up as a tall man passed the car. In the light from the next street lamp, he recognised David Blair. He was carrying a brief case.

"Damn!" Mike emerged from the car, quite sure that Blair was acting without the Police knowing it. He didn't think that the man should be going in alone. When Blair stopped to buzz open the gate and enter the paved forecourt, Mike sprinted to meet the business man, just as the gate began to open, and grabbed his free arm.

Blair tried to shake him off, muttering curses.

"I know you!" Blair suddenly accused. "Are you part of this vile business too?"

"No! I just don't think that you should go in alone."

"Keep out of this, Boy!"

As Blair tried to push past him, the police patrol arrived, and Blair began to protest the 'assault'. Mike calmly identified Blair, and the two men, who knew what Jack and Mike were doing, understood the rest of the story, and took over the task of pulling Blair back.

"Who were you going to see, Sir?"

"You don't understand," Blair protested. "If they think I brought police here, they will kill my son."

"Which unit," the officer insisted. "Quickly."

Blair spat it out, and the second policeman used the radio to request information. Meanwhile the other man said, "They may also want you there to kill you."

Mike slipped away, getting only a look from the first officer. He was back at the car as Jack returned.

"Hey! That's Blair senior," Jack exclaimed quietly.

"Yes. He went past just after you went off, I stopped him going in and the patrol are talking to him now. What were you told?"

"Stay here and watch, but don't get noticed."

"Translation?"

"This time I will take it literally. He had discovered that Blair had eluded his minders. So when the patrol report, he will have reinforcements sent here. Then, I think, we will be able to go."

"Should he be using us this way?" Mike asked.

"Huh? Probably not. But that didn't stop him letting my uncle get in deeper and deeper with Costa all these years. Good. They are taking that fool off with them."

One of the officers was approaching. "Avery," Jack greeted.

"Good work. Can you stay here a bit longer? Someone will be out to see you."

"You are not exactly keeping our presence discreet," Jack remarked. "What if our quarries are watching?"

"It won't be for long," Avery promised.

"I'll move the car," Jack growled.

"I'd keep it close," Avery advised.

"In case of what? If anyone comes out, we aren't trained to follow them," Jack protested.

"You won't be expected to do that. It's in case you need to get word to us. Do you know the number for D24?"

"Yeah."

The officer strode off. Jack waited until the police car drove off before saying, "I don't think that Avery is bent, and Grandfather said much the same as he told me, but my gut is telling me that I don't want to stay here."

"We still have the bikes," Mike suggested. "What if we get them out, and then take off as if we had guilty minds, and when we find somewhere to hide them, sneak back and stay out of sight?"

"I like how you think, friend of mine."

From behind one of the well grown street trees, Mike had a good view of the front of the flats. Jack had done a quick scouting foray to confirm that there wasn't a back way out, and done something to cause a malfunction with the auto door of the tenant's parking garage down under the flats.

When he returned, he told Mike, "I hope if the people want to get Blair away, they will have to come out the front. And I have positioned a nail, in front of the outer rear tyre or our car. Remind me to remove it before we drive off?"

"What was that in aid of?"

"Maybe nothing," Jack shrugged. "Just call me paranoid." He moved back to the last tree and watched across the street. He lounged there, watching the passing traffic as well as the front gate of the flats. He ignored the few pedestrians braving the intermittent rain, and walked as far from him as possible. In a moment when there was no one nearby, Jack called to Mike, "How long is not long?"

"What are you expecting? A parade of screeching police cars?"

"I am assuming that – but they had better hurry."

"You think they might try to run?"

"If Blair was on his way there, and buzzed the flat he was heading for, whoever was there must be getting pretty nervous."

"Do you think the younger Blair is there?"

"Depends if they needed their hostage to be seen before Blair would pay."

"So you jammed the garage," Mike prompted. "And their plan b would have to be coming out and stealing a car, and our car is oh, so handy."

"And we won't be in it," Jack confirmed.

Mike shivered. "I don't mind helping the police, but I was not cut out to be put in too much danger."

"Unless you have a more personal reason," Jack told him. He saw someone approaching and warned Mike to silence. Jack wandered over to Mike's tree.

"Is that why you are doing this?" Mike asked when the person had gone.

"Yeah. Peg and I don't have a rat's chance of a long happy life until Costa and his cronies are history. This is peripheral to that, but might lead to getting him."

"Jack!" Mike gestured to the flats.

Mike spotted the man beside the hire car, gesturing to someone. "The other bloke has Richard Blair," he hissed.

"I'm hoping the car won't get far," Jack said. "Let's head to the bikes, in case we do have to try to follow."

The reeling form of Richard Blair was being hustled into the back seat of the car. The helper got into the front passenger seat, the other man got behind the wheel."

Moments later, the driver had hot wired the car and it was revving hard. It took off fast, but in that first instant the tyre blew out. The car swerved, tried to maintain a straight track down the road, failed, side swiped two cars, mounted the nature strip and hit a tree.

Mike and Jack were cycling to the wreck, as two police cars turned on lights and sirens to come to the scene. Their concern was Richard Blair, and getting him out while the abductors were still in shock or knocked out. Quite likely, they would be armed.

Blair was conscious, although very doped up. He was already aware that he was no longer tied up where he had been, and was trying to get free.

With words of reassurance, Mike and Jack helped him out, dealt with the linen strips that bound his hands using Jack's pocket knife, and led him to the nearest police car. The officers, seeing he was being helped, went to deal with the abductors.

Jack didn't expect to hear his Uncle's voice. "Help him in and get lost!"

"What? You expect us to walk home? They told us to leave our car outside the flats. That's the one those crooks took and crashed. Have you called an ambulance?"

Mike had the feeling that Jack didn't trust his uncle's presence, even though he assumed that Jack's grandfather had okayed it. He, personally, just wanted to see Blair on his way to be checked at the hospital. He moved back to keep a general eye out all around.

The driver and front passenger, had come around and were being dragged from the car. They had bleeding cuts on their face from flying glass, but they were handcuffed. The men were put in the divisional wagon, just as the ambulance arrived.

"If we are going to get a lift, we need to go get the bikes," Mike said as the ambulance carrying Blair moved off.

"I'd rather ride back to my car," Jack admitted. "Uncle drives like a maniac when he's in a mood like he is now. I only made that crack about a lift to keep him here."

"Why?"

"Because I saw several people about that I saw when I went with him to see King."

"You expected them to try to snatch him back?" Mike asked.

"Well, let's say that was what I thought."

Jack went to the driver's window and spoke to his uncle. "We need to get the bikes."

"What bikes?"

"We had them in case being in a car was too obvious."

"Then ride back!" Justin Taylor snarled, and he took off fast without them.

"Bastard!" Mike swore.

"Ungracious sod," Jack corrected. "I made sure that Costa's other crooks knew why he couldn't act to help them get Blair back. I won't bother, next time."

"Will they be mad with him?"

"You know what? I don't give a shit," Jack admitted. "And if they do, it's his own damn fault. He wasn't meant to come here."

Chapter 25

The phone was ringing when they entered Jack's flat. Mike went to answer it, as Jack locked the door.

"Who was it?"

"They hung up just as I got to it," Mike said.

"If it's important, they'll try again," jack decided. "It's almost midnight. I doubt that Peg would ring this late."

"You told her not to ring," Mike reminded him, expecting the growl that Jack responded with.

"Wouldn't stop her! You hungry? Why don't we have a snack and a beer? After all we've done tonight, I need to unwind."

The phone rang again, just as they were thinking of turning in. Once again, Mike went to answer it. "Hello?"

"That you Lover Boy? Or are you the one I met in Matlock?"

"It's Mike. That you Les? What's up?"

"Tell your friend that his arrogant relative, the spineless one, won't be home tonight."

"Right. Do we need to worry?"

"Nah! His majesty is just taking out his bad mood. I reckon the guy got a kicking out for that way things turned out."

"Are you anywhere near where you met Lover Boy?"

"Nah! The worm is at a park near his place. I got told to hike it. You wouldn't like to come and get me would ya? I'll make it worth your while. His majesty doesn't care where I find my fun and he'd probably be too rough with me tonight."

Mike put his hand over the mouthpiece. "It's Les Shaw. King is roughing up your uncle. Told her to nick off. She wants a pick up. Promises it will be worth it."

Jack groaned. "You can borrow the car if you want."

"Les? Where are you?"

"Phone box. A block from the bloke's place."

"I'll find you," Mike promised and hung up.

"I don't know if I want her here," Jack admitted. "In case she is loose lipped around King or Devlin."

"Yeah, a point. However, I think she really is on our side, or rather on Peg's side."

"Maybe. Go get her. I'll call my grandfather."

"He's at a park near his place. What's the address?"

Jack told him.

"You don't have to wait up," Mike told him, taking the keys that Jack had dumped near the phone.

Mike found Les, but she was in no rush to leave.

"Park down the street. Let's watch what happens, huh?"

Deciding that Jack would want to know, even if he claimed he didn't care, Mike did as suggested.

It wasn't long before a police car with lights flashing turned into the street and cruised past and stopped at the park. Two uniformed officers got out, glanced up and down the street, and then trotted into the park. Two more police cars, one unmarked, arrived from the other direction. Those police headed for Justin Taylor's house.

"Oh to be a fly on the wall," Les murmured.

"Why?" Mike asked.

"I don't like cops. I like crooked ones even less."

"I don't think he is," Mike said, trying to be fair. "I think he's stringing King along."

"I didn't mean he was on the take," Les contested. "But I reckon he did something illegal, and the crooks caught him at it. Why else would the worm do what his majesty wants without being paid for it?"

Mike didn't want an argument. "He's trying to find—"

Les abruptly leant over and silenced him by kissing him hard. Moments later, yet another police car cruised by. Mike wriggled to get his mouth free.

"Maybe this isn't the best place to be."

Les chuckled. "Look who is being led across the road."

Whoever it was, had a jacket on, but the street light revealed pale legs.

"It isn't right to laugh," Mike told her. "What if that were you?"

"It has been me! It's been Peg, too." Les was suddenly angry. "And you said that worm let his majesty do it to Peg. So why do you care?"

Mike felt himself blushing. "It's just not right."

"You're an odd one, ya know that? What would you say about someone who, if he isn't bashing his kid, is fornicating with her – like my bastard of a father?"

"He was sick."

"And if that kid decided one day to bash him back?"

"He probably deserved it…"

"But?"

"But doing that – I feel for the kid. Doing that and becoming like him."

"Did you ever hate your parents?"

Mike thought hate might be too strong a word, but he said, "My mother left my father before I ever got to know him. Then she dumped me with her parents and took off to suit herself. I rarely saw her. I don't even know if she is still alive. My grandparents had me until I was 13 and then I was fostered out and lucky to be adopted. Sometimes though, the grandparents' strict church ways slip out."

"Do you know what I think about that? Screw them."

Once again, Mike was glad they were parked halfway between the nearest streetlights. He made no return comment. He wasn't used to girls as forward as Les Shaw, whose hand was now brushing his pants. He tried to wriggle away from her. This was worse than the girls in Matlock who only flirted brazenly with him.

With a sigh, Les drew away from him. "I don't get men like you. Would you be interested if we weren't here?"

"Les, I don't want to upset you, but…"

"You've never done it and you are how old?"

"That's my business."

"Trouble is, seeing Harry bashing people reminds me of my dad. I really wondered what it would be like to have sex with a gentleman. I wanted to forget all that."

"You been doing it with King?"

"A few times, but he's a Neanderthal, and he likes to hurt."

Les decided the lie was justified. Mike would be scared off if she admitted how horny she was feeling. Though it was true about King liking to hurt her first – like Mick Devlin. Those two were like clones.

"I've got no experience," Mike admitted. "I'd be boring."

"Not you, Church Boy."

"No, I'd better not."

"Okay. I think the show is over here. Let's go back to Lover Boy's place."

Mike was glad to get moving, though he didn't race off. If one of the police noticed him, they might follow to see if he saw anything. Though once around the corner, Les undid her seat belt and slid across the seat so her leg was touching his. Then her hand began moving again and he felt himself reacting.

"Les, not while we are driving."

"Then pull over somewhere and I will teach you what you're missing. Jack won't care unless he's horny from not being able to screw Peg."

Jack heard Mike return and the low whispers as he spoke to Les after finding a spare pillow and blanket for the couch. He heard him tell her where to find towels in the bathroom but later decided that he must have dozed off for he hadn't heard Mike's door close. He continued pretending to be asleep when he heard noises from the other bedroom. It didn't take much to interpret them and he grinned to himself. Mike was a great guy, a good friend, but about some things, he needed to loosen up. At least, Les had seen a lot of life, didn't have disapproving parents, and wouldn't have seduced Mike if she hadn't wanted it. He certainly didn't see Les as the kind to cry rape and expect Mike to marry her. He didn't see her wanting kids either. No, this was probably need…

Les might have tried this on him, had she not known he and Peg were married. That said something for her. Though if she didn't leave in the morning, and kept the antics up, he was going to start feeling damned uncomfortable.

Les wasn't a morning person, but she had woken when he and Mike got up to be ready for his Grandfather's make work.

"I should get back. His majesty might want me for something," was her reply when Jack had wished her, "Good Morning."

While holding onto a cup of coffee, Les asked, "Did Church Boy here tell you about last night?"

"Not yet," Mike said quickly, not sure exactly what Les might say. "What more can you add?"

Les considered. "Harry got a call that really riled him. Swore he'd 'kill the bastard', grabbed his keys and told me to come. Had me ring the guy's doorbell, and when he opened the door, Harry barged in. Before he shut the door, he told me to take a hike. I listened for a bit."

Jack forced himself to ask, "What did he do?"

He was talking low and menacing. That's what he does when he is real mean angry. I heard, "you'd be dead now mate, except the boss ain't ready to kill you. You wrecked a real sweet deal, finding Blair. He wanted to know how he had found out where the bloke was."

Mike and Jack exchanged a look, both shared the same worry. Les, sensing something, drew out the telling.

"Someone saw you around, Lover Boy. He wanted to know if you had found the place."

She sipped her coffee then until Mike demanded, "Well, what did that twit Taylor say?"

"Oh, he just said you were sticking your nose in police business as usual. He got hit for that. Harry spoke up a bit and said, 'You tell me mate, or that video of you will go to your old man. He won't be able to cover up for you after that.'"

"I knew that bastard had done something" Jack muttered. "And I am sure the old man doesn't know of it."

Mike urged, "Go on."

"The cop said he'd had police admin aides looking through official records. They found four of five properties in Costa's name. All were being checked and it was fluke that Blair was seen."

"Anything else?" Jack demanded.

"Not that I heard. Harry began to bash him then and I left."

Mike went on, "He must have been dumped across the road, in the park. We saw him being walked back with just a jacket on."

"In that case, I will definitely not going to be anywhere near him today," Jack vowed.

Jack began to eat his milk soaked weetbix before adding, "I am not even sure I want to go to work today."

"Okay," Mike agreed. "Do you have something else in mind?"

"Yeah. Heading bush."

"Might be smart," Les agreed, reaching for the cereal box. "Got a dish?"

While Mike drove Les back to a spot near where she was staying, Jack began packing an overnight bag, and collected the notebooks and exercise books related to their archive searches. He also grabbed the official police aide ID papers. As an afterthought, he added the little instamatic camera that had been with Peg's stuff in the storage place. He would see if he could get a film for it somewhere.

Les's warning about getting away, he took only half seriously. However, he considered the few personal things he kept in the flat and took his few photos of Peg as well. Nothing that he left there would tell anyone anything. When he finished, he checked the time – nearly eight. His grandfather was usually awake by then, so he called the house.

The servant answered. "No, Master Jack. He had a disturbed night, Might I take a message?"

"Ah, just tell him that Mike and I are going to be away a day or two, checking details of some country properties."

"And where might he call you?"

"I'll check in," Jack promised, and he received an acceptance.

That done, he went to tidy up the couch, which was where Les had been when he got up. He grinned, sure that she hadn't been there long at the time.

"So, have you decided where we are going?' Mike asked on his return. "Matlock? Or further north?"

"What? Oh! I'd like to see Peg, but I had only thought to see what I could find about that place her aunt had there. Anyway, Peg's heading to Goulburn, I think, for her next gig with Carson. She hasn't told me where they will be staying yet."

"If she is not to call you, how will you find out?"

"Post card. Hopefully it will be waiting when we get back."

Although they started out travelling in silence, Jack's mind was still on the puzzles he was finding in the archives. He started thinking aloud, bouncing ideas off Mike.

The latter didn't object, for he knew that Jack wanted Costa out of the way, or he and Peg could never have a normal relationship. After the previous night, he had a better idea of what the separation was doing to his friends.

At Mansfield, they stopped for fuel, food and a toilet stop. Jack also went looking for a place selling films for the instamatic camera.

When they were back in Jack's car, Mike commented, "This place is quite busy."

"I'd noticed. Seems they have their major horse racing meet tomorrow."

"A good place to leave, then," Mike suggested.

"Or we could stop here and see if we can work at the races," Jack countered. "Peg and I did that in Mildura last year."

"What did you do?" Mike asked.

"Me? I waited on tables in the public bar. Peg was helping in the stables. Got me to put a bet on some damned horse. I thought she was crazy, but the damn thing won at 20 to 1. I wonder if that beast is running here."

"I wouldn't bet that it would do the same here," Mike heard himself say.

"I reckon if Peg was here, she'd try it. Do you know, she reckoned she talked it into winning?"

Mike was laughing as Jack tried to start the car. It fired, then conked out. When he tried again, nothing happened.

"Now what?" Mike asked, sobering.

"Know anything about cars?" Jack asked, frustrated that he didn't.

"Nope. Never had a car. Ian doesn't know anything either. He reckons it's the reason he got in with the RACV."

"That's a thought," Jack brightened. "My Mum paid that for me as a birthday present. I'll go find a phone. Are you staying here?"

"Might as well," Mike agreed.

Half an hour later, Mike and Jack were squashed in next to the tow truck driver who was towing the car to a garage. The RACV bloke had diagnosed a blown fuel pump. The driver, when asked, had recommended Bluey's garage as their best option, as the owner could get a new pump up from the city overnight.

It seemed that they had little choice about staying in town for the night.

Slightly mollified by the promise of having his car fixed next day, Mike and Jack followed the directions of the garage mechanic and headed for the nearest motel to book a room.

The man had chuckled when he told them, "The Fielder's Inn is usually the last place in town to fill right up."

Jack had asked, "Is it that much of a dump?"

To which they'd been told, "It was done up a dozen or so years ago. I don't rightly know why it's not that popular."

After a twenty minute walk through the outskirts of town, carrying their overnight bags, Mike eyed the motel. "Looks okay. Perhaps the room service is lousy."

"If it's just for one night, that hardly matters," Jack told him. "The important thing is that it has a vacancy."

They had walked past two other motels that had already been fully booked out.

Jack went into reception to arrange a room. Mike browsed the attached shop, intending to buy a few necessities.

"We have just the one unit left," the manager, a man in his 50s with a receding hairline, told Jack. Then he asked, "Are you superstitious?"

"No, why?"

"No reason. It's just that some people won't rent it because it is No 13."

Mike moved closer. "Are you serious?"

"Cross my heart," the man said. "I've had some guests roust me in the middle of the night saying the place is haunted."

"It's in their heads," Mike snorted. "Anyway, why don't you renumber the units and not have a 13?"

"Tried that, but the regulars all know."

"Well, we need somewhere just for tonight, while my car gets fixed," Jack said firmly. "We'll take it." He paid for the rental, accepted the key and directions. Mike brought cereal, milk and a copy of the local paper.

Mike asked, "Where's the best place to eat around here?"

"Fancy? Maybe Ferdinand's – just down the street," the man considered. "But for good and cheap, try the pub."

With that in mind, they went to check out the room. It was right at the far end of the row, next to the property border that was a row of well grown pine trees.

"It will do," was Jack's comment, even though it only had a double bed, along with a table, two chairs, a bench and TV, plus a small fridge, a kettle and a toaster. The small ensuite had a toilet and shower.

"A double bed?" Mike commented doubtfully.

Jack turned to stare. "So? We can each keep to one side."

Mike kept staring, Jack decided to prod him in the ribs.

"A double bed does not mean that the occupants have to do anything but sleep." Jack noticed his friend blushing bright red.

"What will people say?"

"Does it matter, Mike? We are only here for one night and anyway, how would it be different from if two women shared it? Before my dad died, when we went away, I shared a single bed with him, and my sister shared with Mum. It was cheaper."

Mike had a strong memory vision of his grandfather's disgust when he had asked a friend over and they had slept in his single bed. "Sorry, Jack. Old memories."

"It's forgotten," Jack said. "Anyway I'd rather share a bed with Peg. Or better still, one like they have in caravans. It's cuddlier."

"Yeah, I guess you would," Mike admitted. He had almost said that a single bed would be cuddlier still. He hadn't got over how it felt sleeping naked, next to an equally naked Les. He told his conscience to 'Screw it!'

"What do you reckon we should do now?" Jack said. "We have the afternoon to kill."

"Can't you lighten up, Jack?" Mike challenged his friend. So far, he hadn't shown interest in seeing a movie matinee, or having a drink at the pub, or hiring bikes to ride around. Instead, they had been walking for an hour, mostly in silence, stopping finally at the local offices of the North-East Advertiser newspaper.

"Do you think this place has an archive of old newspapers?" Jack asked abruptly.

Mike knew where his mind was. "It's printed here," he confirmed, adding, "It does cover a lot of the NE region of the state."

"Let's see if we can look at old papers," Jack suggested, already heading for the door.

"What do you want to look for?" Mike asked, jogging to catch up.

"Local news," Jack grinned, pausing to glance back.

"Okay. What time period?"

Jack considered, "Say, 15-25 years ago."

"And what reason will we give for our interest?"

"How about trying to trace the movements of family members when they were young?"

Mike shrugged, not sure exactly what he had in mind. He'd wait to find out, and to see if they did find anything useful.

Although very few people had ever made such a request, Jack's police aide ID papers made the request seem official. Within a very short time, they were within a reading room – windowless, but well lit. They had already been given actual physical copies of papers from 1947. They had also been given soft white gloves to wear to handle the pages.

"I'd expected more microfilm," Mike admitted, when the last of the six volumes from that year was brought in by a staff member.

"The bosses are talking of that, but it costs a lot to get someone to do it," the woman told him.

"See if you can get the local historical society interested," Jack suggested. "You might get volunteers to do the labour."

"Not a bad idea, that," the woman agreed, and with a smile, she headed out.

Jack was already opening the Jan-Feb folio of the paper. Mike reached for the next in sequence and pulled on the white gloves.

Even with the need to handle the papers carefully, Mike found looking through the actual paper easier. He could quickly scan a whole page. He had to hope that anything of importance to his and Jack's work for Eugene Taylor, would leap off the page at him.

"I'm looking at news, births, deaths, marriages as well as property for sale or sold. Anything else, Sherlock?"

"No Watson, you have the idea," Jack grinned faintly and finally decided to open up his thoughts, what there were anyway. "My notions are vague. Basically, Peg grew up in Matlock. Ida Jessup lived there. Peg's mother died up this way, I presume, from where her remains were found. "

"I hardly think Ida would have made the paper, and if there's been reports of accidents, or missing people, the police would have checked them to try to identify the girl."

"You are probably right, but we might see a mention if Ida bought property," Jack suggested. "Anything else…I don't know. This just seemed like too good a chance to pass up."

"Alright, alright," Mike agreed.

Half way through the 1948 issues, Mile found the first item of interest. "How's this, Jack? Property on Ridge Road sold. It was an auction on a deceased estate. I am not sure if Ida's place had a number or not."

"What else does it say?" Jack produced, like magic, a tiny notebook and a pen.

"Sold for … doesn't say who to, but it had been the property of the late Sylvia Lomax."

"Does it give the property registration number?" Jack asked.

"Would that be it?" Mike asked, moving so Jack could get in to look.

"Yes. Now where have I heard the name Lomax?"

"Probably from Peg. There is a big vacant spread up in Matlock, locals refer to it as the Lomax place."

"That'd be it. Peg said something about it having being vacant forever. I might look into this."

Once they had figured out the paper's layout, they both got into a rhythm of flicking through from news to personal ads, to property. It was not until they reached the end of 1954 that they found an article that arrested their attention. It related to the very motel at which they were staying. Jack read the sensational article and gave a loud snort - part laugh, part sneeze.

"I think I found out where that business about our motel unit and superstitions came from."

Mike looked up. "Oh, yeah?"

"Apparently," Jack stressed the word, "That room was found to have had blood everywhere, when the cleaner went into clean it. Not only had the woman that rented it gone, but bedding was missing as well."

Mike felt the hair on his head prickling him. "What date was that?"

It was Jack's turn to feel the sensation. "Shit! November 20th, 1954."

"What else did it say?"

"Not much. Police withholding the name of the woman. Wouldn't confirm if they thought a murder had been committed there."

"Let's check later issues," Mike urged. "There might have been a follow up."

The staff member returned to take away the folders they had finished with, and to tell them they had only got another 25 minutes.

"Not that one," Jack stopped the woman taking the Nov-Dec folder. "Can I get a copy of an article?"

"I can give you a request form."

"Yes, great!" Jack said, although his attention was on the later papers. Mike had found another article and Jack was scribbling down the information given.

While he was doing that, Mike continued looking for other related articles. When the woman returned, Jack asked Mike, "Find anything else?"

Mike shook his head.

The woman passed the request form to Jack. "It's a dollar fifty per article."

As Jack filled in the details of the two most useful articles, Mike wordlessly found the coins to cover the cost.

"How long will it take?" Jack asked. On being told up to two weeks, he asked, "Can we have the copies posted to us?"

"Yes, just add your address to the back of the form."

Jack didn't want to use his address, as the mail boxes weren't that secure. "Mike, can I get it sent to your place in Matlock?"

"Yes. Mrs Castle will look after it." Mike gave him the address.

Handing the paper to the woman, Jack thanked her for the help, but added, "We may need to come back."

Once away from the newspaper building, Mike gave a low whistle. "I am not surprised that the police never found the woman. Megan Swan wasn't her name."

"No, and I think we can be pretty sure who it was. And there was one witness who saw a pregnant woman there," Jack confirmed.

"So maybe the blood was from the baby being born," Mike continued the thought.

"Police checked the hospitals. No one went there. So did that mean that mother and child were okay? And they went onto where they were headed?"

"Not if Margaret Blair or Megan Pearl, as Ian knew her, was dumped in the waterhole just after giving birth. Ida Jessup was living in Matlock then," Mike said.

"Or, Megan died from the birth and Ida decided she had to hide the body?" Jack suggested.

"Why? I mean, if the death was from that, she could have called a doctor to confirm it," Mike thought aloud. "She might have panicked. I can't see her moving the body, particularly if she had the kid to consider. And she may have thought that they'd take the kid off her."

"She didn't have to take the kid on." Jack countered.

"Okay, how's this – she was helping the girl and promised to look after the kid if anything happened."

Jack shook his head. "It's all conjecture. I'm pretty sure it was King who dumped the body. So I reckon Ida called him when the girl died. Why, I don't know. Or maybe Ida was helping the girl runaway from Costa and King caught up about then. Thing is – Ida had stuff that was the girl's, and Costa only recently found that out. I'm thinking of those damn shares. However, if King knew where the girl died, why didn't he tell his boss?"

Mike shrugged. "When you next talk to Peg, ask her about what her aunt said that day I reckoned that King was calling her from outside the café."

"That won't be until after we get back," Jack said.

"Or I could call Ian and see if he can find out where Carson's next gig is."

"Ian was seeing the Blair girl, wasn't he? I wonder when he started seeing her? I know my uncle thought the kid might have been his, for a while."

Mike thought back to things he knew about Ian. "Well, Ian was arrested in April that year. He didn't know at that time that his Megan was pregnant."

Jack nodded a few times. "That would fit."

"What would?"

"Ian could be Peg's father. Even if Peg came early. What occurred to me is that Stan recalls Ida coming home with a squalling brat. He was old enough to know that she hadn't been pregnant. But from all accounts, Margaret Blair was an addict, and that may have been part of the reason she died. I suspect that Peg's weeks of crying was due to her being born addicted."

"Jack! Do you know what you are saying? That means Peg might be my half-sister."

"It's possible," Jack confirmed. "But don't go running to your dad yet. Peg's mother was still a whore."

If there had been a handy bench, Mike would have collapsed onto it. The idea of Peg as a sister was as dumbfounding as discovering Ian was his dad.

"You look like you need a drink," Jack suggested. "My shout. Come on, we can discuss what we found later."

They had tea at the pub, and lingered over two beers apiece. The town was coming alive with the pre-race day party crowd. After five minutes of someone's raucous laughter, Jack glanced at Mike and shrugged a shoulder towards the exit. They stood up to leave.

Talking was impossible until they stepped outside, and the noise became merely audible.

"Caught a glimpse of the kidnapped guy on the TV in there," Mike commented. "Couldn't hear what was being said."

"We can watch the late news on the TV at the motel," Jack said. "I don't know that I'll get much sleep tonight."

"Reckon the ghosts will appear?"

"What ghosts? Whoever reckoned that must have been drunk."

Mike wobbled. "I think I am."

"You shouldn't be. I made sure we both ate first. Are you going to call Ian?"

"Yeah. Though if he's not at his place, I will not be calling your Grandfather's place."

"No. I would rather keep what we found out just between ourselves for a while."

"Fine by me. Do you have any change for the phone? I used all I had paying for the copies you wanted."

"I might as well say I do, since I did say this evening was my shout."

Mike did catch his father at home, and after stating his request and giving a flip answer as to why he wanted to know, ended up listening for a long time before hanging up.

"Will he do it?" Jack asked first.

"Said he will. I'll call him again tomorrow about that. Do you want to know what else he told me?"

"If you ever get to it!"

"Where to start? Okay, Richard Blair suffered no great harm. He was able to give a good description of both of his kidnappers, who were not the ones guarding him. Each had a record and both were picked up. Naturally, they are not talking."

"Probably only paid muscle," Jack predicted. "What else?"

"Your grandfather had David Blair around. Closeted in that room he calls an office. Ian said the discussion got heated for a while, but they both emerged later, unscathed. The talk had been about the ransom that Blair had been about to pay."

"Okay…So?"

"Blair owns half a dozen houses in St Kilda, where they are planning to tear down a lot of houses and build better housing. This area is something of a slum at the moment."

"What's the betting Costa also owns property there and wants to get a monopoly?"

"Like he's doing in Melton and wherever?" Mike asked. Jack nodded. "I don't know about that, but the old man wanted to know what was so special about those places. Our research came in useful. Apart from the development angle, Blair's properties used to belong to a subsidiary company of Costigan's."

Mike had got used to Jack going silent and thinking. So he kept on walking back towards the motel, nudging Jack when he began to stray off course.

"I can't figure out how or why that area might be important," Jack admitted after a while. "Surely they aren't the reason why Costigan's wanted to take Blair over. If he'd won, all those properties would have been his."

"Or someone suggested the take over as a way to ensure Blair has a cash flow problem," Mike suggested.

"It has to be more. That takeover was more like a personal vendetta against Blair," Jack muttered. "What else did Ian say?"

"Apart from saying he's glad the old man has a leash on your uncle, there was something about getting a special forensic team to look at those properties before any demolition is done."

Jack's eyebrows disappeared into his hairline. "I wonder what they think they may find?"

"Considering who we think is behind Costigan, and the fact that they used to own those properties, I'm guessing bodies."

Mike only stated what Jack was already thinking.

"Hopefully, it is a chink on Costa's protective screen," Jack said. "I don't know about you, but I don't think I am in a rush to go back to town."

Chapter 26

Having decided that McMaster's advice was to be heeded, Peg was in a toned down version of her stage persona when she and Wayne Carson arrived at the hotel in Goulburn. There was a crowd of people at the front door, the younger girls being the most vocal. All had eyes only for Carson, which suited Peg since she still didn't feel comfortable in a crowd.

The difference this time, was that the young guys working as bell boys, caught her eye and winked. Since the contrast between their behaviour and that of the girls was amusing her, she grinned back. It never hurt to respond to the fans.

Carson didn't mind the attention, so Peg kept beside their manager as he was escorted to the suite reserved for them. The unobtrusive quartet of body guards kept a watchful eye on Carson.

Clair McMasters expressed relief at being out of the crowd with an exaggerated sigh.

"It is always a performance, arriving at or leaving a venue. I am ready for morning tea."

Peg looked around the suite, each new place was different. This one had four side rooms, one of which was the bathroom. The window gave her a rather ordinary view over the roofs of shops.

Carson arrived a few minutes later, grinning. "I think it will be a sell out tonight."

Peg laughed. "I hope it won't be an all-female audience. I had the bell boys winking at me."

"What about that boyfriend of yours. Is he the jealous type?" Carson teased.

"Nah! Anyway he's in Melbourne, and I was just being nice to the fans."

"Okay, settle down," McMasters tried to sound stern. "We have use of one of the smaller rooms for rehearsals, and our first show is tonight at eight. The dinner show."

He went on to outline the perks being provided by the hotel – mainly a reduced rate on the suite, and free meals, drinks and room service."

Then he turned to Peg. "I hope you will keep your wanderings to daylight hours. Goulburn isn't quite the same as where we were. In fact, it would be better if you did not go off by yourself. You are becoming a valuable commodity."

The lesson from near the Illawarra Club was still recent enough to be a warning. However, having to go out with company did not appeal to her.

"I'd still like to be able to look around. I've never been here before." Peg kept her voice even, as if she had accepted the advice.

"You'll have time to do that. Just not today," McMasters assured her.

Peg was still learning the ropes regarding being on tour. Her case and guitar were carried in a truck with the band's equipment. That should arrive soon. It left after the limo that McMasters had hired for the trip down. In fact, he went down to see if it had arrived and to see where they were to perform. She went down later with Carson, and listened to what he explained they needed to be aware of.

One of the young male staff members attached himself to their group. "In case there was any way he could help."

He edged next to Peg and confided, "I play guitar a bit. But I am nowhere near as good as he is."

"Keep at it," Peg advised. "The more you play, the better you get."

The guy stuck around, but since he wasn't trying to push himself at her, she mentally relegated him to the 'safe' category, and went back to listening to what McMasters and Carson were discussing.

The day was busy, but Peg found an hour in which she could explore the hotel. She was alone, since she had promised not to leave the hotel. Her excuse was to make she knew where all the exits were, in case of a fire. Her real reason was the simple one of needing time to herself. Now she wondered if her postcard to Jack had been delivered yet. She almost decided to ring him, but realised that he would probably be working.

On the ground floor, she walked right past the friendly bell boy, since she was not wearing her long black hair wig. She didn't notice the older man who spotted her and began to trail after her.

Word of the petty pilfering from various guest's rooms reached Peg, as did the rumours that someone in Carson's band or crew were responsible.

McMasters simply said, "So, we draw a crowd. The hotel is making good profits. We can't be held responsible if no-goods are attracted too. We just need to be vigilant and careful. That is what I told the management."

Peg had to agree. The first three nights had been sold out, and they had agreed to do a short afternoon gig in the beer garden.

On Sunday, she was thrilled to get a call from Jack, but in the suite, she couldn't talk privately. So she told Claire she was going to call a friend from the public phones.

"So, you got my card at last?" she greeted Jack when he answered. She already knew he was staying with Mike in Matlock.

"Actually, no. I got Ian to find out where Carson's next gig was."

"Well, after here, its Canberra, Wagga Wagga and Albury. We're doing a tour of country towns on the way to Melbourne. So, what have you been doing? I heard the missing guy was found."

"Yeah and it was your mention of Annie Simmons that helped," Jack went on to explain. He didn't mention his uncle's misfortune, though. Instead, he asked, "How long can you talk?"

"As long as I want. McMasters has some kind of prepaid phone chit."

"Good. I have another question for you. Do you recall overhearing a conversation your aunt had on the phone with someone who might have been Harry King?"

"Ye….es, why?"

Jack's hesitation alerted her that he knew something that he wasn't sure about sharing with her.

"In short," Jack said, "I want to pinpoint who that guy really is. I'm trying to figure out if he'd double cross his boss, given the choice."

"Well…" Peg told him what she remembered. "I still think he was on about those shares, but I assumed, because Gianni wanted them – even then. What aren't you telling me?"

Jack chuckled. "It's back to Annie Simmons again. I found a reference to a property on Ridge Road, Matlock being sold. It had belonged to one Sylvia Lomax. So, I followed it up. Your aunt bought it dirt cheap, since the owner had died. I was thinking, that maybe that other Lomax place, the deserted one, might be available dirt cheap too."

"You might be right, but should I try for it now?"

"It's at least worth thinking on, but there is probably no urgency," Jack decided.

"I'll think on it. Maybe let things settle down. So, what else have you heard?"

Jack mentioned the properties in St Kilda, switched topics to his plans for a break in Matlock, and his hopes that nothing else would break on his car on the way back.

When Jack hung up, Peg had forgotten her feeling that he had been keeping something from her. She was just elated that she had finally had a chance to talk to him.

Peg knew that staying in the hotel between shows would soon make her feel like she was back in Meredan. It was the reason for her walking around in Bathurst – to reinforce in her mind that she was free. The first two times she went out, she had gone with one of the bodyguards, looking like a casually dressed Megan Arthur. A few people did recognise her, and it was fun to chat to them. It gave her the feeling that she was important and special.

Not at any time during those walks, did she see any reason for McMaster's paranoia. Her mind told her that Mick Devlin would not likely stick around the town he had escaped from.

However, the presence of her escort made her feel like a tourist, when she'd prefer to blend in like a local.

On her third time out, the young bell boy was just finishing his shift, and he attached himself to her and her escort, and offered to show her the places he liked. While it pampered her ego, Peg wished it was Jack with her.

The boy, Robbie, left her near the hotel, going off to get his car to drive home. Her escort, moved slightly ahead of her to act like a path maker through a crowd of people entering from a tourist bus.

Then, just after her escort glanced back to ensure she was following him, Peg found herself yanked sideways, unable to call out due to a hand over her mouth. Even though she struggled and kicked out, no one paid any attention for just inside the hotel foyer, a loud drunken argument had just broken out. Two people were shoving her along one of the service passageways. Neither were allowing her to get free or fight them. Along the way, her black wig was yanked off.

The irrelevant thought, of her teasing Jack for his paranoia, came back like a slap. She'd started a habit. The first two times that she had gone out, she had ducked her guard/escort the moment she was back in the hotel. Now, her minder would simply think she had done the same again, curse her, and expect her to turn up in the suite in a short while.

When she was pushed into a room that looked to be for ironing linen, she tried again to get free, but succeeding only in wrenching both arms. She did manage to get off one scream before being gagged again.

"Try that again, bitch, and you'll be sorry."

The face of the other man who loomed in front of her was unknown to her.

"We've a job to do bitch. And a message to send," that one told her.

"What?" Peg tried to say around the hand on her mouth.

"That you had better not interfere in things that ain't your business."

"You hurt me and the police will be after you!" Peg threatened, wrenching her mouth free, only to be gagged again

"You ain't that important, bitch."

"Who's going to tell them who we are?" her captor added.

The other man grabbed a clean pillowslip from a pile, then produced a sharp knife and proceeded to shred it. When he had ribbons of cloth, Peg was pushed onto a stool, and her wrists were grabbed. She tried again to fight them free, but the man was too strong. She felt them tying her wrists to the uprights of the stool. When he tried to tie her feet, she kicked out. The man made a swipe at her face with his knife. She threw herself back, instinctively, unbalancing the stool and falling backwards.

Her head hit the floor, hard, and her vision began to grey out.

"You're just making it easier for us, bitch."

The pain in her head forced her awake. Lesser hurts added to her discomfort. She groaned, and memory returned. She expected to still be tied up, but she wasn't. Where she was, was dark with just enough light coming in through a window to show basic shapes, but rolling over told her she was on a hard floor. Her nose was full of the acrid stench of bleach, no, of peroxide. She knew that smell. Her hand felt her hair. It was damp. Worse, it was as if she had been given a crew cut.

Any instinct to cry was channelled into anger. "Bastards! A message, they said."

Peg forced herself into a sitting position. At least the men hadn't molested her as well. But why the haircut and bleach?"

Shit! Do they know who I really am? That thought terrified her. The only people likely to want to send a message of non-interference was Gianni Costas gang. But Jack had told her that Harry King thought her dead. His uncle, King's lapdog, thought her dead. He thought Megan Arthur was just a brainless wannabe that Jack had shacked up with. Unless Blair had said something in the wrong place.

That made her think of the time. She had a show to do. Her head throbbed harder as she slowly forced herself to her feet. She stood, breathing carefully, until the threatening darkness receded. The door wasn't far away, and she moved carefully, reaching out for a table to help her balance. The light switch was just beside the door, and she turned it on. She had to close her eyes from the initial glare, and then slowly open them.

Her mind compared the scene she now saw, with what she remembered. There'd been a stool. There wasn't one now. A ripped up pillow slip, now no sign of it. Why had they released her?

The concrete floor had damp patches, but if they had cut her hair, where had they put that? She turned her head slowly, looking around the room. She saw something black, thrown onto a pile of towels…her wig! She forced herself to go to it, and put it on. The short hair made it easier, and having it on made her feel better. The results of her stupidity were hidden. She returned to the door, it wasn't locked. The passageway outside was deserted.

Her mind recalled the need to know the time – seven thirty! Damn.

The show would start in half an hour. She had to get upstairs, get ready. The back ways were quicker, and she would use the service elevator.

In the busier sections of the service area, people were moving purposefully. At this time, everyone was busy and ignored her. She wasn't challenged, as both she and Carson used the back ways to get to the stage unseen.

When she emerged from the elevator on the seventh floor, people were milling everywhere. The four bodyguards were keeping an eye on a group of media reps. They were taking the opportunity to see what they could.

The hotel manager was talking to two of his security team, with McMasters intent on their conversation. No one had noticed her yet, and as a spur of the moment idea, she took the wig off and went to the cleaner's cupboard, and donned one of the apron like over frocks and picked up some towels.

Acting like she had a job to do, she walked around the people and into the suite. It seemed empty, so she slipped into the bathroom, and re-donned her wig. She had just finished when Claire McMasters walked in and gave a loud exclamation.

"What happened to you?"

Peg looked at herself in the mirror, and took in a bump on her forehead, and her paleness. How had she got that lump, when it was the back of her head that was throbbing?

She didn't know what to say, so reverted to, "I tripped."

"Come and sit down," Claire urged her. She helped Peg get to her room in the suite. "Stay here. I will go and get Alex."

In the few minutes that it took for her manager to arrive, Peg come to the conclusion that she had to keep what had happened to her a secret. Her new career would get flushed away if word got around as to who she really was.

The need to get ready to perform, forced her back to her feet, but her manager walked in, red-faced and ready to vent his anger.

The ruddy flush paled. "You are in no state to perform. What happened?"

Peg repeated what she had told Claire.

McMasters stared as he considered what had to be done. "Where was this?"

"Linen room, ground floor."

"Why the heck were you there, girl? No, tell me later. Sit down. Don't try eating anything, and if you drink, just take sips. I'll get a doctor up here, but first, I have to tell Carson he's doing a solo. I will get that crowd outside sent away, and get to the bottom of this."

As her manager stalked out, Peg shivered, glad she had escaped a lecture.

"You ducked away again, did you?" Claire commented quietly. "At least, that is what Charlie said. We were worried when you took so long to get back here."

"I'm sorry. I came as soon as I realised the time."

"I think you knocked yourself out. How is your eyesight?"

"Okay. The light is hurting them a bit."

Clair dulled the lights on her way out.

Peg was dozing when McMasters returned. As she woke, she thought he had only brought one person with him. The stranger was a doctor, she assumed, due to the bag he carried.

When he had the lights turned up, she closed her eyes again. She was happy to let her manager answer the questions of how long she had been missing.

The doctor's examination of her head was gentle, but even so it made her head throb harder. He asked questions, she did her best to answer them, and left him to consider his diagnosis.

"I don't think you have a skull fracture, young lady. I believe it is only concussion. However, to be on the safe side, I will make arrangements with the hospital for you to have an x-ray there tomorrow. In the meantime, you need to rest, and not answer too many questions. If you have any concerns during the night, do not hesitate to call. You can have paracetamol every four hours if needed."

Peg didn't notice the other man until the doctor had gone, and then only when he came closer and asked her a question.

"I heard that you tripped and fell. Is that what really happened?"

Not wanting to move her head, Peg only answered with a soft, "No."

As much as she hoped to keep things to herself, a habit so ingrained from childhood and Meredan, she had decided she was not going to be like that anymore. She would tell this man everything…well, nearly everything. It had to be her punishment for helping the kid.

"Did you purposefully slip away like in the past two days?"

"No. There was a disturbance in the foyer. Charlie went in first and I was right behind him. Someone grabbed me."

"Did you get a good look at the person?"

"Yes, and there were two of them."

"Could you describe them?"

"Yes, but not right now."

"Okay. Can you tell me what happened?"

Peg kept it short. "I was pushed into the linen room, down where the ironing gets done. They told me that it was a warning. For me to mind my own business."

"What did they do?"

"They were trying to tie me to a stool, but I wasn't having it. I think I unbalanced the stool and fell. When I came to, I wasn't tied up. When I could, I came back here."

"I wonder why they released you?" the man mused.

Peg had no answer for that. She wasn't going to mention the bleached and shorn hair.

"Sergeant, maybe it was because she knocked herself out," Claire suggested. It was likely.

Peg managed to say, "Maybe it was to show me that they could have done worse."

"A point I have been trying to make…" McMasters sighed.

"What would prompt such a warning?" the sergeant asked aloud.

McMasters summarised the events in Bathurst, and then suggested that further questions should wait. Peg was glad. She wanted to sleep.

By morning, the headache had subsided and Peg got dressed, and fixed up the black wig that had come askew in the night. When she emerged, it was to find only Carson in the suite. He stopped strumming when he looked up and saw her.

"It seems that I missed all the fun last evening," he said neutrally. "That's a right shiner you have there."

"You've heard all about it then?"

Carson nodded. "I was relieved when I heard you were okay."

"I'm sorry." Peg really did mean that. "I know I have been pushing the limits a bit, but I can't stay cooped up in here all the time."

"Maybe you should invite your boyfriend up?" Carson suggested.

The comments caused all sorts of regrets to surface. "It would be nice, but he has important work to do down in Melbourne."

"I thought he was working on a farm, up north." Carson didn't look at her, just idly tunes his 'A' string.

Peg bit her lip. She shouldn't have said that. She'd have to watch her tongue in future. "He's in Melbourne now."

"Well, you will need to rest up a bit. I don't think you should perform tonight, but if the x-ray shows nothing, we will see how you feel tonight."

"I'm a bit hungry now," Peg tried to change the subject.

"Oh, Mac had them send up one of those continental breakfasts. It's in the bar fridge."

"Where is he?"

"Out squashing rumours that you were drunk, or doped out yesterday."

"Is that what people think?" Peg had second thoughts about breakfast.

"One of quite a few rumours, I heard."

"Is Mac mad at me?"

"Relieved, I think. Was there more to that warning, do you think?"

With mental fingers crossed, Peg told him, "I think I made someone mad, that's all."

Carson studied her for a while and then went back to strumming chords from her 'Captive' song. "Megan, if you need to talk, I don't mind listening."

"I do know that," Peg told him.

"Then call your friend," Carson suggested. "Mac won't be back for another half hour, to collect you for your x-ray. You can use the phone here."

At that, Carson carefully put his guitar on the table, and stood up. "I need to talk to the band."

It was a tacit statement that he would not try to hear her conversation. Peg didn't move for a while, even after he left the suite. She wanted, more than anything, to have Jack there, right then. He would come like a flash if she asked him to, but they had decided they were safer apart. Talking would help, but she didn't exactly know where he was. He had been going to Matlock, would he still be there?"

Forgetting all about breakfast, she decided to try one number – the place where Mike usually stayed.

She asked for Mike, and felt stupid for not recognising his voice. "Megan, how are you?"

"Is Jack with you?"

"No, but he should be back soon. Is something the matter?"

"I just want to talk to him." She didn't want to share this with Mike, so she asked, "How long are you two going to stay there?"

"Well, I think until Jack thinks it safe to be near his Uncle."

"Huh? What now? Is this related to you finding that guy?"

"Yeah, I guess. But it wasn't Jack's fault. His uncle turned up at the place where the guy was being held. I think he was meant to have stayed at his father's place and didn't. He offered to drive us back, but went off in a temper instead."

"And he's still mad?"

"Well, the other side took their anger out on him. Stripped him, beat him up and dumped him in a park."

"I shouldn't laugh, should I?"

"No, but I was with Les. She told me about it. She thought he deserved it too."

Megan/Peg knew how her friend thought, but didn't comment. "How is she?"

"She's okay. I took her back to where she's staying."

"Jack didn't tell me about his uncle. What else has been happening? Have they opened that tin box yet?"

"Dunno. But Jack did say he wanted to know what was in it."

Peg heard a voice over the phone that sounded like Jack, but Mike suddenly covered the mouthpiece. There was a wait before Jack came on.

"Hi, how are you doing?" Jack greeted her.

"You're in a good mood," Peg said without the same enthusiasm.

"What's up," Jack asked, sensing from her tome that she wasn't happy.

He listened with his expression turning to a frown.

"I haven't told anyone what they did with my hair."

"I think you should," Jack said soberly.

"But what if they know who I am? I look like Peg Jessup this way."

"If they know, you need to be protected."

"I'll be arrested!"

"It might be a coincidence," Jack suggested. "That it is punishment for helping the kid. I can't see how they would know it's you in particular."

"But the hair!" Peg wailed.

"It could be to hit you in your vanity. How would all the wannabees react in this situation?"

"Yeah. Maybe then but…"

"Look, Peg, just for now, stay with your manager or one of the guards. Okay?"

"Alright. What about that deed box?"

"I haven't heard. I have been putting off ringing the old man, since I left the message telling him I was going bush."

"Oh."

"Okay, I'll ring him. I can tell him that your aunt bought her house from the Lomax widow and ask about the box and key."

"Yeah, I want to know. Oh, why did you ask about the phone conversation?"

"I was thinking about those damn shares," Jack said quickly. "How, until recent times, they had not thought that your aunt might have them. Mike mentioned that call, and what you said. It made me think that Harry had thought your mother might have given them to someone. And maybe he thought he had been swindled."

"Like he thought he could have had them all these years. Him, not his boss?"

"Something like that."

"Odd thought. I somehow can't imagine King doing anything without Gianni's say so."

"Now, maybe, but this was eighteen years ago."

"When he wasn't settled into being bossed?" Peg suggested. "I wonder how those two met? What's the connection. Has Les managed to get anything with King's prints on?"

Peg heard Jack ask Mike the question, and his negative.

"Are either of you able to suggest that she does?" Peg asked.

Jack sounded amused as he answered. "Maybe. We let her stay with us the other night and she was being less of a bitch than usual. I don't think she has met anyone as open hearted as Mike."

"No, she's used to bastards like Devlin. Is King using her the same way?"

"Off and on, or so she said," Jack told her.

"Then I reckon she is out to fix King. I can't think of any other reason why she would let him shag her. He'd better watch out."

Peg heard the suite door being unlocked. "Jack, gotta go. Can I call you later?"

<h1 style="text-align:center">Chapter 27</h1>

Peg hadn't considered the pins she had used to keep the wig in place. They had to come out, and even though she kept her hair covered, the wig still slipped.

The technicians didn't say anything, but Claire McMasters, standing back behind a shielded window, discovered her newly bright blonde hair, and the rough haircut that had most of her hair little more than half an inch long. She realised what had happened when Claire came over and wordlessly helped her fix the wig back over it. There was no use trying to make her keep it secret. She'd tell her husband. What happened then, she couldn't predict.

During the wait for the x-rays to be developed and examined, Claire asked, gently, "Why didn't you tell us about that?"

"It was embarrassing," Peg said, looking at her hands. "Does it matter? I mean, the rest of it was bad enough. It doesn't alter the crime of assault those two guys are on. You'd hardly call this grievous bodily harm. Me hitting my head was that."

"Okay, we'll leave it at that," Claire agreed quietly.

McMasters took her to the police station after the doctor had confirmed that she had no fracture, and provided something for the headache. She was introduced to the sketch artist and was soon amazed by the man's skill, taking her description and putting it to paper. In the background, McMasters was talking to the sergeant, and it sounded like the continuation of an earlier conversation. The policeman was passing on what little results they had so far from the investigation.

Peg kept her attention seemingly on the artist, hoping she wouldn't be asked if she had ideas why she was targeted, or rather by whom. Her manager was ready enough to mention the affair in Bathurst, and the sergeant had heard about that and agreed it was a likely reason.

A stampede of shivers shot down her back at the policeman's next statement.

"Do you know of a woman named Peg Jessup?"

"No, I don't think so. Who is she?" McMasters probably wasn't lying.

"An ex-con, recently released from a training centre in Victoria late last year. Was involved in an armed robbery."

"Ah, Wayne was doing some mentoring at Meredan. He was teaching some of the girls to play guitar. What has that got to do with anything?"

"We found a lot of prints in that laundry room and they have been identified as Jessup's."

"She might be working there," McMasters proposed. "Are they the only ones you identified?"

"So far…"

"Nothing from the two men?"

"We are still checking the others we found."

"I really can't see the Jessup prints as significant. If she were involved, surely she would wear gloves?" McMasters objected.

"Some criminals don't think," the sergeant commented. "If Jessup was one of Carson's students, the cause might be jealousy. She could have put the men up to it."

McMasters seemed to consider that idea, and gave no further objection. "So there are two possible motives?"

"This might have been opportunistic. Jessup's brother, is due to be brought back here this week. We have been warned to expect an attempt to free him again."

Peg felt her gut spasm. She took a few deep breaths, not wanting to throw up. It was just as well she had eaten nothing that day to bring up. The artist was starting on the second face, and she tried to concentrate.

Did those men know who she was or not?

"What about the hair, Miss?"

"Keep the side burns, but make it shorter at the sides and longer on top," Peg told him.

The whole attack had to be payback, or they would have been told to kill me.

A niggling voice kept saying, "Why bleach my hair?"

Clair had accepted the idea of 'to humiliate her' but that type of punishment was more likely to be the idea of a girl or woman.

The third option was mentioned a moment later, after she had made more suggestions about the second man's face.

"We will be keeping an eye out for the Jessup girl, particularly with her brother expected up here. However, there is another concern. Bathurst police are looking for someone matching Jessup's description for a spate of robberies there and we are getting similar reports here, from the hotel."

By the time they left, Peg was pale and sweating. Her manager was concerned.

"I'm feeling sick," was all Peg admitted.

"You should lie down when we get back to the hotel," McMasters directed. "You are definitely not going to be performing for several more days at least."

Peg wasn't going to object. Not when all she wanted to do was run and hide. So when she went into the suite, she made a beeline for her room, and changed into a tracksuit. The clothes she wore out when she was being Megan Arthur, were not suited to curling up asleep.

Her door hadn't quite shut and she could hear McMasters telling his wife, and Carson, what the police had told him. She pulled up a blanket and hid herself.

"Do you know that Jessup girl?" McMasters demanded of Carson.

"Yes," Carson's acknowledgement was only just audible in Peg's room. "And I am certain that she was not the cause of the attack on Megan."

"Why not? She was involved in an armed robbery."

"Mac, she was fifteen. And all she did was try to warn her brothers to get away."

As much as she wanted to dig herself deeper under the blanket, she owed Carson and her manager the truth. She stood up, opened her drawer to feel for her beanie and encountered a bag of hard round objects. Using a small torch, she looked at the bag, and then felt the need to rush to the toilet. The bag contained some rings, a bracelet, earrings and several watches. In her mind, she knew what would happen. An anonymous tip and the police would be after her.

She walked out of her room and slipped into the bathroom. No one seemed to notice her. They were still involved in their discussion of the police information. There was no way she was going to be able to win in this situation. At best, she could apologise to the three people who had helped her make a new start – to tell them the truth.

When she walked to join them, they all stopped talking and looked at her. Before she could plan what to say, she blurted out, "I can't stay here."

"Megan? What's the problem?" Claire asked. "Sit down. If you are in trouble, you can tell us. We're on your side."

For now, Peg thought, obeying the direction to sit.

"I think I can guess, now, why they did this to me," Peg said, yanking the beanie off, and looking at Claire who already knew about the hair, but hadn't mentioned it. She probably hadn't connected the bleached hair with the Jessup suspect. Her husband was more on the ball.

"No one mentioned a description. Do you know that Jessup girl?"

"Yes, but that isn't the issue."

"Okay. So what is?"

"Someone is telling the police that someone who looks like this is guilty of a lot of little robberies," Peg stated.

"How can they think you…," McMasters began, but he saw Peg's face and let her speak.

"Because someone has put stuff in my drawer."

"Why don't you put your hat back on, Megan?" Carson suggested.

"It could be that Jessup Person trying to discredit it you," Claire suggested. "That bleach job is more like an act of spite from a woman."

"No," Peg said flatly.

"Her prints were all over the linen room," McMasters pointed out.

"My prints were there," Peg told them.

It took a moment for her manager and his wife to understand her meaning.

Carson, who had stayed silent, asked softly, "Are you afraid of the police? You were released."

"It is not the police," Peg told him, understanding that he had known who she was all along. "I have not done anything wrong, except running away. And that was not because I didn't want to answer questions about my aunt's murder."

She saw her manager about to speak and went on, "I did not kill my aunt! I know who did and I don't have a hope in hell of proving it. However, they will probably come here soon, on a tip off. Then, as soon as they insist on fingerprinting me, they will have to take me in."

"If it is not the police who you fear, who is it?" Carson asked.

"Better you don't know," Peg told him, believing it.

"They won't be able to make a robbery charge stick," McMasters insisted. "We can testify that Megan's hair wasn't like that until yesterday."

"That is kind of you, but even if they didn't expect the charges to stick, the damage to my reputation will be done. Likely, once the rumours become public, and they will, they will expect you to drop me. After all, you have to think of both Wayne's reputation and your own."

"Then they don't know me," McMasters stated.

"The police were asking about you in Tamworth. Is that why you took off there?" Carson asked.

Peg nodded. "And there are some people who, if they know I am not dead, will be after me."

"You will have to explain the logic there," McMasters admitted.

Carson intervened. "Since I knew Peg Jessup quite well, I took notice when I heard her name mentioned on the news. Yes, they wanted to ask her questions about her aunt's death, but then they believed she was dead." He looked at Peg and asked, "Did you do that on purpose?"

Peg shook her head. "No, but I very nearly was. Disappearing then, was the best thing."

"Surely, you should sort all that out?" Claire advised.

"No, the people I was hiding from have police on their payroll."

"So, do you think those who attacked you, knew you were Peg Jessup?" Carson asked.

"I really, really, hope not," Peg said with a shudder she couldn't control.

"And you think this is because you helped the Blair boy? Did you know who he was? That business seems to be a nasty one."

"I know, and both hindsight and Jack were quick to tell me that I was an idiot to get involved. But, I knew who was behind it, and in another way, I am involved in it, and the kid didn't deserve to be terrorised, abused or killed."

Peg looked at each one of her audience and wondered what they were thinking. McMasters was keeping his own counsel. She didn't know if that was good or bad.

Carson asked, "So is that why you and your friend are keeping apart?"

Peg nodded. "His uncle is a policeman, and I don't trust him. He knows Jack and I are friends, but he is convinced that I am either dead, or fled. He dragged Jack back to Melbourne, he said it was so the other guys wouldn't come at me to force him to do anything."

"Maybe he is not trying to hurt you?"

Peg just shrugged.

"I think you should talk this through with the Sergeant," McMasters said finally. "If as you say, you have committed no crime, it should all be easy to sort out."

"I doubt it," Peg told him. "But I am not going to run away. I've had enough! I'm sorry I am going to wreck the act, but I can't see a way out of the mess I am in."

The reminder about the act had McMasters shooing Carson off to get ready, but he paused long enough to wish her luck, and she said softly, "Jack's number is under my pillow. Can you call him later?"

Carson nodded, and disappeared into his room.

The Story continues in
Holder of Secrets
Part Three – Unrepentant

Other Books by Margaret Gregory

WANDA: FROM BAD TO WORSE

If she was going to die young, like her mother, Gwen Willard was determined to die rich and she had very few years to do it. Her first step was to leave home. She met Hooch, who taught her some exciting and illegal skills. She was the Draco's lucky mascot until she came to the attention of the police. Then her uncanny knack for predicting trouble, warned her to flee to the city and change her name.

Life wasn't easy. She was 15, had little money and no regular job, but her new skills came in handy. Then she crossed the path of an evil and unscrupulous man and she didn't want him to have his way.

WANDA: CHOOSING CRIME

Wanda was free. She was never going back to jail. But she was homeless, almost penniless and Harrison Franklin had a long and vengeful memory. Jim Phillips had a long memory too, and Wanda had saved his life. Could he save her from Franklin?

WANDA: RISKING LIFE TO LIVE

The euphoria of successful heists were what kept Wanda Dean alive. At 23, she was crime boss Harrison Franklin's top agent – well paid for absolute obedience. That's all that mattered. Until she met Mike Johnston and her boss ordered him killed. For that, the Franklins were going to pay. In *Risking Life to Live*, justice conflicts with loyalty and the penalty for betrayal is death.

WANDA: A NEW LIFE - HIDDEN SECRETS

Even before beginning as a covert agent for the US Government, Wanda is abducted by a foreign operative. After being rescued, there are signs that she had been subjected to hypnosis. With an important government gathering imminent, her handler must ensure she is not a security risk.

Can Wanda's psychic extra senses help her recognize and resist the implanted commands and clear her for secret work?

WANDA: A NEW LIFE - FIRST MISSION

On her first covert mission for the US Government, Wanda calls on the skills that made her a skilled thief to convince a revolutionary general that she's an ideal recruit. When her team mates' covers are blown, it is up to her to ensure that two missing scientists and confidential Government documents are not smuggled out of the US.

WANDA: FULL CIRCLE

Three generations after the alien Kumatan left Earth, their own world is suffering from alien invaders. In desperate hope, one returns to Earth seeking help - little knowing they had left one of their own behind.
Wanda, a child of the third generation, answers the call.

ERIN: THE FORCING OF WISDOM

For years, Erin has used the intricacies of cyberspace to banish unwanted emotions. Others call what she does hacking, and her manipulations criminal, but now her skill was exceptional - in, out, traceless. She was wrong. Someone betrayed her.
Travis has dangerous plans. He needs an electronics expert – one he can coerce through fear. Erin was perfect.
With the inescapable threat of prison looming, Erin accepts his offer of sanctuary. When she realises his intentions, she is in too deep. But the terrifying of innocents is unforgivable. She cannot walk away. She is an empath and shares their distress. She has to help them, even if it means prison, and insanity…

ERIN: THE CALL
including
ELISABETH AND TANYA: BLOOD CALLS TO BLOOD.

Elisabeth's sister, Wanda, had been missing for half a year. Multiple authorities had found no trace of her, or her two colleagues. Yet she knew her sister was still alive and had answered a call for help from an alien who had once lived on Earth.
Elisabeth, along with her newly found cousin Tanya, have started to sense things from her missing sister. Enough to know that she is in dire trouble, but not enough to help her.
While looking for traces of the aliens, Elisabeth makes some unexpected discoveries about her family. Yet even with the help of a second newly discovered cousin, she fears she is not strong enough to help her sister and the others to return.

ERIN: THE CALL

Convicted cyber-criminal, Erin Mason, is startled into awareness in an unfamiliar place, with no memory of escaping and only vague memories of getting there. Voices in her head were urging her to go west, and they were getting more urgent.

After a chance meeting with covert agent, Jim Phillips, when she helped save his mission, he realised that she might be the key to another, more personal quest – to find three missing state department agents.

All he must do is keep Erin safe, and hide her from an intense police search, until he can introduce her to cousins she was unaware of.

However her uncontrolled psychic gifts conflict with a logical mind that prefers the ordered intricacies of computers and electronics. She only wants to shut out the voices and the madness she sees looming.

Can Phillips convince her to help him, before the forces of the law find her?

KORVU: THE BEGINNING
The prequel to The Wild One

Jai Ansuni was the first female Atapi sorcerer for thousands of years, but she dare not reveal it. However, when tribal sorcerer, Stacion Ansuni escalates the enmity between Atapi and Kumatan to an ominous level. Jai and her womb mate, Con, try to mitigate his atrocities but can two young Atapi, not even a score of years old, win against the powerful sorcerer?

THE WILD ONE

Sixteen year old Jai Cassidy thought she was finally free of her family until she is discovered by her other relatives…the ones that aren't human. Jai uses her natural perversity and cunning to escape their control, but catapults herself into the middle of a deadly feud between two alien races.

ATAPI SORCERESS
The sequel to The Wild One

Jai Cassidy is beginning her mission of reversing the decline of the non-humanoid Atapi. As a sorceress and an Atapi-Human hybrid, she is vehemently disliked by the male Atapi sorcerers and the humanoid rulers of Korvu. Her task is complicated by the treachery of a group of alien engineers, who are inciting insurrection and harsh reprisals.

THE TYMOREAN TRUST BOOK 1 - POWER RISING

The Tymorean Trust - When peace rules Tymorea - Peace reigns in the universe.

Chosen to be the Advocates of the mystical and incorporeal Guardians of Peace, twins Tymos and Kryslie must first learn to control and use the power rising in them - or it will destroy them.

On Tymorea, only the ruling Triumvirate Governors are powerful enough to guide the strong-willed alien-bred twins until they have mastered their power.

THE TYMOREAN TRUST BOOK 2 - GREAT ONES

The peace of the Guardian Planet, Tymorea, is in deadly peril. War there will create ripples of unrest and destruction throughout the settled universe. Tymos and Kryslie, still adolescents, have barely mastered their power and Llaimos is still less than a year old, but they are the three chosen to be Advocates of the mystical Guardians of Peace, to safeguard the Tymorean Trust.

THE TYMOREAN TRUST BOOK 3 - RETURN TO EARTH

Even before the war on Tymorea, the Elders foresaw that Great Ones Tymos and Kryslie would have an imperative mission on Earth.

But as the Tymoreans prepare to build an Earthbase to support them, they discover that specifications for two vital protective shields are missing.

Now, nearly a century later, Tymos and Kryslie must find his work and build the generator before the base is found.

THE TYMOREAN TRUST BOOK 4 - EARTH MISSION

Just before their graduation from the prestigious WSRA Washington University, Tymos and Kryslie Ward deliberately disappear.

The Great Ones have foreseen the capture and death of the new Tymorean missionaries and discovered that the leader of the Eastern Imperium plans to undermine the United World Nations.

Tymos and Kryslie must protect their kin and prevent a potentially devastating world war.

THE TYMOREAN TRUST BOOK 5 – ALIEN CONTACT

Tymos and Kryslie Ward, hide their Tymorean intelligence and abilities while working as low ranked technicians at the WSRA's lunar base. When an alien ship arrives at Lunar One, pursued by a powerful enemy who will stop at nothing to get what he wants, only the two Tymorean Great Ones have the knowledge and abilities to overcome him, but to do so they must risk their sanity, and their souls.

THE TYMOREAN TRUST BOOK 6 – INVASION

Great Ones Tymos and Kryslie go to rescue the crew of Earth's first deep space mission – and discover that Ciriot space pirates have discovered Earth's location. When the Ciriot invade in force, the Great Ones reveal themselves so that Earth can gain vital help. However, Kryslie becomes the victim of Ciriot, who want to control her mind and make her betray the people of Earth.

TRICKS

Tom and Jo Dwyer had a reputation for playing tricks – and getting detention. They didn't seem to care about that, so long as they made their class laugh. That was until someone began to turn their tricks against them, and it was no longer funny.